4·4·4

A Breakthrough Book

4·4·4

Short Fiction by Laurence Gonzales,
Grant Lyons, and Roger Rath

Foreword by William Peden

University of Missouri Press
Columbia & London
1977

Library of Congress Cataloging in Publication Data

Gonzales, Laurence, 1947–
  4 • 4 • 4: short fiction.

  (A Breakthrough book)
   I. Lyons, Grant, 1941– joint author. II. Rath, Roger, 1942–
joint author. III. Title.
PZ4.G64933Fo   [PS3557.O467]   813'.5'4   76–56873
ISBN 0–8262–0207–1

"The Home Country" by Grant Lyons first appeared in Occident.
"The Trim" by Roger Rath first appeared in The Carleton Miscellany
(Spring/Summer 1973); "The Model" first appeared in Tri-Quarterly,
no. 36 (Spring 1976); and "The Sportsman" first appeared in The Carleton Miscellany 15, no. 2 (Winter 1976).

This book is being published with the assistance of an award from the
American Council of Learned Societies.

Foreword

4·4·4 is the first of what is hoped to be a continuing series presenting a sampling of short fiction by three young American writers. The concept is not new. Twenty years ago New Directions published a paperback volume of fifteen stories by three then little-known authors, R. V. Cassill, Herbert Gold, and James B. Hall. The following year Scribner's inaugurated an equally admirable but short-lived series introducing the stories of four similarly little-or-unknown young writers, which was to include the likes of Richard Yates, Arno Karlen, Seymour Epstein, and Robert Creeley. Today, even more than then, similar encouragement of the talented younger writer is imperative. Confronted by inflation, recession, the virtual disappearance of a competitive magazine market and increasing competition from television, film, nonfiction, and the New Journalism, the short story is fighting for survival. There is nothing really new about this, either.

From its great beginnings with Irving, Poe, and Hawthorne, the American short story in book form has tended to be a financial failure despite the enormous popularity of short fiction in periodicals during the heyday of the mass-circulation magazine from, say, the 1840s to the 1950s.

But the form simply refuses to die.

The short story remains the province of the young and the seasoned professional alike. In spite of the increasingly harsh realities of the contemporary publishing situation—it has been estimated that of the some thirty thousand books that will be published in the United States in 1977 fewer than fifty will be "first" short-story collections—it seems to me that there are as many good, young short-fiction writers around today as ever before. Indeed, the adversity inherent in the situation has eliminated most of the mediocrities and the hacks; in such a climate, only the genuinely talented and persevering writers are likely to endure.

4·4·4 is a modest attempt to encourage such writers of short fiction. From its beginnings, the University of Missouri Press has been receptive to short stories. *The White Hound*, the first book to bear its imprint, contains eight of what I would unblushingly label as superb short stories by Ward Dorrance and the late Thomas Mabry, along with an impressive introduction by Caroline Gordon; more recently, its Breakthrough Series has presented outstanding annual first collections of short fiction and poetry. Similarly other university presses, noteworthy among which are the annual collections of short fiction begun by Louisiana State in 1968 or the more recent projects of Illinois and Iowa. In such undertakings there is hope for the future; the university presses conceivably may be able to render to the short-story writer the encouragement and stimulus they have given to younger poets in the past.

In spite of their differences in background experience, subject matter, and technique, the three writers represented here possess much in common. They are young: the oldest is thirty-five, the youngest twenty-nine. They have published in a variety of magazines ranging from obscure "littles" to major quarterlies, but this is the first time their stories have been collected in book form. They are skilled practitioners of a difficult genre; they know and respect their craft. They are individuals; each speaks with his own voice and without pretentiousness. Each *knows* his own particular segment of the universe, ranging from an Australian suburb, the American South-Southwest, or a lake resort in Missouri, and each writes about it and its people with understanding, insight, and compassion, whether his concern be the doomed and violent world of Laurence Gonzales's "Running Dog"; the quiet character revelations of Roger Rath's " 'The Young in One Another's Arms' "; or the drab hopelessness that destroys

the husband and wife of Grant Lyons's "Across the River."
They will be heard from in the future, these young authors.

The Authors

Laurence Gonzales was born in 1947 (Capricorn) and
raised in Houston, Texas. He worked as a trumpet player and
singer with Johnny Winter and others, was director of the
electron microscopy department of Children's Memorial Hospital in 1965, and edited *Tri-Quarterly* in 1970–1971 with
Charles Newman. He is now Senior Editor Non-Fiction of
Playboy magazine and foreign correspondent for *Spit In The
Ocean*, published by Ken Kesey. His short fiction and poetry
have appeared in numerous small magazines, including
Poetry and *Minnesota Review*. His nonfiction and humor
have appeared in slick magazines including *Playboy*.

He calls his fiction "bizarre, dirty stories inspired by para-
noia" and admits to having written "six widely rejected
novels." He plans "a big, big book next year. Unfortunately,"
he adds, "no big, big publishers share my plans."

Grant Lyons lives and writes in San Antonio and has lived
in Texas much of his life. Born in Butler, Pennsylvania, in
1941, he attended Tulane University on a football scholarship,
graduating with honors in philosophy. He has a master's degree in history from the University of New Orleans. He has
been messboy on a Swedish tanker, a teacher in Israel, and a
journalist in California. His stories have appeared in *Red-
book*, *Northwest Review*, and a few "obscure literary magazines." He has written "a novel and a half" and is the author
of two books for children, *Tales the People Tell in Mexico*,
and *Andy Jackson and the Battle for New Orleans* (both published by Messner). He is married.

Of the stories in *4·4·4*, Mr. Lyons writes: "I regard [them]
as parts of a whole, a whole that is not complete . . . but of
a single cast. They are dominated by the Spirit of Place—the
sullen marsh country of the upper Texas gulf coast and
neighboring Louisiana; [they] focus on individuals who find
themselves . . . isolated and forced into an effort of self-

definition . . . it is the environment in which these figures grope toward this rather fundamental *rite de passage* that determines the gloomy cast of these stories. . . ."

Roger Rath was born on April Fools' Day, 1942, in Sydney, Australia. He graduated from the University of Missouri and the Writers' Workshop at Iowa and has been teaching writing for the past ten years. He is presently at Johnson State College, Johnson, Vermont, where he directs the Green Mountains Workshop. His work has appeared in *The Carleton Miscellany*, *Tri-Quarterly*, *Esquire*, and other magazines. He is married and has one daughter.

"My characters," Mr. Rath says, "persist in talking directly to the issue of the story; their self-consciousness provides whatever movement there might be and, in the novel I'm working on now, the same thing holds true. To convey their often shaky sense of gravity and consequences, I try to set up an uneasiness in the reader through prose rhythms meant to slide through the usual distinctions made between narrative and interior monologue. It's a limited and limiting way to work, a myopic way, a re-writer's way, and it may or may not be successful. Whatever, I'm at its mercy and command and, just as often as not, grateful to be able to pay it obedience."

W. P.

Contents

Laurence Gonzales

Running Dog
A Bowl of Texas Red
Rainbow
The Grand Prize

Laurence Gonzales

Running Dog

Years later Jesse Sky would take a man hunting and then nearly get into a fist fight on account of stopping him from shooting a particular white-tailed deer. The man was deep in concentration, honing for that deer and taking careful aim, when Jesse caught the barrel of his rifle and brought it to the ground, where it fired in the mud, cracking the still wet air and scared the daylights out of man and deer alike, sending the latter bounding off through blackberry and silver beech, flat out in fear.

The man—a neighbor by then but not yet (or necessarily ever to be) a friend—was furious and could not understand when Jesse offered no more by way of explanation than to say, "You don't shoot something that's running like that. You scared him too bad. Shoot 'em when they're standing. Shoot 'em when they're peaceful."

The man ranted and raved and even coughed up a few threats, but Jesse wasn't really listening by then as they walked along in search of another deer—one they both knew wouldn't show that day. Jesse was already remembering when he was no more than eleven years old down along the Texas gulf coast, running like that whitetail.

The first time the boys chased him with rocks and baseball bats—not a week after he had moved into the middle-class, white neighborhood—Jesse had known panic. Something beyond fright, beyond even terror, had entered his body at a point midway between his navel and his vocal chords, which were suddenly frozen in a rush of icy air, even though the day was hot and oppressive, as it usually was in Harris County, Texas, in the month of September. How the thing got into him, Jesse didn't know, but it took hold in his chest and something switched on that he knew he couldn't control. So he ran.

As he felt the first dull pain of a rock in the center of his back the thing in his chest changed, opened up, and his legs moved faster. The boys were hollering at him but the sound faded, merged with the slipstream of wind on his ears until the voices were nothing, unintelligible. All he could sense clearly was his feet not so much hitting the ground as moving above it, making a whoosh with each pass through the grass.

It couldn't have been more than two hundred yards after he began running that he saw the fence ahead. He didn't turn to see how much distance he had put between himself and the boys who were chasing him. In fact, he no longer even thought about them. The thing in his chest was in complete control and Jesse wasn't even afraid anymore. He was totally caught up in the singular purpose of moving forward with the greatest possible speed, as far as he could. Several yards before he reached the fence he already knew which foot he would be on when he attained it, just how much energy to give to that leg, and what the arc would be like as he sprang headfirst, leaving the earth behind. He came toward the ground as if he were going to land on his head and then twisted at the last moment so that one shoulder hit the grass, and he rolled out onto his feet without missing a stride and kept on moving, leaving divots of grass where his footprints began again, interrupted only by the chain link fence, which looked as if it had been built across his path long after he had gone by.

By that time there was no way the boys could have caught him. They had no things in their chests and ran under the weight of rage, not uplifted by the light flashing of panic. They were far behind. And seeing him vault the fence in a somersault like that—knowing they would have to climb it—they had given over to a slow walk, vowing to get him the next time. Jesse had no mind of this though and kept running until he dropped, several miles later in a field near the bayou that ran by his house. As he lay there on his back, staring up at the bright hot day, he saw as if peering through a dark tunnel and knew he was passing out. The dark crept quickly from the edges inward covering his eyes like scars. When he came to, no more than a minute later, he was breathing hard and had a painful stitch in his side. But the thing was gone from his chest. He felt tired but good. He had not only beaten them; he had beaten himself in a way he knew they never could.

He knew his neighbor did not understand these things about a man or about whitetail. He didn't care if the man understood, but he wasn't going to let him shoot the deer wrong if he could do something about it. Besides the man was not a good shot and had no business fooling with a gun anyway. The man would have gut shot the animal. Jesse had nothing against killing for eating. Somebody was going to have to kill something if he was going to eat—he might as well do it himself and do it right. But Jesse learned hunting from his grandfather, and the old man had been very careful about how he killed his food. It was almost like being a kosher Jew. If you didn't kill it right, you couldn't eat it. And to waste it was the worst crime of all. So Jesse had spent summer after summer with a .22 rifle and then with a heavy old .44–40 Winchester saddle rifle that had belonged to his uncle, who was a pig farmer in Mexico—and then with a .30–'06 and a .270—until he could put one in a whitetail's spinal column at three hundred yards. And when he had shown his grandfather his achievement, his grandfather, whose name was Big Sky, had said, "That's fine. Now learn how to find the animal." And Jesse had spent another series of summers tracking with an unloaded rifle until he could stand just about at arm's length from the animal, take careful aim, pull the trigger and hear the firing pin fall, see the animal turn with a puzzled look on its face and calmly go back to eating without ever knowing it had just been killed—and killed outright with a 180 grain Springfield Core-Lokt bullet in the brain.

But years later, he found that hard to do with his neighbor crashing through the woods like a tank crossing enemy lines. Jesse went with him to be polite, that was all. But he wasn't going to stand by and let the man do something foolish. Besides, he didn't even like the idea of being out in the woods during deer season, much less risking putting out wild shots of his own into a forest that was as surely full of trigger-happy hunters as it was trees.

"Let's go have a beer," Jesse said to the man after they'd walked another hundred yards without seeing an animal. He knew the hunters—all of them thrashing around in the undergrowth—would have scared anything as smart as a whitetail away for a week. They turned and started back toward the truck. Jesse felt like running but didn't for two reasons. One, his neighbor would have been puzzled and offended at being left alone (and probably would have gotten lost, though they were only half a mile from the truck). And two, anything running in those woods during deer season was subject to draw more fire than John Kennedy waving in Dealy Plaza.

Walking back and wanting to run, Jesse felt the squared off muscles on the front of his thighs flexing and clicking like compact little motors, tuned up and idling. The forest floor was springy under his feet, just right for the kind of traction he wanted. Jesse wore only moccasins, had since he was a kid, which had also branded him: Not only was the bastard a half-breed, part Indian, part Mexican, but he flaunted it by wearing those things on his feet. Couldn't even try to at least act like a white man, now that they'd let him into a white neighborhood and a white school to be taught properly by Catholic nuns and priests.

Jesse would have worn moccasins anyway. It was the only way you could feel the ground. What was the point of being on the earth if you couldn't even feel where you touched it all day? And it was the only way to run. He couldn't understand people who put on hard boots for hiking, rubber shoes for running—a man wasn't a car. You don't put rubber on your wheels unless you're a car, he thought. Just put some skin between you and the ground—a little something to toughen the skin you've already got—and you'll get there on time. Anyway, when he was five, a horse had stepped on his right foot and crushed it flat and he couldn't really wear hard shoes. He still had the foot but it wasn't the prettiest thing in the world. And since moccasins were pliable, the right one would conform to his lopsided foot.

Years later Jesse put this little college teacher down on her back one night for about six hours behind some white dust he'd picked up from a dirt track motorcyclist from South America whose face had been beaten so much and so badly from landing on it in the dirt that he looked as if he had no nose at all. Jesse had asked him how he could (or why he would bother to) put the magic dust up his nose when it was in such bad shape already, and the cyclist had replied that a man can rise above himself in the face of great danger.

"What danger?" Jesse asked.

"The danger of not being high, man."

Jesse and the girl lay exhausted on the bed in her little college teacher's apartment, and she told him he was like George Gordon (Lord) Byron.

"That one of your fag friends?" Jesse had asked.

She explained that Byron was a poet who had a clubfoot but was otherwise very beautiful. She told Jesse how Byron used to hold court, arrive at parties hours early so that he could prop himself up in the right place, and not move until the guests had all left so that he could socialize all he pleased without anyone ever seeing the way he walked as a result of the foot.

Of course, Jesse could walk fine but the lady thought it was an interesting analogy, though Jesse neither wrote poetry nor was self-conscious about his foot or about anything else.

"Fuckin wheel's a mess alright," Jesse had told her. "It's for shore a recap if they ever was one. But shit, we got two four-barrel Webers in here behind four hundred horses, child, and she'll get rubber in three gears if you want her to."

Jesse liked to jack with her mind. She took her poetry so seriously. She read him some Byron and he said it was nice but that was about all he said. She told him about Byron's tragic ride to his death on horseback in Greece and he allowed as how Byron was probably pretty much an asshole, if you left aside the fact that he was a historical figure and regarded highly as a poet. The girl was disappointed that Jesse couldn't appreciate Byron properly, especially since they both had a bad wheel and a beautiful body and face.

How Jesse had come to meet this teacher was that he

worked part-time as a hunting, fishing, and walking guide to pick up some extra money. The lady's boyfriend had insisted on taking her hunting to show her what real living was all about. As they walked along through the woods, the lady was almost as quiet as Jesse, picking her steps carefully, while her boyfriend thrashed about, getting entangled in brush and branches every ten feet or so and swinging his .30–'06 around so wildly that Jesse insisted he either unload it or take more care. But worse, the boyfriend kept commenting to the lady how, "This is how it was really *meant* to be. Stalking *game*. This is how they *used* to do it. Ask Jesse there. He's part Indian. Isn't this where it's *at*, Jesse? The *hunt*? The smell of the *woods*? *Picking up the scent*?" And on and on until Jesse, with a short barreled 30–30 slung over his shoulder, started seriously considering putting one in his back just to give him *the feel of the hunt*.

In the end, though, Jesse reasoned that this guy was doing him a favor. Because it was the lady's first real chance to see what a clown he was, even though he taught college philosophy courses. And when she saw, she began exchanging glances with Jesse while the boyfriend went crashing ahead, blabbering away about the greatness of Hemingway and hunting and Faulkner and on and on until, when it was time for him to get back to teaching, the lady left Jesse with her name, address, and phone number in Austin where he could drop over anytime, which he did.

The time she told him about Byron it was eight in the morning before the coke ran out and they got to sleep. About noon she woke up and hit the shower. When she came out, drying her hair, wrapped in a robe, she stood dumbfounded for a full minute watching Jesse, who was still asleep because he was running in his sleep, like a dog will sometimes do, making funny grunts and breathing hard, his legs ticking out the rhythm, his arms swinging ever so slightly in counterpoint. Then she woke him and he sat bolt upright, accidentally knocking her onto the floor, where she sat on her ass for a moment before Jesse realized where he was and what he was doing. He apologized and picked her up but would offer no explanation of his strange behavior other than, "I must've been dreaming."

"But people don't dream like that," she said, "only dogs dream like that."

Jesse shrugged and stood under the shower until the hot water ran out. Then he let the icy water run over him for a few minutes, his heart feeling as if it would burst from the shock. During breakfast she asked him several more times to explain what had been going on in his dream but he would say nothing. He left saying he'd be back or give her a ring the following weekend but she never heard from him again. She showed up during the next hunting season but Jesse was out at the time. Finally she gave up on him, still wondering what it was all about, still wondering why he had never called back.

He didn't much have to worry about men that way. You don't sleep with men. They don't get to see you like that. Or else if you're camping out or something, you can go sleep away from them, you can go sleep in the truck if you have to or else get so drunk with them that none of them would wake up if you ran a herd of buffalo through the camp. But his college teacher wasn't the first lady he'd left like that. That's why he ordinarily tried to get out before falling asleep. Sometimes it wasn't so easy if he'd been running dust up his nose and drinking hard liquor all night. Sometimes he just succumbed and then it was all over. Then he just had to hit the hooks and disappear. But he was getting better and better at not slipping up, at slipping out before he fell asleep.

It was the same with his bad foot. It was something he didn't dwell on too much. There was nothing he could do about it and he just went along and did the best he could do. Big Sky had told him the right thing, Jesse knew that. His grandfather was a good Apache of the Mescalero tribe, and though he loved Jesse as much as a man could love a boy, he had known that there was only one thing to tell him, only one thing for Jesse to do. And that was just stick it out. They had tried to do something about it but even traveling up into Arizona to other Mescalero Apache tribes didn't help. There was apparently no one.

Brother was the name by which the Yaqui sorcerer was known in that area. No one was sure why he was called that, though there were many versions of the story of just whose brother he was. When Jesse was a little boy, Brother lived in a cabin near Jesse and Big Sky. Brother kept a very bad horse known as Se Quema because his mane was red like fire and because he was wild and dangerous and nearly impossible to ride. One day Brother's son (whose name was Juan and who was rumored to be someone else's son altogether, who had merely been apprenticed to Brother) taunted Jesse until he agreed to mount Se Quema and that's how Jesse got his foot crushed. At that point no one thought Jesse would ever walk again, so badly was his foot damaged. Learning what had happened, Jesse's grandfather had taken his rifle and shot Se Quema in the head and killed him.

Brother was furious and in revenge told Jesse and Big Sky that he was going to change Jesse into a running dog. Soon after that Jesse's foot began to get better and he found himself able to walk around with the aid of a stick. Though his foot was badly deformed, a few months later he could walk and run with no noticeable handicap. In fact, he could run better and faster and farther than anyone else and became known among Brother's family and friends as R. D. Jesse Sky, R. D. standing for Running Dog, though no one would call him that to his face.

Throughout the rest of his childhood Jesse experienced no ill effects from what Brother had said. In fact, Big Sky had begun to feel guilty about shooting Se Quema because it seemed Brother had actually cured Jesse's foot. But just about the time Jesse's adolescence was over and he was starting to turn into a full-grown man, the dreams began and he started running in his sleep. Some nights it was worse than others. Sometimes he would just wake up with his legs ticking out the rhythm and the same group of hunters after him as he easily loped along outdistancing them, leaping over fallen logs and fences with ease, until morning. On other nights, though, they gained on him, sometimes using jeeps and other dogs to track and keep up with him. On nights like those Jesse frequently woke up lying in his own blood having rubbed the sides of his legs raw from running. And all around him would be the tatters of what had been bed sheets, ripped to shreds by his pumping legs.

When he was twenty-one years old, he took to sleeping apart from others. He had to put a plastic cover on the bed in case he bled too much and ruined the mattress. The dreams weren't often that bad but when they were, the mattress had to be replaced and he couldn't afford that, couldn't afford to take the chance. After a while, he developed a tough layer of calluses on the sides of his legs, which helped keep him from rubbing the skin off during the bad nights.

❀   ❀   ❀   ❀

As Jesse and his neighbor entered the bar, several men sat drinking beers and shots in the midafternoon. They all knew both Jesse and Ronnie Parker, the neighbor, and waved or nodded.

"Boys get anything?" one large middle-aged man asked. He wore a lumberjack shirt and a John Deere cap.

"Would've," Ronnie said, pulling up to a stool, "but the goddamn *guide* wouldn't let me shoot it. Nice eight pointer."

Jesse said nothing, taking the stool next to Ronnie's. The bartender brought two beers without asking what they wanted. They always wanted beer. All you had to do is specify if you wanted the beer with or without a shot, Slim Jim, beef jerky, or boiled egg.

"Yeah," the man in the baseball cap said, "a nice eight point cow." The other men in the bar laughed. It was an old joke. Older than the one about the zebras, but even so, the farmers in the area did lose on the average a dozen cows a season from the deer hunters who insisted on using firearms that could send a projectile up to eight miles.

"Hey, Jesse," the man with the John Deere cap called across Ronnie, who was sulking in his beer, "ain't that pointer bitch of yours come in yet?"

"Could be in today," Jesse said absently. During bird season Jesse used a dog if the hunters insisted. He didn't need one—didn't even care to have one along—but sometimes a hunter just wouldn't feel like he was really hunting unless you brought along a dog, and anyway Crystal, his pointer bitch, was pretty good.

"Well, is my dirt eater gonna get a shot at her or not?" the John Deere cap wanted to know.

"Sure, Clovis, we'll go over and try her anytime you like. But while we got witnesses here just remember it's your idea not mine and I don't want you hittin' me up for no stud fee."

"Two picks'll do her, Jesse," the man said draining the last two inches of warm beer in his glass and motioning for a fresh cool one.

"Two picks, my ass." Jesse stood up on the rungs of his stool and leaned over the bar to draw himself another beer from the tap rather than wait for the bartender to do it. "I told you months ago when you first asked me. I don't particularly want to breed Crystal. Takin' care of all them shittin' puppies, gettin' 'em wormed and shot and all. . . I'd as soon not. You want one pick, it's worth my while. You take two picks, hell, we don't even know how many there's gonna be. She's never thrown a pup before."

"Jesus." Clovis spoke to the room in general. "Here I am offering this half-breed the best six inches of my pointin' dog for nothin' and he's trying to jack me around." He turned slowly around to face Jesse. "Listen. I'll tell you what. I take one pick, just one lousy dog. But I take it when it's three months old and that way I know for sure I'm gettin' the best one."

"You can't tell a dog by the time it's weaned you might as well forget it, Clovis," another man said.

"Jesse there can tell 'em when they come out, I've heard," Ronnie seemed to have forgotten about his eight point mistake.

"You think I'm gonna try and give you anything less than the best one, Clovis, then don't do business with me." Jesse said.

"You a hard man, Jesse," Clovis said and everybody in the bar knew that Clovis would get only one pick and that he would take it when it was weaned and like it.

"Well," Jesse said, taking down half a glass of beer, "might as well get to it."

The men all tossed bills and change on the bar and left in a group, each one saying something to the bartender as he left. Ronnie had his station wagon there and went home. Clovis and Jesse got in Jesse's Chevy pickup truck with the whip aerials and the twin spotlights and pulled away kicking up dust. The other men followed in their trucks down the two lane toward Jesse's farm. It wasn't actually a working farm to speak of (when asked what he raised, he usually said, "A ruckus.") but he did have a couple of pigs, three beef steers that he raised himself, and half an acre of high corn with rows of marijuana planted in between so it couldn't be spotted from an airplane. He also had two riding horses, one good quarter horse for himself and a gentle mare for guests. Jesse had found that making friends was often a good deal easier if you first introduced your guest to the simple pleasure of locking between your legs something that was essentially an enormous trained muscle, in the same sense that a locomotive is just a giant motor to which someone has attached wheels.

Crystal was in a chicken-wire pen beside the barn. The minute the men pulled up Clovis's dog was out of the truck and over to Crystal before anyone could stop him. Then the two dogs were smelling around each other like blind people feeling the beauty of each other's faces, and Jesse let the male in to be with Crystal. Clovis, Jesse, and the three other men stood around in a circle while the dogs got acquainted, waiting for something to happen and, sure enough, pretty soon Clovis's dog started to mount Crystal, whereupon she swung around and bit him right on the nose, growling and baring her teeth.

"Mustn't be in," one of the men said.

"Supposed to be today," Jesse said, looking at his watch, which had the day and date showing on the face of it.

"You may know that," Clovis said. "And my dirt eater may know it. But old Crystal don't."

"Show her your watch, Jesse," one of the men said and the others laughed.

They fell silent to watch as the dog again tried to mount Crystal, but she reacted even more emphatically, and a spot of blood appeared below the male's right eye where Crystal's teeth had laid open a gash in the skin.

"Well *hell!*" Clovis said, taking the dog by the collar.

"You can try her again tomorrow," Jesse said. "Should be in by then for shore."

"Can't do anymore with her today," Clovis said.

"I'm gone," one of the men said, moving toward his truck.

The little gathering broke up. Jesse locked the kennel and went into his house. It was a converted barn.

A great, uninterrupted space presented itself as he entered: Raw joist and plank, high vaulted barn ceilings, oiled down hardwood floor. Jesse went over to his chair in that part of the space he referred to as the living room. He took a deep breath and leaned his head back. He held his right hand flat out in front of his face, palm downward, and watched as it trembled. He wondered what was wrong, couldn't figure it. I drink a lot, he thought, but not enough to give me afternoon shakes. Not yet, anyway.

When, after ten minutes of sitting still, the feeling had not gone away, Jesse went to the part of the room he called the kitchen and took a bottle of sour-mash whiskey from the cabinet. He poured two brown inches of the liquid into a water glass and drank it off straight away, steadying himself against the counter top, bowing his head as the whiskey seared down into him and flushed his skin. As it worked its way through him, he could feel the shaking subside slowly, as if, with a small lead weight, he had balanced out a wheel that shimmied too badly on the open highway. He went to the refrigerator and popped the top on a can of beer. He took about a third of it down to drown the whiskey burn. He leaned against the refrigerator and listened to himself to hear what was in there. The shaking had stopped. All he could hear were normal sounds, like a series of erratic ticks —an engine that has been run hot and then shut off abruptly.

Though the shaking had stopped, Jesse still felt the strangeness. It was not something he could pin down—just as he could never pin down the thing that had entered his chest from time to time. The good computer in his head that ran its smooth tape day after day, the good angel had gone for the afternoon and the demon had arrived unexpected. The very concept of a "train of thought" was gone, for the conveyance—whatever it is—jumped and skipped with no ballast, no rudder, no weight of its own, no destination. He wasn't afraid that he would do something dangerous or irrational or foolish. He was afraid because he had no idea what he would do, great or small, right or wrong. There was a severe lack of focus. But there was nothing to take for that. A man could stop shakes by knocking back a couple of shots. Or could jolt himself awake with strong coffee or a cold shower. He could go down to Seguin and get his cookies crumbled at Beth's for $35 if he needed to. But if he felt strange, just a plain old case of the horror-show-can't-help-its—there was no medicine for that, not even the magic dust.

So he shrugged, said, alright, I'm going to feel strange, and went outside to feed the pigs and horses in the running sunlight of the late afternoon. He went into the barn, took up a big sack of number four hybrid cracked corn (which cost him but made the pork taste better), and walked out into the long shadows and bright cones and spokes of light slowly turning and slanting in from the west like a big, rolling, rimless wheel of light. Halfway across the yard he stopped and sniffed the air: Something he couldn't identify, something sweet like a supper cooking, though there wasn't a neighbor close enough. He gave the pigs some corn, still trying to identify the smell. Pollution, he thought. Well, if it's going to be pollution, it might as well smell like supper.

After he made sure there was water for the steers and hay for the horses, Jesse went back inside. He stood by the kitchen sink thinking: Can't be any pollution around here. There's nothing around here that *makes* anything. Nearest thing to a factory was in Lockhart, thirty miles away, and all they did there was bolt together those twenty-five cent lockboxes for selling rubbers and shit in gas-station washrooms.

He shrugged again, picked up the opened beer can, and went back to his chair. He watched the television: The news, a rerun of *Ironsides*, and then turned on a movie with Michael Caine called *Zulu* in which they showed more bare tit than he had ever seen in one place before. Jesse didn't know bare tit was allowed on television. In fact, it isn't, unless it's black, because television people think your blacks are not real people.

In *Zulu* there is a line of girls—no more than teenagers—all dancing around, maybe two hundred of them, with their firm, freshly formed breasts sticking out, jiggling. They wear almost nothing below the waist. When this scene came on Jesse actually leaned forward on the edge of his chair to make sure he was really seeing what he thought he was seeing.

"I can't hardly believe it," he said out loud and turned the brightness control a little.

He felt a ticking in his groin as they danced and danced with their beautiful breasts and their young strong thighs pumping out the Zulu rhythms that the nearly naked men on the screen were beating out with spears against their wooden shields. The cameras pulled in close on one of the best pair Jesse had ever seen and lingered there for a full few seconds while the girl did things with her hips that hurt Jesse to watch. At first he thought maybe he was getting one of those freak electromagnetic radiation conditions, where radio signals bounce off the Pleiades and pick up broadcasts from Mars or something. Then he thought maybe he had become part of *The Twilight Zone*. But finally Danny Thomas came on with a very important message to all parents and following that there was a woman talking to a man in her toilet bowl and Jesse knew it was just a real movie on the TV that somehow had slipped through with all the tits still in it.

Fighting a definite urge to drive down to Beth's in Seguin, Jesse finally went to bed and fell into a sound sleep. About three in the morning he sat bolt upright, suddenly wide awake and vividly aware of two things. One, he had not been dreaming. It was the first time in years that he had not awakened from the dream of running. His legs were still. And two, the smell from that afternoon was stronger than ever. It was as if someone were cooking right in his bedroom (yet another area of the big room).

Jesse slipped from under the sheet into the still, stale air and walked across the dark room, sniffing as he went to determine where the smell was coming from. At the front door he stopped, sniffed, and then went out. The moon and stars seemed painfully bright and made his eyes feel the way they do when he got up in the middle of the night, feeling through the darkness and then turned on the bathroom light. He walked nearly naked into the yard. The smell was stronger than ever. He stood, letting his eyes adjust to the brightness of the moon and stars. And then he heard Crystal.

She was at the gate of her pen, whining and whipping her tail back and forth. Absently, Jesse went over to her pen and opened the gate. Crystal seemed so happy to see him that she boiled around him with the fury of six dogs. Only now Jesse thought he knew where the smell was coming from and bent down, calming Crystal so he could make sure.

But how, he thought, could it be everywhere? He continued to take in the smell, wondering how it could have gotten into the barn and the house and have covered the entire yard like a blanket of ground fog. And then he began stroking Crystal all along the length of her spine, and she arched her back toward him, and he had a sudden urge to just hold onto her, so he took her with his arms under her forepaws and pulled her toward him and he was inside her and she was moving, his shorts around his ankles, and he was on top of Crystal and sliding inside her and he looked up at the sky and saw the moon and all of the stars and thought, am I doing this? Am I really doing this, or has my dream just changed now into something good and fun instead of having to run every night? And he moved and moved, thinking, well, as well this as being hunted down, and lowered his head from the moon and took Crystal's neck in his teeth and bit down hard until she howled.

❖   ❖   ❖   ❖

"Goddamn it, Jesse," Clovis said, "You wanna rent me a room. I'll come out here and do this with you everyday."

"Well, shit, Clovis," Jesse said, watching Crystal snap at the dog again and again, refusing to let him mount, "what do you want me to do? I told you I wasn't any too keen on the idea anyway."

"Well, *hell*," Clovis said, taking his dog's collar again, "I don't know."

"You know Ken up the road north of here?" Jesse asked, pointing.

"Yeah, I know him."

"He's got a good pointer bitch. Why don't you try her?"

"Yeah, I heard she was due to come in right about now." Clovis mumbled, dragging the dog, which was turning and fighting to get back to Crystal. "But she still ain't the dog Crystal is."

"Sorry, Clovis," Jesse shrugged, closing the gate on Crystal and came out into the yard. "Ken's bitch'll throw a good pup for ya."

"Shit," Clovis said and got into his truck and drove off, spitting gravel back at Jesse.

*　　*　　*　　*

"Doc," Jesse said, squinting under the bright light of the examining room over the stainless steel table, "I already told you she was locked up inside of a chicken-wire pen the entire time. And I also told you Clovis come up with his dog and she wouldn't let him mount her even right on the day she was supposed to come in."

"Well, Jesse," the vet said, lifting Crystal off the examining table onto the floor, "that's all fine and good but, hell, you know how dogs are when a bitch comes into heat. They always seem to find a way. And Crystal here is pregnant whether you like it or not. Something slipped into that pen and got to her. Maybe some kids left it unlocked or let her out to play, I don't know. All I'm tellin you is *some*-thin' slipped in and got to her and that'll be five bucks for my sayin' it."

Jesse paid the vet and drove home slowly with Crystal sitting in the front seat beside him. She was unusually quiet. When Jesse got home, he took Crystal into the barn and tied her to the side of the horse stall. He went over to unlock the tool closet and took out an old double barreled shotgun and fired both barrels, point blank into Crystal's skull. At the sound both horses started and the quarter kicked backwards and knocked a slat out of the gate to his stall. Crystal's back legs ran on for a few seconds as she lay on her side with no head. Jesse went inside and put four inches of bourbon in a water glass and drained it off without flinching. He took a beer out of the refrigerator and drank about half of it while leaning up against the counter watching the far wall and trying not to think about what Crystal looked like with her head gone.

He went to the front door and stood looking out. The yard was still. The shot must have scared the animals and insects because everything was very quiet and it was the hot part of the afternoon when the bugs usually get up. He walked around to the back of the house and dug a hole six feet deep and four feet around. It took him nearly an hour. When it was dug, he went into the barn, trying not to look, and threw an old horse blanket over Crystal's body. He carried her out and put her in the hole and covered her up with dirt.

As he stood over the mound of freshly turned earth, he could not put his thoughts together. His body felt as steady as it could feel but his head was reeling. He stood trying to pull it together, trying to line it out so he could see what it was. Then in the middle of dusting the dirt off his hands he hit on it: He could still smell the same aroma of that sweet something cooking.

Jesse jerked around and ran to the door at the front of the house. Before he reached the bathroom he had stripped off all his clothes. He jumped into the shower, hit the hot water and lathered himself up from head to toe with Dial soap, and then went over his whole body again with Safeguard. When he was done he toweled himself down and carefully smelled his hands and arms. They smelled fresh and perfumed like the soap. He even bent down and smelled his knees. Then he sat down and picked up his bad foot and smelled it. It smelled just like Safeguard soap.

And that's when he first smelled Ken's bitch. Sitting there on the closed toilet seat, a pink towel draped over his square shoulder, his broken, deformed foot pulled all the way up to his face like a dog about to scratch its ear, he let the foot fall to the floor and sat very still for a second with his nostrils working. Clovis was probably over there right this minute with his dirt eater. But Jesse could tell from the smell that Ken's bitch was not ready. Not yet.

As quickly as he could Jesse got dressed in some old jeans, a T-shirt, and his moccasins. He locked the front door on his way out and went behind the house. He looked out over the field for a minute, studying the rippling surface of the long grass between his land and the forest. Then he bolted and ran, leaving two holes in the grass where his feet had been.

A Bowl of Texas Red

Steven carefully cut two pounds of meat into cubes the size of the tip of his smallest finger. Half of the meat was round steak, half venison from a whitetail he had shot a month earlier with a bow and arrow in Michigan's Upper Peninsula. He held the handle of the large hunting knife in his right hand, placing the palm of his left hand on the dull top of the blade for each cut against the chopping board, the surface of which had started to go spongy from years of lacerations. The fresh meat made a crisp ripping sound each time he cut through it again and Steven felt it as if the knife were cutting his own flesh—his cheek perhaps.

There was a large cast-iron pot on the stove with some olive oil in it. The low, blue flame beneath had started it crackling as water vapor came out of the porous metal and fried off like shots in the hot oil. Steven dumped in the chunks of meat and the pot made a sound like applause heard from far off—the roar of Carnegie Hall a mile away. Steam and the smell of frying meat filled the kitchen as Steven took an onion the size of a baseball from a gear hammock in the pantry and, with sure gentle strokes, cut off either end and flayed the dried skin away, leaving only the white slick ball smelling of acrolene. He ran water over it to reduce the lacrimating effect and slowly bisected it, flipped each half onto its freshly cut face, then made twelve cross sections of each piece and twelve more sections perpendicular to those, parallel to the bilateral midline, leaving a large pile of finely diced onion.

When he had finished the onion the meat was crackling

brown and he felt a sense of relief putting down the knife, which he had stropped before each use for eight years and which was consequently sharp enough so that if he happened to cut himself accidentally, he would go to the hospital. Once to demonstrate to a lady who had come to stay with him the danger involved in using this particular knife, Steven had taken a piece of flank steak, so tough it could only be used after hours of marinating and after tenderizing it with enzymes, and he had thrown this lightly into the air and split it in two with a single stroke of the knife (apparently without disturbing its descent toward the floor, because he was able to catch the two pieces before they landed on the tile). The lady decided to do her chore with another knife Steven kept for people who were subject to cut their fingers off given anything sharper than a spoon—a fancy looking stainless steel knife that wasn't worth a dime as far as Steven was concerned beause you couldn't put an edge on it without a machine shop and even if you bothered, the knife wouldn't hold it through a single cooking job.

Steven ran cold water over the knife blade, gently wiped it with a towel, and slid it into a wooden scabbard cut in a board that hung above the sink, where a quick and careless hand would not find its edge. More: The knife had an ivory handle. Its blade was eight inches long with the classic shape of a hunting knife. On a fishing trip in Canada eight and a half years ago Steven had fallen through the ice into three hundred feet of water. He had been plucked freezing from the water by his guide but he had lost his favorite hunting knife with no hope of ever seeing it again unless he wanted to wait until summer and get a bathyscaphe and some underwater floodlights. It wasn't *that* great a knife. But the guide, whom Steven trusted purely out of instinct and faith in his ability to judge men, especially outdoorsmen, told him he could replace that knife with one the likes of which Steven had never seen before and would never see again. He told Steven that a man by the name of Briar who lived, appropriately enough, near Yellowknife, was seventy-four years old and had been making knives since he was ten. He was taught by his uncle, who had been a blacksmith. The guide said it would be expensive but for a man who hunted, fished, trapped, and generally stayed outdoors as much as Steven did it would probably be a sound investment. The guide then slipped off his glove and held up his left hand, which was missing the first joint of the index finger and grinned at Steven.

"I was drunk," he said as if it were a joke of some kind. "If you get one of his knives," he continued, putting the hand back into its glove, "never try to use it when you're drunk. I'd sooner use a chain saw drunk. These knives have an edge that can only be matched by breaking glass. Once in British Columbia I took a professor on a fishing trip like this. He was from the University of Victoria doing some kind of biology there. I showed him my knife and we talked about edges. He said in his work in order to cut tiny things that were hard—things from animals—so that he could look at them under a microscope, he had to take a diamond marker and scratch on glass, then break the glass with pliers until he got a certain kind of edge, which was the only edge sharp enough to give him smooth slices that were thin enough to see in the microscope." Steven had dried out by a big fire the guide built and they were sitting close to it sipping from a plastic water jug full of whiskey. The authorities didn't allow anybody to go into that part of Canada with containers that could be thrown away, such as beer cans. So everyone who went on these fishing trips took along a big plastic container of whiskey and sometimes skins of wine. The guide bubbled the bottle loudly, passed it to Steven, swallowed with a wince, and went on. "Well I showed him some tricks with my knife and he examined it. He touched the blade like people do to see how sharp it is and he drew blood. Just a little touch, like this," the guide made one finger into a knife and ran his right index finger over it ever so gently, panto-miming the pain, as if he had touched a hot stove, drawing his finger quickly to his mouth and sucking, then replacing his gloves again.

"The professor—Aarie was his name, Professor Aarie—told me he'd pay me extra if I would go back to the university with him and let him look at the blade under a microscope and so I said, hell, I was going back that way anyway and he could look at it all he wanted if he just put me up for the night, which he did, and in a pretty nice place too. Had a big modern house on the channel there, and his wife was as sweet as a woman could be, cooking us steaks and potatoes and then in the morning making eggs and bacon and a big pot of coffee and standing by the stove just humming to herself and calling me 'Mister Wolf.' He had a son about eight years old and he came in that morning and asked me who I was and why I was in their house so I told him, very serious like this: 'I'm the subject of an official scientific study, son.' Just like that and he gave me a look like I was asking him to play the shell game with me, so the professor told him about the knife." Wolf reached for the bottle and Steven handed it to him.

Steven could see lights in the sky behind Wolf—the aurora borealis. He felt good and calm, almost as if he'd worked out hard and he thought it was probably because of falling in the water, the shock of every single muscle in his body suddenly tensing to its limit, if only for a moment. He liked the easy way Wolf told a story and thought he could have listened to the guide recite names from the phone book and just sit there in northern Canada drinking whiskey by the fire. After Wolf had bubbled the jug once, he passed it again and went on.

"Well, this kid went nuts over the knife but I wouldn't let him handle it because I thought, well, after his mother had been so nice and his father had put me up it wouldn't be right for me to end up letting their boy cut his thumb off, which I figured he was likely to do, being fairly excitable like most boys are." Wolf pulled a stick out of the fire and lit a cigarette from a pack of Camels Steven had given him when he had seen that Wolf rolled his own from a bag of Bull Durham. Wolf was not old, perhaps thirty-five, but he held the cigarette like many old-timers, for whom smoking is an act in itself, during which you do not do anything except smoke, having learned in a time when it was a chore to smoke because you had to go to the trouble of rolling it up, with the paper and the sack and so on. Now so many people hold cigarettes so casually because all they have to do is whip one out and plug it in. And there seems to be little joy in it. But for Wolf, smoking was still an object in itself. When he wanted a cigarette, he would say, "I'm going to smoke a cigarette." Then he would put down whatever he was doing and go about the job of smoking as if he had said, "I'm going to build a fire," and started chopping wood. He held the factory-rolled Camel between his thumb and index finger, looked at it carefully, studied it, lit it, drew a long draft of smoke, and blew it into the still air. Only then did he continue talking.

"Anyway, after breakfast we went down to the university there. I had never been to a university. He showed me a little of the—what do they call it? The land there?"

"Campus," Steven said. His voice sounded strangely resonant in the cold clear air. He realized he hadn't said anything for a long time and Steven first became aware that though Wolf wasn't whispering, he was speaking very quietly. Steven's own voice sounded out of place, loud compared with Wolf's gentle monologue.

"Campus," Wolf said, "that's what he showed me. Beautiful campus. A lot of people, all walking around, all with books. There must have been thousands of dollars worth of books there. Everybody had books. Professor Aarie had a whole wall covered with books, right in a room all his own." Wolf took another thoughtful awkward pull on his Camel. "And machines like you've never seen before. I couldn't even tell you what they were, even though he explained them to me. Big things for taking pictures of things so little that you can't see them without a microscope. He had one that had a camera on the top of it. You put a slide in it and look at something. If you want a picture then you just snap—and there it is." Wolf cocked his head at a noise coming from the wall of trees fifty yards to his left. Steven looked over at the trees, then back at Wolf.

"Bear," Wolf said flatly. "And of course he showed me the machine they used for cutting up the stuff with glass knives. It's kind of like a baloney slicer, except it uses this very little blade and cuts things no bigger than the head of a pin. So we rigged up this vicelike thing and clamped my knife into it and then the professor looked at it through a microscope that had two things like a pair of binoculars and he just said, 'Boy,' like that. So then I looked and it just looked like a straight edge to me only you could see the edges sparkling like there was something shiny buried in the steel. So then he put in one of his tiny little things that he wanted to slice, and with my knife clamped in there instead of a piece of glass he turned the crank and off came this slice of something thinner than paper, and so small it just looked like a speck on the blade unless you looked into the microscope. Under the microscope it looked gray and smooth, like a sliver of mica. He took that and put it onto a screen almost as little as the slice itself. Then we went into a room down the hall where there was a thing he called a microscope of some kind but it wasn't like any microscope I'd ever seen. It had a screen inside of a glass box that glowed green when you turned it on. It was about eight feet tall and made of burnished steel with things sticking out on all sides and a control panel with as many dials as a cockpit of an airplane. Looked like some of the machines I'd seen on a submarine when I went aboard to visit a buddy of mine who was in the Navy at New London, Connecticut. Had cables as thick as my wrist coming out of the top and this little holder on the side inside a door maybe four inches square that was like a hatch on a sub. Well, he put the screen with the slice on it into the holder and shut the hatch and when he turned the machine on there was a picture of I don't know what on the green screen in the glass box and the professor got all excited about this and said he'd never seen anything like it before. I asked what it was pointing down at the screen and he said, 'Oh, this? This is just liver.' And I asked him what was so special about liver and he said that wasn't what he was talking about. He had never seen metal cut a slice like that. Then he went into this long speech about what a big deal it was when they realized you could cut thinner with glass and then later on with diamonds because metal had not been good enough, no matter who they went to or what kind of metals they used, they could never get anything sharp enough to do work like this. He said the glass blade is so much sharper it makes the razor blade seem like an ice-cream scoop. And he said this slice he'd cut with my knife was better than the slices he got with glass and immediately offered to buy my knife from me. Well, I told him I liked him a lot and was glad to help but that this knife was sort of my life, being that I'm a guide and all. I told him, you know, what if I give you this knife and then I go out and get stuck in the middle of nowhere with no knife? I'll die."

And Steven thought maybe he was easy to listen to because he was oddly articulate. He was only half literate but spoke as if he had spent a lot of time around educated people and then Steven thought, of course he spent a lot of time around educated people. Or at least around people with a good deal more money than Wolf had because he was a guide for the kind of trips that only people with money could take. You weren't going to find Wolf up there with a gang of workers from a steel mill in Indiana. He'd spent years hanging out with judges, doctors, Ernest Hemingways.

"Well, this went back and forth and finally I told him that I'd put in an order with Briar if he wanted, so Briar could make him one just like this. We finally settled on that and I took down the professor's address and he gave me a deposit on the knife to give to Briar and we shook hands and that was that." Wolf had taken only a few puffs of the cigarette but it had burned down to his fingers and he threw it into the fire after trying unsuccessfully to get one last puff out of it. Steven offered him the jug of whiskey and he took it and just wet his lips before going on.

"At least I thought that was that because Briar wouldn't make one for him. Said his knives were hunting knives for hunters and that he didn't want any goddamned professors coming around studying him or his knives and he didn't want any of his knives in any goddamned lab-bore-uh-tory— that's how he talked, lab-bore-uh-tory—and the old man is pretty set in his ways so I didn't argue with him. He just flat refused to make one for the professor. Said the bastard was probably trying to steal his secret and patent it and make a million bucks, which I knew wasn't true. Professor Aarie wouldn't do that, I don't think." Wolf pulled his hands out of his gloves and held them close to the fire for a moment. He reached around behind his back and picked a log without looking and put it on top of the fire.

"Why do you think he'll make me one?" Steven asked.

" 'Cause you're a painter," Wolf said as if it were the most obvious thing in the world.

"Lithographer," Steven said. He rarely painted anymore.

"Call it what you want, old Briar paints and he likes other painters. He's not too good but he enjoys it. Been doing it for years and years. If I tell him you're a hunter, angler, woodsman, *and* a painter, he'll make you a fine knife for sure. A lot of the old boys up there make fun of Briar for painting. They've been making fun of him for probably forty years. There's not another painter, good or bad, around that place for a thousand miles. Aren't hardly any pictures for that matter. Briar writes off to a mail-order bookstore in Seattle for picture books and the old boys make fun of him for that too. Of course, it's all in fun but I think deep down Briar would like to meet with another painter once in a while. I think all along he really wanted to be a painter instead of a knife maker or a blacksmith, no matter how good and he knows he's never going to amount to anything as a painter so while he doesn't let on that it bothers him, I think their poking fun at him sometimes does bother him."

Wolf squinted now, suddenly, as if something had stung him. He shot a hard frowning glance at Steven. Then conspiratorially, he posed a question. "You wouldn't consider giving Briar a picture would you?"

Steven shrugged, raising his eyebrows: "Sure," he said, "why not?"

"Goddamn," Wolf said, hitting his knee with a balled fist. "I bet that would just knock the old man smooth out. Do you realize what that would mean to him? A real painter from the States, who makes his living painting, I mean actually supports himself and probably in pretty good style?" Wolf was clearly excited by the proposition. "Goddamn, that'd surely do it. No telling what he'd do."

"Consider it done," Steven said. "I'll pick out one of my best prints and pack it up. I'll send that and the money to you to give to Briar." He sat there and Wolf abruptly stopped, as if he had never been talking in the first place because the matter, as far as he was concerned, was settled. Steven put his hands out to the fire and warmed them. Then he smoked a cigarette with that casual indifference of people who smoke a lot while working. He listened to the Canadian night and watched the northern lights. The bear came back by their camp later that night and stopped nearby, still hidden in the trees. Then it moved on into the woods, crashing as it went. Steven and Wolf built up the fire and slept in down bags close to it. Wolf kept a twelve-gauge shotgun loaded and cocked next to him, though there was little chance that anything like a bear would come near their fire.

❀   ❀   ❀   ❀

In his kitchen Steven watched the meat and onions sizzling now in the olive oil and took in the aromatic steam. From a rack he took cumin, oregano, garlic powder, chili powder, curry, cilantro, celery salt, and cayenne pepper. He put some of each into the pot, first crushing the oregano and cilantro in the palm of his hand until it was as fine as the garlic powder and then dusting it over the onions and meat. It was his own recipe and he didn't tell those who ate it how it was done. It's a bowl of Texas Red, he said when asked, just an ordinary bowl of Texas Red. He stirred in the spices and smelled the pot to see if it was right. He didn't have to taste it. He knew from the smell if it needed anything, except salt, which he couldn't smell but could add later if he needed. After sniffing the pot twice he took out the chili powder again and spooned more of it over the meat and stirred it again.

The mixture was very red now and rusty looking. Steven put the spices back on the rack and opened the refrigerator. He took two Dos Equis beer bottles and opened them. He put one up to his lips and bubbled it several times and set it on the table next to the stove. He took the other bottle and poured it into the cooking pot. The beer foamed furiously at the heat of the pot and a thick head five inches deep rose out of the pot. The ugly brown foam was flecked with patches of chili powder, which looked like a blood-rust fungus spreading on the surface of a septic pool. The immediate effect of adding a fresh, cold beer to a pot of Texas Red was truly disgusting, but after the foam went down about two minutes later and the pot looked normal again, the smell was just right and Steven knew the beer would do something that would insure that special flavor all the other Texas Red cooks he knew could not achieve.

He wasn't sure exactly what the beer did but one night

after drinking considerable amounts of Dos Equis while the pot simmered, he had, for no particular reason, poured the last beer into the pot, saying, "Here, old Red, you're doing all the work, you have one on me." He had been alternating the beers with shots of tequila and he saw no reason that his old buddy, Texas Red, shouldn't at least have a drink. "You must be thirsty from eating all that chili powder," he had mumbled, tossing the empty bottle into the trash, then promptly sat down on the couch, fell asleep for an hour, and awoke with a splitting headache. He remembered the pot of Red and ran into the kitchen, but the pot was alright. The addition of the extra liquid in the form of beer had saved it from burning while he slept. And when he tasted it, he realized that he had stumbled on a truly unique Texas Red ingredient.

So now that the beer was settling down in the pot, he took tomatoes and peeled them, chopped them finely, and added them to the mixture. He knew that many of the finest men in this business likened the use of tomatoes in a pot of Red to putting catsup on filet mignon in a fancy restaurant, but Steven knew how he liked his Red and no one seemed to object too strongly when he served it to them. Besides, he wasn't trying to please purists, he was simply trying to make a good bowl of Red.

Steven took the stairs two at a time, holding the beer in one hand and entered the studio he had set up on the second floor in the room with the most windows and best light—a room probably intended to be the master bedroom. Laid out on a long workbench before the windows was the stone on which Steven had drawn about half of the composition. In photographic detail the head of a beautiful woman was completed. Sketched out beneath this was the body of a rhinoceros beetle, with claws extending up before her face. She observed the claws with detached, bemused curiosity, her head slightly cocked as if someone were showing her a mathematical equation she was attempting to understand. Near the workbench was a large press for printing the stone and along the walls were racks for drying the prints and thin, wide drawers for filing them. Above and among the furnishings, hanging at Steven's eye level were several of his prints.

One of them was the first of twenty-five impressions of a picture he had made for Briar, a picture of a hunting knife that would have been forty yards long in real life, slicing open a low slung, ranch-style home in the suburbs. The home stood among others just like it and in the driveways were Cadillacs and Lincoln Continentals. The home was cleanly split in half through the dining room. A startled husband, fork lifted with a piece of meat speared on the end, stared in disbelief at his terrified wife across the chasm left as the dinner table was split by the blade, which had continued on through the floor and foundation, making a perfect split in the earth large enough to swallow a city bus. Out in the driveway their Cadillac was sliced smoothly from bumper to bumper and the two halves were lying on their doors like the precisely bisected chambered nautiluses one can buy in curio shops by the sea.

After returning from the fishing trip with Wolf, Steven had decided that he would make a print especially for the old man instead of simply picking an existing picture. When he finished it and mailed it off to Wolf with a deposit of $100 for the knife, he brought it to the gallery that handled his work—a prestigious place in midtown Manhattan—and George, the owner, had immediately put a price of $750 on it. In the first week that it hung there, George sold four of the prints, and Steven wondered about Briar, sitting up there in (Steven imagined) a log cabin with a potbellied stove, working away on a hunting knife that normally sold for $300, with a $100 deposit and a fancy, $750 New York gallery lithograph in a frame that Steven picked himself that cost another $75. He saw the picture hanging there in the Yellowknife Canadian wilderness, and the old boys coming into Briar's place and looking at it and he wondered what they would say or think. He imagined Briar painted landscapes—that's what most amateur painters do. Maybe some portraits or a deer, a moose, some ducks.

Of course, he didn't know. Didn't know who Briar was or what he painted. Wolf had said Briar was no good at it but he hadn't described the work, nor had Steven thought to ask: So many people paint as a hobby.

Five and a half weeks after the print and money order were mailed off to Wolf, a letter came back from Wolf with the money order in it. It was printed entirely in uppercase on lined notebook paper in a deliberate hand:

BRIAR LIKED THE PICHER SO MUCH HE WOULD NOT TAKE ANY MONEY. HE IS BADLY BACK OR-DERED ON HIS KNIVES BUT HE SAID HE WOULD MAKE YOU ONE IN A MONTH.
ROBERT B. WOLF.

When Steven received the check and note from Wolf, he sat down at the typewriter and wrote back to Wolf: *Dear Bob— Tell the old man I appreciate his kindness and am glad to have my work admired by a fellow artist. Also, tell him that if he is ever down this way for any reason I will be mighty offended if he doesn't come have dinner with me. Hope you're doing well. Don't feed the bears. Best, Steve.*

He had originally asked Wolf for Briar's address but Briar had none. In the summertime you could get a letter to Briar by mailing it to him in care of general delivery, Yellowknife, because the local postmaster knew him and would take it out to him or give it to him when Briar came into town for supplies. During the winter the mails were a different prob-lem. The roads were closed early in fall and not opened again until late in spring. Mail was flown above Yellowknife to places like Anchorage, Fairbanks, Nome, Valdez. But if any arrived in Yellowknife, it was irregular, unreliable, and not very safe if you were sending anything of value. Wolf, however, knew a journalist named Joslyn Phillips who knew Briar. She had been traveling the ice road that since 1964 Ted Betters had been cutting across the hundreds of lakes that dotted the area in order to move supplies with trucks that would otherwise have had to wait until spring. Joslyn was the only journalist Wolf had ever met whom he liked. And even though she worked for the *New Yorker*, she was as tough and woods smart as any man or woman who had been born and raised all his life in the Canadian wilderness. She traveled the ice road two whole seasons to write a book about it and had met Briar through Ted Betters and Wolf through Briar. So, knowing she was coming through on her way north and then back again and up and back all winter, Wolf had arranged with her to stop by Briar's with the painting and check from Steven. On her way back down with Ted and a broken deuce-and-a-quarter Joslyn had returned to Wolf with the letter and check from Briar.

Two months later the knife had arrived, shipped by Wolf from Vancouver by registered mail and insured for $300. It was eight o'clock on a Monday morning and Steven was hung over and in bed with a lady named Marjorie, whose last name he couldn't remember, whom he had gotten to his bed by offering to show her his lithographs. ("Believe it or not," he had said, "that's what I do." She had demurred at first, finally agreeing, seeing that Steven was articulate, well dressed, polite, and not very much like most of the men who usually asked Marjorie to their homes. Once she had seen the prints she was enthusiastic and liked them very much. "How much do they cost?" she asked. She said she wanted to go to the gallery and buy one. When Steven told her they ranged from about $200 up to about $750 she didn't believe him. When they had gotten good and drunk he gave her a small one to have framed. It was a tree frog holding a princess in its paw, which had suction cups for fingers. Then they made love in Steven's bed and fell asleep about three in the morning.)

When the delivery boy rang the bell, it seared through Steven's head, tearing the dumb, drugged, dreamless fabric of sleep that results from drinking too much. Wrapping himself in a ratty robe he'd had for years, he stumbled down and looked through the wide angle lens to see who was there. In his state of disorientation, the boy looked like some kind of weird monster, distorted by the lens. In truth, the boy looked like something Steven would have drawn. He opened the door and the boy said, as delivery people have a way of doing, "Delivery for Mr. Copeland," as if he had not in fact awakened Steven, as if Steven didn't look like something one would cough up in the morning after a bad night of cigarettes and tuberculosis. Steven signed the yellow page held to a legal-sized clipboard and, looking at his signature, saw it as it appeared at the bottom of prints, saw the yellow page with its scrawled signatures and stiff black type as a strange lithograph of some kind, as if he had just signed his name to something he didn't do and he immediately wanted to take it back from the boy and tear it up but the boy was gone and Steven stood watching his back receding. In Steven's hand was the slim, heavy package.

He set it down on his way upstairs and without even wondering, fell immediately back to sleep beside Marjorie, who had not been awakened by the bell and was snoring loudly, her mouth agape, her many amalgam fillings and gold crowns winking like tawdry jewels from the back of her mouth in the sour cud smell of her sleeping innards.

They awoke at a quarter to twelve and the day was bright and extremely cold for New York, barely five degrees. The house wasn't really made for that kind of cold. There was frost on the inside of the windowpanes. Marjorie ground Kivu coffee in a Braun electric coffee mill and ran boiling water over it and through a filter into a glass pot, which sat on a warming plate. At the kitchen table Steven sat and remembered the package. He got up and brought it to the table, seeing that it had originated from Vancouver but not having about him wits enough to connect it either to Wolf or to Briar. He ran his thumbnail along the taped seam and pried open the box, which was filled with tissue. He was barely awake.

Fortunately, probably as a result of previous unpleasant experiences, Briar had packed the knife inside its own custom-made, leather scabbard. Otherwise, Steven probably would have sustained a serious cut, for instead of removing all the paper to see what the box contained, he simply plunged his fingers in and felt around until he got hold of the scabbard, which was handsomely decorated with Canada honkers expertly hammered into the leather. When he realized what the box contained and what he had almost done to his hand, his heart jumped. Steven removed the knife from its sheath. It had an odd look to it, not like any new knives he had seen. It was not shiny but had a clean look to it, a matte sheen, a dull, pale graphite appearance as if a light came from within the metal itself like the light in a Vermeer painting. He looked at the edge. It looked like any other knife edge. There was nothing to see. On the blade where it met the handle, perpendicular to the length of the knife Briar had signed it with an etching tool of some sort. It said "Marshall Briar" in flowing script and beneath: "handmade for Steven Copeland" in smaller script and then a date written out. On the blade was a finely rendered picture of a moose, looking up at Steven from where it stood, knee-deep in a bog with a mouthful of something leafy.

He turned the knife over and over, being careful not to touch the blade and make the same mistake Professor Aarie had made.

"What's that?" Marjorie asked, cheerfully stirring up eggs in a bowl and frying bacon at the stove. The coffee was ready and she brought Steven a steaming cup, set it in front of him with a little pitcher of cream and a bowl of sugar and said, "Oh, you got a new knife."

"Yes," Steven said and set it on the table in front of him. He wanted to use it right away, to see it work its magic. Marjorie reached for it and Steven grabbed her wrist. "It's not an ordinary knife," he said gently. "It's extremely sharp."

"I like to keep my kitchen knives sharp too," she said. "Can I see it?"

"Yes," Steven said, letting go of her wrist and picking up the knife, "but first I want to show you just how sharp it is because I don't want to be taking you to the hospital. I'm too hung over to drive."

Then he went to the refrigerator, took out the flank steak and tossed it up. As it began its descent he quickly brought the knife, blade upward, through its middle. At first it seemed he had missed but he held out his left hand and the steak landed in his palm with a plop. It still appeared to be untouched. Then he picked the steak from his hand and it came away cut neatly in half as if it had come from the butcher shop that way.

"Darn," Marjorie said. "Where'd you get that?"

"A man in Canada," Steven said, handing it to her carefully. "So please be careful. Your hands are too pretty to mess up."

"Thank you, I'll use something else," she smiled at him, putting it down carefully and taking a knife from the drawer.

At the counter she sliced mushrooms to put into the scrambled eggs. Steven put his knife back into the scabbard. While the bacon was cooking Marjorie sat across the table from Steven and drank a cup of black coffee while Steven smoked the first cigarette of the day and drank his coffee with cream and sugar. "What's this mean, 'Kivu?'" Marjorie asked, holding the bag of coffee beans and looking at the word that had been handwritten on a white, stick-on label.

"It's the name of the place the coffee came from. It's Congolese coffee. From the Congo in Africa. Now they don't call it the Congo anymore. They call it Zaire."

"That's where Ali fought Frazier," Marjorie said, pleased that she recognized the name. "Why do you get coffee all the way from there when they sell it right here in the Safeway?"

"I like it," Steven sipped delicately at the hot cup. "Anyway, they sell this right here in the store too. I don't exactly go to Africa for coffee."

"I guess not," Marjorie said and they ate breakfast and made love again on the couch in Steven's living room and then Marjorie had to leave because she was a waitress at a bar that opened at five in the evening and she hadn't brought a change of clothes and had to get all the way to the east side and then back uptown.

It was only after Marjorie had left that Steven noticed the letter from Briar in the bottom of the box. It was written—possibly with a quill—in the same careful script that appeared on the knife, like a wedding announcement, on a page from a sketch pad with the Strathmore watermark clearly visible behind the writing. The note said:

Dear Mr. Copeland:

I am pleased to send you herewith the knife you ordered. It is one of a kind and I trust you will find it useful in your hunting and fishing. The handle is walrus tusk, given me by a man I know in Kotzebue, Alaska. With use, the handle should change color like a good meerschaum pipe and take on a chamois hue.

I wanted to thank you personally for sending me your exquisite lithograph. I've never seen that kind of control of the tusche-water matrix to bring up detail.

I realize that you've already done me a great favor in

sending me one of your valuable and beautiful prints but forgive me for presuming to ask you for another favor. As you know, I live in a relatively remote place and supplies of even the most basic kinds are terribly hard to come by. I noticed that your print was made on Rives B.F.K. paper. Is there any way that you could ship me a small supply of that in the 16 x 20 inch size? I have tried to write the company to place an order and they will not ship to Yellowknife. It would mean a great deal to me as I am now reduced to using ordinary papers such as the one you see before you.

Again, my sincerest gratitude for your kindness and I wish you luck hunting and fishing.

Sincerely, Marshall Briar, Jr.

P.S. I don't suppose I have to warn you to exercise caution in the use of your new knife but I make it a practice to point out to all new customers that it has an abnormally keen edge.

Steven was so surprised that he laughed out loud. Somehow—for no particularly logical reason—he had gotten the impression that Briar was semiliterate and more a woodsman than a man of letters. Well, Steven thought, he may not be exactly a man of letters but he sure could write a polite, lucid letter, in contrast to Wolf's block-printed "PICHER."

He immediately packaged up one hundred sheets of Rives B.F.K. paper in between two stiff pieces of cardboard and sent it off to Briar in care of Wolf, who, two weeks later, gave it to Joslyn, who in another two weeks placed it in Marshall Briar's hands, at the same time placing a kiss on his withered cheek. When the old man opened up the package and saw what it was, a tear came to his eye. He had not seen paper that good in fifteen years. Steven's note read, simply:

My Dear Mr. Briar:

Your knife is marvelous. Please accept the enclosed as an expression of my admiration.

Cordially, Steven.

P.S. I do hope we meet sometime. If you happen to come to the States, let me know and I will make the trip to see you or if you are ever on our east coast, let's have dinner.

When Steven read the note before mailing the package he thought: The man's seventy-four years old. What are the chances that he will ever get down this way?

✿   ✿   ✿   ✿

Steven began preparing to work on his stone. The smell of Texas Red rose from the kitchen, crawled up the stairway, and curled around him. His studio filled with the tingling odor of Texas Red and a warm infusion of sunlight. The limestone shone gray in the sun coming through the window, and for the first time Steven realized that it was the same color as the knife, though he had had the stone for three years and the knife for eight. That was the color—the same as Bavarian gray limestone. He hadn't heard from Briar after receiving a thank-you note for the paper and a promise to visit if they were ever in the same place. The man would be eighty-two years old if he still happened to be alive.

Wolf had died of exposure two years earlier when the plane he was riding in went down near Hudson Bay. It had made a safe emergency landing when, after a carburetor heart valve stuck, his carburetor iced up and the engine of the Cessna 172 stopped. Wolf was both an excellent cold-weather survivor and in the company of a good ex-military pilot and woodsman, but no help was forthcoming and they were not found until spring when a fresh search party was sent out. Wolf and the pilot had done a remarkable job and had apparently stayed alive for quite a while, but the conditions were finally just too fierce and they both froze to death, apparently one at a time, the last to die finding it impossible to go on under the circumstances without the other. After Wolf's death Steven had stopped hunting the Canadian territories. He had never known of or met Joslyn and so had no way of contacting Briar except to make the trip to Yellowknife and ask around, which he was not about to do.

About two years after he had gotten the knife, he was on a grouse hunting trip in central Michigan one fall with some friends and it occurred to him what the single most unusual characteristic of the knife was. With three hunters they had had an exceptionally lucky day, taking five partridge and two woodcocks in as many hours. Back at the house where he was staying, his friends were standing around a stump drinking beer while Steven cleaned the birds quickly and expertly, like a surgeon. The knife moved through flesh as if through water. Billie, the crazier of Steven's two friends, had had someone mail him a kilo of hashish and it had arrived that morning tightly bound in layers of brown paper and string. Now Billie held the package there, near the stump, trying to work the knots and set free the wondrous, blonde genie, but they were tied too tightly and he asked Steven for his knife to cut the string. When Steven handed him the knife, he said, "Be careful it's. . ." and stopped, about to say "loaded," perhaps because he had been handling a shotgun all day long but more so, he realized, because that was how he regarded the knife: It was like handling a loaded gun. And he saw that those two years since he'd had it he'd been treating it with the same quiet respect he reserved for rattlesnakes and firearms. You only make one mistake with a gun and then somebody is hurt—or dead. So you make no mistake at all. And even though he assumed logically that the worst that could have happened was the loss of a couple of joints of a finger, he had still treated the knife as if it could kill.

He had not opened his beer because he was tired from a day of hunting and did not want to concentrate on drinking a beer and dressing out the birds at the same time, at least not with Briar's knife. And another thing: He didn't tell people about the knife unless he had to. His two friends, for example, didn't know about it. He only mentioned its unusual properties for the sake of safety, as he had to Marjorie. And now, looking at Billie with his kilo of hashish and his hand out, he thought, *how can I explain it to him? He's a hunter. He's been around guns and knives all his life. And I'm going to tell him this is a sharp knife? He won't understand. Of course it's sharp. It's a knife. But he doesn't know sharp.* So Steven simply reached over where Billie was holding the box and allowed the knife to touch the top of it where the string was knotted about fourteen different ways. The string fell away. Billie looked twice at it and frowned at Steven, who had gone back to cleaning the birds with sure, deft motions of the knife. The other man had missed the exchange.

❖ ❖ ❖ ❖

Marshall Briar showed up while Steven was in the kitchen getting another Dos Equis, having tasted the pot of Red and added some beer and water because it was getting to the point where it might burn and he wanted to spend a while upstairs working on the stone. Steven opened the door when he heard Briar's knock and saw a large-boned, thin, old man dressed in an ancient but neat suit, a top coat, and a hat.

"Mister Copeland?" The man inquired.

"Yes," Steven said with no idea who the man was.

"I'm Marshall Briar," the man said. "I was in Boston. I thought I'd stop by."

Steven didn't react at first. It was too much of a surprise. Then he shook Briar's hand, smiled, motioned him into the kitchen, and shut out the cold. Briar immediately took off his hat and stood looking around the kitchen, which was done in raw woods and tile. Steven took Briar's hat and started to lead him into the house, but Briar stood for a moment sniffing the air, looking around with a curious expression on his face.

"My," he said finally. "That smells good." He sniffed the air twice more and smiled at Steven, his face shattering into hundreds of deeply cut lines.

"Texas Red," Steven said smiling. "It's almost done. Come in, let me take your coat."

They went into the living room; Steven hung up Briar's coat and hat and offered him a drink. Briar requested a small tumbler of bourbon, and Steven brought a bottle and two glasses.

"I've used your knife for eight years," Steven said, breaking the silence that took over while Briar was obviously resting and composing himself from the cold and (Steven assumed) a walk. Briar lifted his face from the tumbler of bourbon and looked at Steven.

"They're good little knives, aren't they?" he asked thoughtfully.

"There's nothing like them in the world," Steven said.

Briar took another long drink of his bourbon and seemed to straighten up somewhat from where he sat on the couch. He looked around the living room at the lithographs and sculptures, the stereo system, bookshelves, carpeting, and potted plants. Steven didn't say anything. He didn't feel he needed to. Finally, Briar spoke.

"You've done very well," he said. Then he stopped and looked around the room again. After a few moments he said, "Did you hear Wolf died?"

"Yes," Steven said. "He was a good one."

"The best," Briar said. "When I heard he'd gone down, I joined with the search party, though they didn't want me to because I'm an old man. I insisted. Joslyn came with me."

"Joslyn?" Steven asked.

Briar told him about Joslyn, then stopped and sipped the bourbon, which he had been holding with both of his large hands since it was given to him. "When the official search ended, Joz and I hired a plane and continued for a solid week, but it was no use. There was too much ice and snow. Everything was just plain white. A thousand square miles of it." Briar stopped his narrative and set his bourbon on the coffee table. He carefully removed a package of Pall Malls from his coat pocket and extracted a slim cigarette from the red wrapper. Steven took out his lighter and reached across, holding the flame in front of Briar's face. Holding the cigarette with thumb and two fingers, Briar deliberately drew the flame in and started the end burning, watching it as best he could down the length of his craggy nose. He took several long slow drafts and then sat back, holding it carefully, as if it were a cigar. He brought the tumbler to his lips and sighed. Only then did he continue.

"We found them in the spring time," he said. "Joz cried. She and Wolf were lovers for many years. No one knew. Joz was married but she was always away because she loved adventure and because her husband was boring. But she had talked to me about herself and Wolf often. They didn't have much chance to see each other." Briar lifted the Pall Mall and took several long puffs, blowing each one out carefully, watching the smoke as it drifted across the room in the still air, giving definition to the bright spokes of winter sunshine that knifed into the room. He took another drink of bourbon. "Wolf and his pilot did well though and I was glad for them, not because they died but because they had done everything right, all the way up to the end. They had had two .30–'06 rifles in the plane when they put down. They rigged trap lines and baited them. It was apparent that they had trapped a lot of game. They used the rifles in the traps. A moose would come up, nibble the bait, and get his head blown off. Very precise. Joz and I studied the camp. They had rationed their fuel. They had a lot of fuel in the plane and used it carefully. They had good markers out but no one saw them. Trees cut and furrows dug that you could see from the air in winter. We just didn't happen to fly over that spot. They ate well and kept their morale up, just like you're supposed to. There was a very clear and complete log—a very important thing in survival. You keep track of your achievements and reward yourself for them—record them. You keep track of your failures and remember not to make the same mistake twice. That is half of what keeps you alive. But no one came. No one came."

Steven lit a cigarette and took a pull from his beer, then a sip from the glass of bourbon. The sun was slanting into the room now.

"When we arrived at their camp, Dean, the pilot, was still in his bedroll. He must have died in his sleep and Wolf must have left him like that. There was no way to bury him, no way to dig. Wolf may have already been going a little crazy by then anyway. It's hard staying calm in a situation like that. Anyway, Wolf was sitting in what was left of the cockpit, after they'd used it for so long as a shelter. His mouth was open as if he were shouting and he was gripping the wheel as if he thought he were flying. They were both frozen solid." Briar paused then for a full minute. He smoked and drank and looked at the room. "But that was more than two years ago, wasn't it?" Again he stopped and observed the room with that absent pleasure you might see in the face of an old person watching a child play. "At eighty-two it seems like yesterday."

"I think the Red is done by now," Steven said. "Will you join me for a bowl?"

"Ah," Briar said, as if Steven had made a very complicated point in an argument. "That I will."

Briar sat at the dining-room table while Steven brought the pot and set it on a wicker pad. Then he set out two bowls, big spoons, and poured two fresh beers into tall glasses. He went back to the kitchen once more for butter, a dish of crackers, and two napkins before sitting across from Briar. With a ladle they each served themselves portions from the pot. Briar took his first bite and his face brightened.

"Ah," he said, "that is really good." He took another bite. Steven smiled and nodded, eating from his bowl.

Briar ate two bowls and drank his beer. Steven showed him the studio and a number of prints. He offered Briar paper to take back to Yellowknife but Briar wouldn't take it. Finally, Briar agreed to accept a new print Steven had made but insisted that Steven take another knife in exchange. Steven was reluctant but finally took it and Briar left with the print.

❀   ❀   ❀   ❀

Steven put the knife in a drawer for future use, having no place to hang it in the kitchen and somehow the days just passed away and he never took it out to look at it. Anyway, a Briar knife was not the type of knife you just took out to look at. Somehow (at least Steven felt this) it was not to be trifled with, you either used it or you didn't. Finally, in the spring, he was rummaging through a drawer and came upon the second knife. It was early in the morning and he sat down at the table before a cup of coffee and withdrew the knife from its sheath, realizing what, he thought later, should have been obvious at the time. There, on the blade, was Briar's own mark and a small picture of Briar himself, more or less as he had appeared that day he stopped by. It was an incredible job of etching, a small self-portrait, shaded with minute raspings of the metal and signed with Briar's own hand. It read (almost a parody, Steven thought): "Marshall Briar—His Own Knife."

Steven was so startled by this that for the first time he forgot himself in the presence of a Briar knife and turned the blade with fascination in his hand and then, lightly, with the point of his index finger, touched it. The red bead formed immediately and swelled and then broke over the crescent of his nail. There was no pain. Steven brought the knife into the kitchen and set it on the counter. He washed the cut in the sink and put a Band-Aid on the finger, tightening it so the bleeding stopped. And then, without even thinking about it, he was cutting meat again for another pot of Texas Red. An hour later the mail came. There was a letter from Joslyn Phillips. It was written on plain white typing paper in a scratchy, awkward hand of someone who wrote quickly, urgently. It said: "Dear Mr. Copeland: Marshall Briar died May 3. He said to tell you. Joslyn Phillips."

Rainbow

gold

Jane was on a rib. This affected all of us in one way or another. Renata looked at the stars for three nights in a row and came to awaken us in the morning saying, simply, "Gold." Federico knew immediately what she meant. She might have said something more to Federico. She always went back to his bed after waking us. Federico told Jane to make gold. Gold was the configuration, he said; gold had to be made. Jane was adamant. "No gold," she said and walked off to sit in the sun and do her breathing exercises.

I had no opinion about gold except that what Renata saw in the stars was often right. For three nights she saw gold, and when Jane sat by the fire that evening and told us what she was going to do instead of making gold, we sensed something would go wrong.

We were smoking her grass and each of us had enjoyed the benefits of many other potions she had made from various things she grew. We had trusted her for this. But Carla said, "You are wearing the clothes I made for you, and I say you should not do it."

"Each year I make good conditions for you," Steven said, "so that your plants will flourish and give you what you need." He paused and added, almost as a threat, "If you do this, conditions may fail."

"Gold is the configuration," Philip said. "Renata is not often wrong about this." Philip stood and stretched to his full height: well over six feet. "I have made all your furniture," he said, "and I do not think you should do it."

"I've written about this," Lady said. "It's in my book. In the book someone dies. I had a dream about it. Three nights I've dreamed about someone dying. I can't say what you should do but I think Gregory can say. He's the one who counts."

Gregory sat at the edge of the circle of light made by the fire where the night air was warm. Gregory played his flute. I played the guitar, half listening to the argument. Everyone stopped to listen to what Gregory and I would say. My guitar said good-bye to Gregory. The notes that came out knew Jane would go ahead with her plan, and Gregory would not stop her because Gregory trusted Jane. Gregory's flute said trust. The notes hung in the air above us. My guitar said good-bye to them as each of us took one last look. Lisa held onto Steven's arm and cried. Lisa liked Gregory a lot. Neither of them spoke very much and they seemed to understand something very basic about each other's reasons for this silence.

"You can't do it!" Carla shouted. But everyone knew by then what would happen. The stars said gold. The music said no gold.

baby

Lisa was getting ready to make our first baby. Lady and I often spoke of babies. We wanted to have the first one. It was a historical event for our group. No one had babies yet. Federico had been waiting a long time to deliver one. Now Lisa was going to have it. Federico examined her and said yes. We were having lunch. Steven called for a celebration. Renata said she saw something in the stars she didn't understand. She hadn't seen the baby but this was clearly in the stars. Philip promised to make the finest crib he was capable of making. He began talking with Carla about the wood and design. Carla told Philip what fabrics she could weave for its lining, what clothes she could make for the baby. Everyone wanted Renata to look at the stars and say whether it would be a male or a female. Renata promised to do this as soon as it was dark.

Steven said it was his baby and would be a boy. Lisa said

yes, it felt like a boy. Federico said there was no way to tell yet.

We stopped work. Lady put away her papers and I canceled my trip to the city. By nightfall we had smoked a great deal. Federico said Lisa shouldn't have too much grass, that it might not be good in the early stages of pregnancy.

Lady had awakened me the night before to tell me a dream. She dreamed of walking along the road that leads to the waterfall. She walked almost a mile, just a fourth of the way, when she met a young child coming from the other direction. He said the waterfall had frozen. Lady told him it was impossible, the weather was not cold enough. The boy said, nevertheless, the water had stopped falling, it was solid enough to walk on. Lady laughed and asked the boy where he lived, what his name was. He said he was looking for a home, he had none and had never met a person before and so had never been called by any name, that no one had talked to him and so he had no name. Lady told him to come home with her and she would call him whatever he liked. He said he liked to be called Solomon. Lady said she went on and found the waterfall frozen solid. It hung motionless in the air. When she stepped on the water it broke and she fell through.

Gregory played, stopping only to eat and smoke. I played my guitar again. In the air our notes stood like a frozen waterfall. Steven asked Lady what Solomon meant. She said, "Peace." Later that night Lady asked me why we wouldn't have a baby. I said I didn't know. We made love again. She said she knew there were no babies inside her.

city

The next day I went to the city. At the outset we determined I was the only one strong enough to go to the city. The others would have died or lost their senses. I, on the other hand, was considered dead by some, crazy by others, strong by still others, but in each case the one to be sent to the city.

In the shadow of the giant building I stood watching people walk past. A couple coaxing a child between them. Young girls, almost women, their faces bright with makeup, their hair washed and washed until it shone like a stone in the tide. Ancient, weathered men, half erect, gathering momentum for another step, portraits of finity. Working men, twenty-eight, thirty, in clothes clean but trailing threads here and there that betrayed their age. A forty-year-old woman in sun-bright pants, barely long enough to cover the lower fold of her buttocks, making a sad picture of proportion. What must she think of herself?

Next to the giant building I looked about the size of half a speck of something motile and soft. I leaned against the outer skin of the structure and felt its mass, its incomprehensible enormity, its quiverings—so minute for something that size . . . and I knew my size. I placed my hands behind my back, palms flat against the skin and tried to calculate. The building was so big as to be out of the realm of dimensions. It had no size. It was a world unto itself and could only be understood in its own terms. Nearby stood another building, half its size. It too was large enough to be a world of its own, but it was relative to the first building, half the first building. To the building, I was something on the order of a marshmallow in the mouth of a whale. When the building swallowed me, it tasted nothing.

Inside it was cool with lighting even cooler—a vague blue iridescence beyond what the eye perceives as light, an absence of darkness that was not light, a quality of the very air that permitted things to be seen without shedding any light on them. Yet people moved in it as if in darkness. They looked at nothing, their eyes turning down or inward, wandering. And extrasensory message told them where not to look, where to place their feet, how to set their faces.

I felt the building digesting me, referring me on to other spots within its passageways, unaware. The vibrations of its materials were more intense within. The very air belonged to the building. The people within were as bacteria must be in an intestine, serving some function, left unnoticed, marginal. In actual fact, the building was owner and operator of the space it occupied, more space than a human could imagine or use or want or even perceive at once.

Little human things clung to the building at various places inside. Racks of dresses stood against walls. Women with wrinkled faces peered at them, fingering the spectacular materials. Cases bolted to the building's floor offered trinkets, shiny and new and expensive, through their glass faces. Pictures that did not depict anything recognizable hung in frames from the walls. Signs, objects, things appeared and faded as I walked through, feeling the greatness of the building.

A light appeared. Green. Above my head. I entered the cage with others, smelled their minute smells. Their decorated senses. On the others things sparkled, jewels, bits of metal attached to their bodies, to their clothing. The others were just barely there, so well hidden were their bodies. Doors slid silently, shutting them all in. I wedged among them, among their flashing lights. The cage moved suddenly causing my stomach to contract and my knees to give way in a surge of giddiness. I held my breath. I felt my feet sinking into the floor of the cage, my knees straining to keep from buckling, the blood draining from my face. There was nothing to hold onto. I waited. Lights flashed at me from every side. The tremors from the building were reaching a pitch, which I found extremely distressing, as if someone had locked a vibrating machine to my skeleton. I felt my heart trying to pump more blood, expanding, working, failing. Then the car stopped. Everything was still. Distant tremblings came to me through a thick barrier, an exceptional locomotive, charging far away. The doors slid open. Glittering lights around me parted, became diffused like a gas being released, rarefied. Then I was nudged from behind and found myself out of the cage, at the top of the building.

At first I thought the sway would throw me to the floor. I caught hold of the wall beside the closing doors, steadied myself. The building moved pendulum-like, from east to west. I thought for a moment I was going to be sick, concentrated hard on thinking of the boat I used to sail in, the rocking of it in an open sea, how I had learned to master the vertigo, to stand, to walk, to ignore it finally. I sought something fixed to look at but from there I could find nothing that wasn't attached to the building.

I worked my way along the pulsing wall toward one of the

large observation windows. A crowd of people three lines deep throbbed before the staring glass eye. The eye inhaled and exhaled with the winds outside. The entire room moved in a thousand different directions, absorbing us.

I attained the window and forced myself between two older women, desperate for a look at something outside the building. Beyond I saw the lake, vast and molten, steel gray, shivering minutely in the wind, its shoreline advancing, retreating, then advancing again. It threw me into a fit of dizziness. I put my palm on the window, felt its icy, sticky crystalline surface, recoiled as if burned, caught my balance; and my eye, rolling, found a sidewalk, one hundred-and-ten stories below, solid, a small, still rule of white in the chaos of motion. I held onto it with my vision and let its stasis drag me toward shore. It worked. My head cleared. On the sidewalk people moved—specks—but demonstrating the sidewalk's solidity. Even the building's vibrating ceased to bother me for a few moments.

Beyond the sidewalk I could see the very curvature of the earth itself. It too was still, a long, hazy half circle—where I did not know. There the sky met the water and they almost became one shade of blue, green, gray, but remained distinct—barely distinct. And it turned away from me as I looked. It turned at the same speed that the hour hand of a clock turns. You have to watch it closely. But, of itself, it was still, a resting muscle.

My distended bladder presented itself within my body. I felt steady, let go of the window. I felt my sea legs, stood balancing, forward, back, now forward again. Beyond the window, a cloud the size of a lake passed by. I moved away from the window, across the room, feeling the floor carefully with each step. I pushed the door, entered, found a metallic gray stall and locked the door. Looking down I saw the water moving back and forth in regular opposition to the building's sway, an intractable body of material, refusing to play the game. I defiled it and left.

I bought a hammer from a city person. From other city persons I bought wood for Philip; fabrics and yarns, threads and needles, and dyes for Carla; supplies for Federico's medicine chest; paper and styli and books for Lady, strings for my guitar; and Coca-Cola for us all. Sometimes Jane needed chemicals and seeds and so on.

There were many items to be had in the city but it was most dangerous going there and the items brought out carried grave dangers with them. When I returned from the city bearing items, Steven always met me at the lemon orchard on the road to the waterfall about a mile from where we lived. Together we placed the items on the ground. If it was afternoon, we had to wait until the next day. If it was before the zenith, we waited until the sun went high as it would go. At this point we lit a fire and Steven made magic to purify the items. Steven was a good magician and nothing impure entered our dwellings through these city items. Afterwards, we loaded the items again and returned home with them. Lisa met us there and looked at them, touched them, smelled them to make sure they were pure.

When this took place, we spent a long time sitting around talking about the items, about their relative merits and flaws, about qualities evident and remembered. This was an occasion for much diversion and fun and I answered questions about the situation at the city. It was fairly bleak. I related anecdotes for those who could not go there.

rain

The rain came. And with it came snakes and insects, diseases and discomforts. But also with it came a purification of the earth. The dust washed back into the earth so the sunlight could shine that much brighter after the rain. The underbelly of the moon would be polished to lustrous ivory and the ring around it would be gone for another six months.

Beforehand, Philip and I made preparations with Lisa and Jane by mixing a compound from certain plants Jane grew. Everyone then spread this on the inside and outside of the leather covering of his home and Steven slept one night in each home to insure safety from the rain.

Renata again insisted on gold. She said she was wrong before. Jane was not to make gold. Renata said we lived near gold and had to find it before Solomon was born. She looked in the stars and saw Solomon walking toward the waterfall. She said Lady was right. The waterfall would freeze. Solomon would be homeless unless we found the gold. Jane said, I am not responsible for finding it and all this won't stop me from working on my potion for Gregory. Renata said, it doesn't matter now what you make for Gregory, if we don't find gold before Solomon is born.

Lady said she had written in her book that the rain would wash us away this time and we would all be forced into the city. Philip said we could rebuild what the rain washed away. Steven said he had made sufficient magic to prevent our being washed away. The conversation became confused because all Renata wanted was for us to agree to find the gold. I said I would look for the gold. Renata admitted the city was near and gold might be found there. I said I would look anywhere for it.

Gregory and I played by the fire. I played the search for gold. My guitar took me to the city and back, to the waterfall, which was not yet frozen and to all the forests around. The trees stood eight stories high around my guitar. The notes hung in awe of the trees but no gold was to be found. My guitar went on searching for the gold. Gregory's flute found the gold immediately and played death. Gregory's flute went to the city and died in suffering with no body. It went to the waterfall and found it frozen forever, the fish stiff and lifeless, inedible. Gregory's flute visited the forest and found the trees chopped, fallen, stripped, burnt, lifeless. Gregory's flute held before us notes that had gaping holes in them where everything had been taken from him. We sat in silence, fearing what would come.

I went to the city and bought plastic to cover Philip's wood and other things that would be damaged by rain.

It was then the rain came. Lisa became ill. Federico said she would be all right. The rain came heavier and heavier. We had never seen rain as heavy. One night the rain was so heavy we all gathered in my home because we were afraid. Lightning came. It seemed to be right outside my door. Each time it exploded we could feel the shock wave from the air. We smoked more of Jane's grass and got very high listening to the lightning and rain. We fell asleep there.

In the morning when the rain subsided Steven and Lisa had no home. Gregory and I sat in the drizzle near the spot where their home had been and played good-bye to it. Their belongings were completely burned. Lady and I took Lisa and Steven into our home, which was the largest.

Renata could see no stars during the rainy reason and became very uneasy. Federico and Jane combined their efforts to make her easier, but even with pills and potions, Renata could not sleep with the rest of us. Each morning she made a new effort to get us to find gold.

steven

Lisa didn't seem to mind so much about the home being blown away. Philip, she said, would build a new one. The baby wasn't due for months. Steven was convinced that because of gold their home was blown away. He blamed Jane for the lack of energy, for the fact that no one had tried to find gold. He thought it was Jane's fault their home was gone. Whenever I would listen, he told me his thoughts about this. I said, if he was so intent on solving our problems with gold, he should go looking for it. I said this knowing Steven could go nowhere. He had never been able to go anywhere. Even his short trips to the lemon orchard left him weak for days afterwards. And now, with Lisa pregnant and ill, he was not about to risk his life looking for gold. When I saw the look on his face, I tried to make him feel better by suggesting he try to make gold. Alchemy was not, I submitted, beyond his powers.

That night Lady and I watched Steven change mud into soap, quartz into bone, hair into glass . . . he was trying everything he knew but could not make gold. At one point he came up with something that looked very much like gold but we all knew it was not.

Following this Steven tried many other methods of producing gold from more common substances. There seemed to be no simple way to find gold. Some of Steven's experiments proved dangerous to all. After he tried to use wheat in one of his formulas, we discovered the whole supply was infested with a small insect. In another attempt he set our house on fire and, though we saved it, many items were burned.

Steven became more and more distant from us. He refused to speak most of the time and snapped at those who spoke to him. Lisa became despondent and begged Steven to give up trying, to join the rest of us in common work. Steven ignored her and the two of them grew further apart. By the time the rain was half over, they weren't sleeping together. This made life in our house most unhappy. We often heard Lisa crying in the night. Lady sometimes went to comfort her but it was no use. She felt Steven was permanently changed.

bear

Three-fourths through the rainy season I went looking for gold with Lady. Philip and Carla were working on Steven's new house. It was slow work because of the rain. Lady and I knew nothing about gold. We had hardly seen any at all in our lives. It was alien to us. But we searched. The first day we walked through two forests and spoke of what to look for. We both knew that gold was not pure when found outside. We examined many rocks. Some contained quartz, others sulfur. None seemed to contain gold.

On the second day we were approached by a bear. It was a large grizzly. We climbed a tree and waited. The bear clawed at the tree, taking large chunks of wood from its base and shaking the upper limbs. We held on. The bear walked a distance and sat down, poking at the ground occasionally and looking up at us. We climbed down and stood by the tree, ready to climb back up if necessary. The bear made no move toward us.

Lady spoke to me in a whisper telling me of a dream she had several nights ago. She said there was a bear in her dream but she couldn't remember why or what happened. All she knew for certain was that the bear wouldn't hurt her.

We approached the bear. He got up and walked away from us, looking over his shoulder. We followed in silence.

The whole second day we walked with the bear, stopping finally, exhausted, unable to go any farther. The bears stopped about fifty yards away and went to sleep.

The next morning we were awakened by the roaring of the bear. The sun was just rising as the bear stood a few feet away, bellowing in our direction. We were so startled we ran and climbed a tree. Again the bear clawed at the base of the tree and again retreated to sit, pawing the ground until we came down. We followed the bear half the third day and ended up in a clearing surrounded on all sides by dense woods.

In the clearing was a single tree, which had been knocked over by lightning. Beneath the massive stalk of the tree a small bear had been trapped. Its mother was standing guard. When we arrived the bear that led us to the clearing sat a distance from the mother and child, waiting for us to do something. It was then Lady remembered the reason the bear wouldn't hurt us in her dream: She was supposed to do something for the bear; the bear needed her help. Now we were faced with the problem of how to get the enormous tree off of the bear cub.

Our first thought was to go for some tools with which to cut the tree but when we made motions to leave, we were opposed by the bear that led us. Seeing that we wouldn't be allowed to leave until we had done something, we both came up to the log and feigned an attempt at lifting it, falling back in mock exhaustion after some exertion.

We were at our wit's end for a way to get away from these bears, when it occurred to us to direct the bears to dig with their huge claws at the ground beneath the cub, starting back a few feet so as to make a kind of tunnel beneath him. Within a few minutes, with the mother and father digging, there was a gaping hole almost six feet wide and four feet deep extending under the body of the cub, and the dirt was still flying. We stopped the bears from digging and lowered ourselves into the hole. By pulling the already loosened dirt from beneath the cub we soon had him free. The ground was so soft from the rain that the cub was not injured by the tree but only frightened and a little thinner than normal.

Soon we were on our way again, remembering that we had found no gold, even though we had saved a certain bear and perhaps our own lives. We stopped at nightfall and made love. The sky was clearing, the short, violent rainy season nearly over. In the trees, branches and leaves, birds and insects spoke to the wind about something neither Lady nor I could understand.

In the morning I questioned Lady but she remembered none of her dreams.

potion

By nightfall we reached home. Renata's gold was nowhere to be found. Federico met us on the way. He had been waiting all day, he said. He said Renata told him to wait for us and tell us. Federico was the doctor and it was his job to tell us.

The morning after we left, Jane came to breakfast with Gregory and neither of them would eat, neither of them would speak. After breakfast Jane indicated that there would be a potion for everyone, that we would sit while she mixed it. She explained she had made her potion for Gregory already, that it was finished. No one spoke.

When Jane felt a potion was indicated, we always followed her advice. In the past she had done this numerous times; it was her business to do this. And we always had good results from her potions. When Federico and Renata objected, Jane told them if Gregory objected she would not give him the potion. As for the rest, she told them their potion was as good as any other she had given them and was merely to bring everyone together for the occasion.

Steven objected that this couldn't be true, that Lady and I were away and so we could not be together. Jane explained that I was the one who went to the city, that I was their link to the outside world and so it was only right that I should be in the outside world on this occasion. And Lady, because she wrote, was also a link to the outside and, because she was my lady, was a link between me and the others. That I was her man and the two of us should be together.

When the arguing threatened to continue, Gregory produced his flute and played yes. He played each one a different reason why they should keep quiet and do what Jane said.

Each person in his turn listened in sadness to the flute. It said not to cry. It said the rain had cleaned the earth and new plants would grow there. It said that only when the earth was freshly cleaned could the potion be finished, that many months of work had gone into it, that it had its own direction and could not be tampered with. There was good in its work, this work would come, and Gregory was happy to be honored to carry it on. Carla, it said, could not understand it, she was the person who enclosed everyone, she held them in her clothes, that it was necessary but of another world. The moon was open tides of marbled ivory, white on white, an audible silence. Steven could see but not understand, for Steven was a breaker of laws. His job was to make magic that would change for the better the natural way things were; the fact that it made things better was an affirmation, a yes. But the denial of what is was a no, a negation. The flute played that there was no negation in Gregory, that talk was the opposite of being, of life, and Gregory did not talk because of this. Federico, it said, fought death, which was the right and the left hand of nature and saying no to death was not saying yes to life. Renata, it said, could best understand, for she spent her life looking into the stars, from which Gregory took his music. If there were no nights the flute could not play. From those white hot holes in heaven all affirmation came and only Renata's will to control the stars forced her to object, forced her to demand gold, that stars were silver and only light, that when they died they turned red and gold, that gold was the color of death, not natural death but the death of saying no to death, the death of. . . .

Gregory threw up. The flute fell from his hands and Jane passed each person a cup. Drink, she said, Gregory has drunk.

Federico told us there was much grieving afterwards. The potion made everyone calm. Gregory was gone but no one could move to stop what was happening. Federico said when Steven was able to move again he withered Jane's arms so she could no longer make potions or grow plants. Gregory was my brother, Steven said to her, and you have lost him to us forever.

Federico said everyone was in agreement with Renata

now. Renata had seen a star all afternoon. Only gold would help now. Everyone was preparing to look for gold.

doctor

Philip says there is a doctor not far away who lives in a house in which there is a great deal of gold.

Lady and I returned and saw that people were changed. No one was happy. Somewhere inside each of us, what had been flowing froze. Jane would not come out in the daytime anymore, would not allow the sun to touch her skin. They had to feed her by force to keep her alive. Lisa claimed her baby would be born dead. Federico told her she was a ridiculous girl.

Renata followed Philip to the house where the doctor lived and returned the next day. Yes, she said, there was much gold and it was not far.

dream

Lady moaned and turned in her sleep. I lay awake and waited for her to finish. Just before dawn she sat up and told me her dreams.

Jane, she said, was already gone. Jane had gone to the city. I said that was impossible. I was the only one who could go to the city. She said no, that Gregory was gone away and that now any of us could go. Gregory, she said, was music. The flute was an extension of his body, just as Jane's hands were part of her. She said people went to the city who had lost their bodies, people who had turned into ideas of people. These people, she said, either go to the city or kill each other in order to be real again.

She said in her dream Steven's magic turned bad and many people died because Steven didn't know how to use it anymore. When Carla and Philip saw what Steven's magic was doing they ran away and no one ever found them. She said I was chasing them to find out where they were going but I didn't understand what was going on and had to be shown.

Lady said she walked in a field of the most beautiful flowers she had ever seen, flowers that gave off a light of their own from their insides. She stood knee-deep in them and lifted her face to the sun and smelled them. When she looked down again to see them she saw a person lying dead in the flowers at her feet. There was a small hole behind the ear and blood was coming out of it.

She tried to tell me the rest of her dreams but cried and couldn't say anything except that we had to leave right away, we couldn't say good-bye but must just leave, silently, immediately. And she wouldn't have any more dreams, ever. She just had a feeling, she knew.

As the sun was touching the mountain, we were leaving. Renata didn't see us. We walked out toward the city and saw a bear pawing at the surface of the stream for fish. Lady seemed pleased that we were going. She said there were a lot of things for us to do.

rainbow

As the cars went by kicking up a mist from the wet road, we could see a small rainbow behind each one, as the sun heaved red into the morning sky.

breakfast

We reached the road just before noon and walked to the diner. Fine Food—Cold Beer was the name of the diner. On the jukebox Merle Haggard was singing, "I kept the wine and threw away the rose."

I looked at the menu. I whispered to Lady that we should go somewhere else because they didn't have anything we could eat. She smiled at me and told me to let her order for both of us. She ordered steaks and eggs. I had never had steaks and eggs but they were good. Steaks and eggs. They sounded good too. Steaks and eggs. Chicken eggs and beef steaks.

Four big men came in. They had very short hair like a lot of people in the city do. They seemed to be having a good time.

Lady told me we were going to get a place to live in the city and she would sell her book. But I like your book, I said. She laughed. She explained to me about selling books. I asked her how she knew so much about the city when I was the one who had been going there. She said she learned it from books.

fuck

We left the Fine Food—Cold Beer diner and went into the city. People without bodies wandered everywhere. Some of the people talked to themselves as they walked along the street. It all seemed odd to me, as if I'd never been in the city before.

Lady took us a room in a hotel. We went to the room and turned on the television. I asked her where the money came from. She told me she had taken it from a man in the diner. How? Out of his back pocket. How? Just like that.

The man on the television said that seventy miles northwest of here an obstetrician, his wife, and four children were found dead in the swimming pool at their suburban cottage. They had apparently been tied up and shot before being pushed into the pool. He said local residents were being questioned.

Lady called room service. A man came with a bottle of liquor. We drank some of it and watched the television. The sun went down. We made love. Lady unpacked our things and ordered food. We ate and made love again.

I'm pregnant, she said.

A baby? I asked.

Yes, she said.

We turned the television up loud and danced around. We drank more liquor and made love. I asked her what we would do in the city. She said she would write more books. I asked what I would do. She said I could read her books and make love to her. I asked if we could always have liquor. I had never had liquor. She said yes, that we would drink a lot and fuck. I asked her what fuck was. She said it was like making love, only it didn't take as much time.

Laurence Gonzales

The Grand Prize

His wife—call her Christienne, though that was never her name, nor had she ever considered calling herself that; only, David (whose name is pronounced Dah-veed, with the final *d* sounding almost like *th*) had always wanted a girl named Christienne and had never been able to find one. He also longed to marry a woman who was black so he could have black children. David believed black was more beautiful than white . . . at any rate, his wife—who was only a little tan and that from the sun—dreamed almost every night. Though David and Christienne were not really married, they were considered man and wife by society, such as it was. They lived together. They shopped together for the livers of geese, the loins of calves, the tips of asparagus. They had common property. And Christienne awoke each morning to tell David her dreams as he was dressing. She would roll herself up in the maroon satin quilt under which they slept, leaving only her head and fingertips showing. David, his broad back tattooed with hieroglyphics from the rumpled sheets, would lazily pull on pants, socks, shirt, and Christienne would say, "Do you know what I dreamed last night?" And David would say, "What? Tell me."

On the particular morning in question—call it a Friday, say October something, though it may have been mid-June on a Thursday—it may have been February too—after all, Christienne is not her real name, so the real time is of little consequence, though let us say it was a cold day and therefore Christienne was wrapping herself in the maroon satin quilt;

also, it was taking David—who was to go out into the cold —longer to dress himself: undershirt, shirt, sweater, jacket, and so on . . . Christienne, then, tells him this dream:

"I was walking around the house straightening up a bit because we were going to have a special guest," Christienne says, for example. "And two things happened. One was that I discovered a room that we didn't know existed. I opened the door. I went in. There was nice furniture, Victorian. A mahogany secretary—opened—with a number of small drawers and compartments. There was a rocking chair—with a floral design or something. The other dream was that we had a very special guest. It was a man, someone I didn't know. He wore thick, rimless glasses and had long, straight hair. He was very attractive. You knew him and hadn't seen him for a very long time." Christienne stopped there.

"Anything else?" David asked.

"No." She said. "Oh, I had another dream but that was a small one. We—you and I—were in the kitchen and you wanted to throw away my wine decanter. That was all."

These dreams were not so unusual. David went to work, let us say he cut trees for a living, and it was his job to climb up and take off large branches with a power saw that he carried hooked to his thick, leather belt. On his boots he wore spikes with which he climbed. He had tremendous calf muscles from doing this. Suppose that at one time he had worked in Alaska and learned a trick because he was not as big as the other men he worked with. David would jump about four feet into the air, hang perfectly horizontal for a split second, and then kick with both feet, putting two holes; each the size of an index finger, into the side of a Douglas fir tree. This had the effect of discouraging the bigger men from picking fights with David. Perhaps, on the other hand, no one ever considered fighting David. He never knew.

On this Friday in question, even though Christienne's dreams were ordinary, two things happened that made her wonder. One was that an old friend of David's came to visit him in the afternoon.

"My name is Michael," the man said to Christienne, who was home alone. She immediately recognized him as the

man in her dream. He immediately recognized her as someone he would like to fuck, so he accepted her offer to come
in and have some tea with cognac. Or it may have been just
cognac ("You must be cold..." Christienne might have
said). After an hour of conversation they could stand it no
longer and went up the stairs to make love in David's bed.
Before David came home, Michael left, saying he would call.

The other thing that happened was this: David came home,
opened the refrigerator and took out a beer (as he always
does when he gets home). Christienne's wine decanter,
which was on top, fell off and broke on the floor. David
jumped back and watched it gently explode into four hundred small fragments. (Perhaps there were only three
hundred. It makes little difference.) He and Christienne
looked at each other strangely.

"The dream," he said.

"Isn't that odd?" She said, thinking about Michael. "You
know what's even more bizarre?"

"What's that," David said, squatting to pick up the pieces.

"Your friend Michael came looking for you today. He was
the man in my dream."

"What?" David ran a sliver of glass through his right
thumb, winced, pinched it, extracted the glass. "Why didn't
he stay? I haven't seen him in years."

"He had some business." Christienne refused to meet his
eyes. "He said he would call."

"Is that something," David stated flatly, as if it were nothing. "You're sure he was the man in your dream?"

"Positive," Christienne said, taking David's thumb, examining it. "Let me put something on it."

"It's only a cut," he said, squeezing blood from his thumb.
A bright red bead swelled; the surface tension broke and the
drop moved down toward the palm of his hand, shining.

Christienne wanted to tell David about going to bed with
Michael but didn't. She didn't because David was a very
jealous man, though he claimed to believe in personal freedom, claimed not to want to own Christienne. And she didn't
want to make enemies of the two men. And she also didn't
want David to jump up in the air in front of Michael, hang

there for a split second, and put two holes, each the size of an index finger, in Michael's chest.

❀   ❀   ❀   ❀

"I dreamed about teeth," Christienne said the next morning.

"Teeth," David said absently.

"Yes," Christienne said, "Teeth. I also bit my lip while I was dreaming." She pulled a hand from beneath the maroon quilt and drew her lower lip back to show the damage, but David had his back turned, dressing. "I'm not sure what the dream was about, I only remember something about teeth. I think I was at the dentist or something. I also dreamed about a dead bird. It was small and green. Very bright green. The kind of green that shines."

"Iridescent," David said.

"Yes, iridescent green. That's nice. I like that word. Iridescent. At any rate, there was an iridescent green bird. He also had some other iridescent colors on him. Orange perhaps. Blue. He was so small. Dead. Those were my only dreams. Not very interesting."

"They're not bad," David said. "Perhaps today we will meet an iridescent green bird who will die of bad teeth." He said. Christienne laughed.

At breakfast she broke a tooth and David took her to the dentist to have it filled.

"This is frightening," Christienne said.

"I don't know what to think," David said. "Perhaps tonight you could dream that a kind man knocks on the front door and presents us with a fortune. I would like that dream."

"Don't make fun," she said. "I'm frightened. What if I have a very bad dream?"

"I'm sorry," David said. "I don't know what to do. We can't stop you from dreaming. So there's no sense in making ourselves miserable. Perhaps you dreamed about the tooth because your tooth was bothering you in your sleep. And it was bothering you because it was bad. And it broke when you chewed with it because it was weak from being bad. So now your dream has come true."

"And what about this Michael who I had never seen before? What of that?" She said, unconvinced, knowing that David was not the kind to believe in such things as predicting the future with one's dreams.

"Perhaps you have seen a picture that I have of Michael," he said rather unconvincingly.

"And then, coincidently, he comes the next day, right?"

"I really don't know, Christienne. But what are you worried about? That you are predicting the future? Or that you are creating it? If you are predicting it, then it would be no different if you had no dreams about it. What is in the future will happen. If you are creating it—well, perhaps that is different. But maybe we all create the future, whether we know it or not."

Christienne was silent. She was afraid. Let us assume that Christienne has this hobby: She plays flute. That same evening, say, she was practicing the flute, playing from Bach, looking out the window at the sun going down. In the middle of a long, high-pitched glissando, a hummingbird, green and orange, accidentally flew (drawn by the sound) into the window screen, sticking itself by the beak in the mesh of the wire. Christienne screamed, dropping her flute, and ran to the living room, where David was. For a number of minutes she was hysterical. Still shaking uncontrollably, she brought David to see the bird, still hanging from the window screen by its beak, squirming.

"Take it away," she said under her breath. "Get it away from here!"

David went outside and gently pulled the bird from the screen, he placed it on the ground but the bird would not fly. Perhaps it was injured. Perhaps it was not; it mattered little what the truth was. David tried to make the bird fly, urging it on. Through the window he made a shrugging motion, palms upward turned, toward Christienne who was watching in horror.

"Get it away," she said through the glass, but he didn't hear her and stepped closer to the window, cupping his ear. "Get it away!" she said louder. David took one step backward and the heel of his boot came down squarely on the bird's body. His stomach turned as he felt the thing being crushed and he jumped off. But it was too late to matter.

For a long time they sat in the living room without talking. Christienne was mortally afraid of what was happening, afraid of her own inability to control what was taking over, afraid of what things might happen. David was nervous, still not convinced, but edgy, wondering.

"Still," he said finally, trying to sound casual, "nothing really bad has happened. A bottle is broken. This happens all the time and we think nothing about it. A bird is dead. Your tooth is filled. What are those things?" He opened his palms again and Christienne looked away. "Nothing," he answered himself. The sound of his own voice reasoning was reassuring to David. Christienne said nothing. She was terrified. That night she didn't sleep. David sat up with her, trying to convince her that there was nothing to be afraid of. Eventually, he fell asleep on the couch. When he awoke early that morning, Christienne was still sitting there.

"No dreams," he said. "Now you won't know what's going to happen."

"Don't make fun," she said. "Today is Sunday. Let's go to the park."

They showered and dressed for Sunday. It was a bright, cold day and they walked through the park for two hours, holding onto each other like lovers. But when they returned home, Christienne was so exhausted she immediately fell asleep. Some hours later she awoke with a start, coming straight up in the bed where David had carried her after she passed out on the couch.

"What is it?" David asked, more anxious to hear her dreams than he would have liked to admit. "Did you have a—"

"I had a good dream," she said, smiling. "It was a good dream."

"What was it?" he sat on the bed, his hand on her shoulder. "Tell me," he disliked the fact that he wanted to know so badly. It meant that he believed the dream would come true and he detested this notion.

"I dreamed that we won a contest of some sort. It was some kind of thing with tickets that you buy. We were walking along on a beautiful day, like today. It was a street that I had never seen before and there were horses on it as well as cars and bicycles. We bought this ticket, just on a whim. We never expected to win but then it happened. Ours was the right number. We won a lot of money, I think."

"What contest was it?" David asked excitedly, "which one?" And he winced, the two convictions inside him fighting. *How stupid,* he thought. *I don't believe this rubbish.*

"I don't know," she was saying. "I don't think I saw. Or maybe I just don't remember."

"This is silly," David said at last. "It's only a dream." He laughed with some difficulty. "We're acting as if we can just go out and buy a ticket and we'll be certain to win just because you dreamed it."

"But, Dah-veedth," she said, "the bird, the bottle, Michael. What if it is true? We could go on holiday to Switzerland for months."

"We don't even know what ticket to buy. There are all sorts of contests going on. You don't even know what street," he said, thinking: *horses, bicycles . . . where could that be?*

"Did you dream anything else?" he asked.

"I don't think so." She swung her leg over the side of the bed and got up. He followed her into the bathroom where she slid her slacks down to her ankles and sat down. "We could at least find out what kind of contests they give money for. Which ones have tickets that you buy. Maybe I would recognize the ticket if I saw it."

"It would be a waste of time," David said, fighting the urge to rush out and buy a ticket for the first contest he could find.

"Spoil sport," she said, standing, pulling her slacks up. "Will you answer that?" she asked when the phone rang. It was Michael. David invited him over to dinner. When he told Christienne she again tried not to look at David and couldn't meet his eyes while she told him she was going out to buy some food for dinner.

Christienne walked along the street thinking fondly of Michael's body, flinching at the thought of sitting at the table with the two of them. Cuckold was a word that she hated. It sounded small and mean. And the thought of that word would not leave her mind. Her lip curled as she walked along with the word stuck in her thoughts, like a stupid song that won't go away. Her David, strong and handsome and fiery, was not a cuckold. But she had made him that. And so, thinking these unpleasant thoughts, she failed to notice when she took a wrong turn and found herself on a strange street with bicycles and cars and horses. She stopped, raising her head to look around. A smile came to her face. There on the window of a store was a sign advertising the contest. She thought of David. He would call her silly for wasting money. But then, he needn't know.

She walked out of the store, stuffing the little ticket—the familiar piece of stiff paper with the numbers printed on it —into her purse. She walked back the way she had come, feeling like a smart housewife who had made a good investment. The winner would not be announced for a while yet.

"Would you care to criticize my shopping?" She asked as David rummaged through the bags.

"Hm, yes," he muttered to himself, playing for her. "Excellent," he said, holding up a piece of red meat. "Fine, fine," he said stroking a head of lettuce. "A modest Medoc," he held the bottle of wine to the light, pretended to examine the sediment. "Full bodied, mature. This year—ah, yes. That was the spring when, on seven different occasions, seven inches of rain, followed by seven days of bright sunlight, graced the vineyards in the northern ten acres of M. Lucine's property, no?" He peered at Christienne as if over spectacles. "Quite a lucky year." She laughed and snatched the bottle from him. He snatched it back, put it on the table, and snatched her up, carrying her off to the living room where he put her on the floor and stripped her slacks off in one clean motion. While they were making love, a long spoke of sunlight filled with tiny, glittering motes, made its way across their backs and down their legs. When it reached the sole of David's right foot, he rolled over and sat up.

"Would you like to consider criticizing my lovemaking?" he asked.

"Full bodied," she said, "mature, modest bouquet—all in all, not a bad lay," she giggled.

"Christienne! What would your mother say?" he mimicked shock, hand to chest.

"She might say 'A cigar is just a cigar—but a good woman is a. . . .'"

"Now, now," he wagged his finger. "Remember we have a

guest coming. You must be on your best behavior," but the mention of Michael changed Christienne's expression so much that David asked what was wrong.

"I completely forgot," she lied. "I have to begin cooking."

"It's not nearly time," he looked at his watch, which was all he wore at that moment.

"Still," she said, getting up, not finishing her sentence. David watched with admiration as her muscular bottom kneaded its way across the room. A perfect ass, he thought. Incredible.

David dressed and went into the kitchen where Christienne was making herself busy. He put his arms around her waist, his head on her shoulder.

"I forgot to tell you to get me some cigarettes," he said. Christienne made herself very busy. "I think I'll go get some."

"OK," she said.

He slung his jacket over his shoulder and went out the door. Halfway down the block, out in the cold air, imagining as he always did in this kind of weather that he was thinking more clearly, David decided to see if the dream street was the one he thought it was, where six weeks ago he had cut a stout maple from the electrical lines. He walked for about ten minutes and made a turn onto a narrow street. Horses and bicycles were all around him. He searched up and down the street with his eyes but saw no sign of a contest going on. He walked the length of the block without finding a contest to enter. As he was turning to leave the street, however, a small man in a baggy coat approached him with illegal Irish Sweepstakes tickets.

"Win a quarter of a million," the man croaked. His front teeth were badly discolored, with great gaps where others had fallen or been knocked out. The man's face looked as though people had been wiping their boots on it for a number of years. He held up a ticket before David, who immediately pulled out his money and bought the chance. Placing it in a small compartment in his wallet, David left the street, feeling very sneaky and went to the tobacco store.

At home he sat with the paper, not sure whether he wanted to gloat or feel silly for being convinced by Christienne's dream. *If we win,* he thought, *then I will pull out the ticket and say, "See—no sense taking chances."* Christienne, oblivious in her work, had put Michael out of her mind for the moment and was humming to herself, thinking essentially the same thing about the ticket she had secreted in her purse —with the exception that she was not ashamed to believe in dreams.

That evening Michael came in carrying a big bottle of wine and a package. He and David hugged each other, slapped each other on the shoulders, grinned, held each other at arm's length, saying, "You haven't changed a bit." To David Michael gave the bottle, to Christienne the package saying, "It's just something I picked up in China that I thought you might like."

David uncorked the wine while Michael narrated about his travels and Christienne, trying not to show embarrassment, opened the gift. It was a large wild pig carved from some kind of solid, blonde wood, perhaps twenty pounds of it. Typically Chinese, the detail was elaborate, giving the pig a ferocious appearance.

"It's beautiful," Christienne said to Michael as he and David went into the living room to sit and talk. Christienne stayed in the kitchen preparing dinner, glad to be away from them.

Though she worried all evening, nothing happened that gave David any indication of what had been going on in his absence. He and Michael got politely drunk and told each other lies about their past—tacitly understood, tacitly agreed upon. Late, then, let us say that David excused himself to go to the bathroom. At that point—drunk enough to be bold, though he planned it that afternoon without having had more than a glass of wine with lunch—Michael leaned over to Christienne in a conspiratorial fashion, slipped the lottery ticket into her hand and said, "I picked this up for you. Keep it and bring us all good luck."

Christienne's jaw dropped in a caricature of shock and she started to say something but Michael cut her off. "Put it away. Don't say anything about it till we win." And she went to her purse and slipped it inside next to the other ticket, now realizing that she had bought the wrong one, that the one Michael gave her was the one in her dreams—of this she was positive. The color was right. Even the numbers, she imagined, were like the ones in her dream, sixes and threes: That round look somehow seemed right now. The other one, which she had bought that afternoon, had too many fives in it. And it was too big. Now she was certain. And the words "Irish Sweepstakes" looked correct, though she wasn't sure what the ticket in her dream had actually said.

When David returned from the bathroom, Christienne was so nervous that she claimed she was exhausted and went up to bed, saying good night to the men. But when David came up to bed after Michael had left, she was still awake, agitated from thinking about Michael, her dreams, the tickets.

"I thought you were exhausted," David said, cheerful, drunk.

"I thought so too." She watched his back as he undressed balancing unsteadily on one foot to get out of his pants. "I guess I'm just wondering about what it'll be tonight."

"The dreams?" he asked, smiling.

"Yes."

"Well, look what happened last night," he said, slipping under the maroon quilt next to her body, which had warmed the bed.

"That doesn't mean anything," she said, wanting to tell him about the tickets—then wanting to go the other way and say, "We can't win unless we buy tickets"—but she said nothing.

"I bought you a ticket," David then said, lowering his head like a small boy confessing to an adult. "I couldn't resist."

"How sweet of you," Christienne tried hard to say it right but it came out trembling, and if David had been at all in control of himself he would have seen something was wrong. But he was too plastered to hear. He reached out his arm and caught hold of the cuff of his pants, pulling them toward him. From his wallet he extracted the Irish Sweepstakes ticket and gave it to her. Again she tried to smile—again he failed to notice.

"Now we'll find out if it means anything," he said confidently and turned over and passed out.

Christienne threw off the cover and padded out into the

hall, standing for a moment in the moonlight that streamed through the window, her naked body shimmering with heat in the still, cool air. She went to the living room and slipped the little ticket into the compartment of her purse next to the other two, thinking, *I can't stand to wait. I'll go crazy. Ten days to find out who it's going to be*—and then thinking: *This is ridiculous. Three chances out of how many millions? None of us is going to win.*

But she didn't go crazy. She was only somewhat nervous and flared up easily. David and Christienne, let us imagine, had several fights during the next ten days, fights they would not have had otherwise. But the day came. And they survived. David was getting quite nervous as well because Christienne had been having more and more dreams that came true— though nothing since the lottery that made any difference. Since then she had dreamed about a package from the post- man: a gift arrived from her aunt, who was traveling in the United States; a terrible disaster: a Turkish Airlines DC–10 crashed the next morning outside Paris, killing 346 persons (they were very relieved that day); something about police- men: David was fined for a traffic violation; and other things equally unimportant.

But on the night before the winner of the contest was to be announced, she dreamed that David found out about her and Michael. And she was frightened. She had no idea how it was going to happen. In the morning she told David that she hadn't had any dreams.

"Well, I suppose nothing will happen today then," he said, in a good mood. "Or maybe it's because today's the day we become rich and you've already dreamed that, so there was no need to dream anything last night. We already know what's going to happen." And he pulled out his wallet and unfolded the piece of paper on which he had written the number of the lottery ticket he had given her. Then he read it to Christienne and she knew that it was not the winning number. She knew Michael's ticket would win.

And when it did, Christienne was much more convincing about being disappointed than she had been about covering up her secrets.

"What good are these dreams of yours, if all they can do

is get me traffic fines and break wine decanters?" David said, not really upset at all, more relieved that at least one of her dreams hadn't come true, as he crumpled the piece of paper and let it fall in the street.

Christienne fingered the winning ticket Michael had bought her, knowing she would never redeem it. It was in her pocket and as she fingered it, she began shredding it at the edges, walking beside David, joking, thinking about all that money—wasted.

"Well," she said, "maybe that means that nothing really bad can happen either." She turned sideways, the ticket mutilated beyond recognition and dropped the little pieces into the street as they walked along. The slight breeze that was blowing from behind scattered the bits of paper before them and David and Christienne walked over the scraps, chatting.

That night when David picked up the phone, Michael said, "Congratulations, old goat, now you can take that trip to Switzerland you've been bullshitting me about for years," assuming that, by this time, Christienne would have redeemed the ticket and told David.

Grant Lyons

The Water Tower
Across the River
The Assistant
The Home Country

Grant Lyons

The Water Tower

"God!"

"C'mon, man, don't be afraid, you ain't gonna fall."

"God*damn.*"

"C'mon."

"I . . . I can't!"

"Whattayamean you *can't.* You gotta."

Artie stopped climbing to listen. The voices rose from below like wisps of smoke. He looked down: three pale blurs wavered in the blackness. A great silver circle surrounded them, and beyond it strings and clusters of lights—the town. The dark seemed to have contracted, thickened in some way.

"Man, I just *can't!*"

"Move your ass!"

The ladder was still now—Danny must have reached the catwalk.

"Shitfuck. What are we gonna do? He's froze."

"Get Artie down here. It's his baseball buddy."

"Artie!"

"Artie!"

The two voices were several tones apart and made a chord. Artie looked down again—his own hands were slimy with sweat. The ladder, shining silver, made a curve backward into the dark circle. What happened if you fell from here? Squish. Nothing left.

"Come on down, Artie, we got trouble." He was in the shadow, they couldn't see him.

"What's the matter, cops?" Danny shouted from the catwalk above.

"Nothing like that. Never mind. Just get Artie down here."

"What's the matter?"—Danny again.

"Artie's buddy just panicked, that's all. Froze hisself to the ladder and won't budge."

Artie began to climb down. The ladder shook with each step.

"No, no, no! Don't *let* him . . . ."

"What's the matter *now*?"

"Don't let him . . . come *down* on me!"

"Christ."

"Get ahold of yourself, man—we been up and down this thing dozens of times." Cal was tightening up his own nerves. It seemed to Artie that he could feel Larry's fear, rising through the cool air like waves of warmth.

He stopped a few rungs above Larry. "OK, what's the matter?" he said. He saw Larry glance up quickly and then press himself to the ladder.

"What's going on down there?" Danny called.

Artie looked up. The ladder bent back now in a graceful curve above him, then ended abruptly. The shadow, where he had been. The great silver globe throbbed with light—it looked as though it floated in the air. For a second Artie felt himself let go, fall slowly through the air, through black space . . . .

"I just can't . . . can't *move*," Larry whined. "I don't know what's the matter."

"You don't know what's the matter?" Jason said. "I'll tell you. You're scared shitless. You're *chicken*."

"Fuck you."

"Oh yeah? How's this?" Jason pounded the ladder with his feet.

"No, no, *please* . . . ."

"Thinks the ladder's his mommy."

"I'm getting tired of holding on here," Cal said. To Artie he was hardly more than a blur, below Jason.

"Why don't you lay off him, Jason," Artie said. Then to Larry, "Look, Larry, you're gonna have to go down, sooner or later, right? So just do it, that's all. You can wait for us in the car. They'll get out of your way. Just go on down."

"But I *can't*!"

"But I *can't*," Jason mimicked.

"Lay off, Jason!"

"I'm going down," Cal said. "This could take all night."

The ladder shook again with Cal's steps. Larry made little moans.

Artie stepped down one rung. "Come on, Larry," he said, "there's nothing really to be afraid of. You got up here, you can go down just as easy."

"Hey come on, where is everyone?" Danny yelled from the catwalk. "I'm getting *lo-o-onesome*."

Artie twisted so he could sit with half a buttock on a ladder rung. He took a deep breath. The quiet seemed so perfect, so deep—yet delicate, like fine glass. Looking up again he saw the shafts of the tower, silver in the light of the half-moon, like thin beams of light, converging at the tank. At this angle the tank looked like a quarter moon itself, brilliant, unreal, dazzling. It was all a luminous abstraction, a geometric design in silver and black that stirred him strangely. He wondered what Danny could see from the catwalk. Could he see them at all?

Larry was breathing oddly, in irregular sigh-like gasps. Artie felt responsible; Larry didn't know the others at all. He wasn't really a friend, they played together on the same baseball team.

"Larry, look," he said very softly—as though trying to pry something open, some secret, very quietly—"you just got to think about it, that's all. *Think* about it. You can't stay up here all night, right? You can't stay up here forever. You're gonna have to go down *some* time. So you might as well start. Take your time. Make sure of each step. But you have to . . . to *start*, right?"

"I feel so weak, like with a fever or something," Larry said. "Man, man, I don't know what I'm gonna do!"

"Hey! Hey! Where is everybody!" Danny shouted from above.

"This is a drag, man," Jason said.

"I just want to die!"

"OK, man, that's easy. Just let go—and fly! All your troubles will be over."

"For Christsakes, Jason, will you lay off!"

"Man, my patience has done run *out*."

"Larry, why didn't you tell us you were afraid of heights?"

"What? How did I know, man! I never been up anyplace like this! I mean, I never even *thought—*"

"Never been on a water tower before?" Jason asked in mock disbelief. "But man, it's the greatest! From the catwalk up there you can climb up on this little teeny ladder that curves back up around and over the tank. That's where the red light is. You know, the one you said you were gonna snatch, remember? Only there's no safety rail at all, and the wind—"

"Jason! Shut the fuck up, will you!"

"At this point I'd just as soon he did panic and drop off. Plop. Get him out of my way."

Artie was getting angrier. Why did Jason do it? Didn't he feel it? But if he didn't feel it, then why climb at all? Without the fear it was nothing, there was no point.

"Larry, look, don't look down. That's the thing. Just don't look down. Move one foot, just one rung at a time, and look *up*. At the tank up there or something, think about something else . . . ."

"No! No, no, that's just *it*. The ball, that thing, that whattayacall it, tank, it looks like it's gonna fall, *down* . . . ."

"OK, so don't look *up*," Jason said. "Don't look anywhere. Close your goddamn eyes! But *move*."

There was a long pause as the three of them waited. Then it was Jason who spoke: "I'm coming around."

"What?"

"I'm coming around! I'm tired of waiting."

"You can't do that! He's scared enough as it is. Don't be an asshole."

"You're the asshole! Who asked you to bring this jelly-guts!"

Jason swung around to the inside of the ladder and climbed past Larry. When he came up even with Artie he grinned at him.

"I ought to push you off," Artie said.

"Oh no, you can't do that. I might take along your buddy down there on my way."

Artie waited until Jason reached the catwalk and the ladder stopped shaking.

"Larry, do you think you can move—just one step?" he asked. "Just one. Try."

"I just never knew . . ." Larry said.

"No, I know."

"I just never knew." Larry pressed his face to the ladder. For an instant Artie felt the cold metal against his own face, and he felt his strength rush out of him—toward Larry. Then it came flooding back. Below them, the pattern of girders disappeared into blackness, as though into a pit. Why did they do things like this? Water towers, or sometimes breaking into some place for no reason. Excitement, risk, for the fear. Tonight, when he cleared the high fence with the double strand of barbed wire and dropped into the shadow, he looked up, and it completely overwhelmed him, the whole incredible thing. The pattern of silver lines, so geometric, the eerie gleaming tank . . . it made him catch his breath. He felt, deep down, that he wanted it, wanted to conquer it, to possess it in some way. Somehow to absorb it. It wasn't at all like breaking into the high school last week—there had been nothing there, nothing to do. This was different.

"Just *concentrate*," he said. "Concentrate on taking that one step, Larry. Just one. I mean, in your head you *know* that everything's going to be all right. It's just a *feeling* you have. That's all. Nothing. You have to lick the feeling. Listen, I was scared too the first time."

"Yeah?"

Artie hesitated. The actual truth was not so easy to say. He was afraid now, in fact. But the first time—the first time it had not been pleasant at all, not till it was over and they were driving home. Now something pulled at him both ways. A fear and—and something else.

"Sure," he said, finally, almost in a whisper, as though telling a secret. "Jason too, don't let him fool you. Everyone is. But—but you have to *think*, you see? You have to think—climbing down this ladder is a lot easier than, say, hitting .350. I mean, you *know* you can do it. So you take one step, don't think about anything else."

Larry said nothing. The two of them were silent for a long time, suspended in space, waiting above the glitter of the town.

Finally Larry made a movement.

"That's it, Larry. One step! If you can make one, you can make them all . . . ."

❖   ❖   ❖   ❖

When Artie reached up to the catwalk Jason pretended he was going to step on his hands.

"About time," he said. "What did you do, hold his hand?"

"He all right?" Cal asked.

"Yeah, he's all right." Artie pulled himself up onto the catwalk. "I thought he might be sick though, when we got down."

"Not in the car!"

"No, no."

"He waiting?"

"No, he went home."

"He can sit in his momma's lap."

"Jesus, Jason, what's the big deal? He didn't know, he didn't know what would happen."

"I thought he was some kind of baseball star. Isn't he? That's what I hear. A stud."

"He's a good baseball player. A whole hell of a lot better than you. He's just as surprised as anybody."

"Big baseball star."

"OK, forget it."

"You're too late for our contest," Danny said.

"What contest?"

"Pissin' contest. I won."

"You bastard, you saved up since this morning I bet," Jason said. He wrestled Danny toward the edge of the catwalk. They struggled a few seconds, carefully, and made noises as though they were falling off, their voices trailing away.

Artie walked away from them to look around, all the way around to the other side of the tank where the ladder went up to the top. He looked at the ladder and thought for a moment about trying it. But he knew he never would, none of them would.

He could see the street pattern of the town in rows of blue lights, the moving headlights of cars, and far away the black patch of the lake. On the lake a single boat was moving from right to left, or a light at any rate, pale green. It was easy to imagine flying, taking a leap out and flying through the dark, floating above the town and lake, turning and swooping . . . . Feeling a little dizzy, he leaned back against the tank. The metal was icy cold. He moved to the edge of the catwalk and unzipped his fly. His fingers were cold, a little numb, as though they too were made of metal. The urine shot out into the moonlight, a silver arc, and then spread out as it fell, like a spray of stars, or embers, burning out and down into the dark.

It must cool by the time it reaches bottom, he thought, hardly more than a mist.

Danny came around the tank. "Nothin', man, nothin'," he said. "You wouldn't even a been close."

Artie laughed. Suddenly he felt—triumphant. "Piss on it," he said exultantly.

The others came around. Their faces, pale and ghostly, looked like fat white balloons, and this made him laugh more—the sound seemed to ratchet the dark, shredding the silence.

"Piss on you—piss on the world!" he shouted, as loud as he could. "You hear me—*piss on the whole fucking world!*"

Across the River

When Beejee and Chris came back from their first year at the university Doug was married. It was a shock, they hadn't heard a thing about it. Of course, they didn't write letters ordinarily and they wouldn't have expected Doug to—but married!

"It's like he's ashamed," Chris said. That was after they met Lily.

Lily was ridiculously misnamed. A heavy, dark girl, with coarse black hair, grainy skin, a thick, flattish nose—she claimed, with a certain hauteur, to be "of Italian extraction." She wore no brassiere and her large breasts flattened on her chest, as Beejee observed, like hot-water bottles. She took an immediate dislike to Beejee and Chris. Whenever they came around she seemed to start simmering. Sooner or later she would blow, and the wildest profanities spewed over them like pus from a squeezed boil.

Doug admitted Lily had been pregnant when they got married—so what? She was due in August. He'd have married her in any case, he assured them. She had him by the scrotum. "Man, you guys will never really understand," he said. "You'd have to get in the sack with her. You just can't imagine. She may not be so much to look at, but *Christ*, she's a goddamn tornado with her snatch."

They weren't inclined to doubt it. Lily did exude sex in some inexplicable way—like an odor, almost. A heavy, funky sort of earthiness. She was built for hard wear, if not for speed, Beejee said.

The fact was, Beejee and Chris felt betrayed. Before they

left for Austin there had been the three of them. They had waged high school together. Doug's folks couldn't afford to support him away at college so he couldn't go. But the triad was supposed to hold. One of the jokes they had shared was "teenage marriage, the local disease." And here was Doug, up to his neck in it! It was as though he had somehow gone over to the enemy.

In any case there was nothing to be done now. Neither of them expected the marriage to last. But the kid—what about that? That was the stone they couldn't dislodge. Once the kid was born, it wouldn't go away. Doug would be tied to it one way or the other all his life. And so, somehow, would they. Or so they felt. Doug's imminent fatherhood threatened *them*—and they weren't ready for it.

Doug and Lily lived in a tiny garage apartment in an "ambiguous" part of town. That is, near the leading edge of Negro residences. Their landlord was a Mexican. Lily worked but she didn't make much money. Doug was still in the local junior college, foundering and cursing. They had countless cockroaches and a rat or mouse somewhere between the ceiling and the roof.

Lily was surprising in some ways. Chief of these was her painting. Doug made a big point of this. In fact he made too much of it, as though salvation—his, hers, and *theirs*—lay in just this hidden talent, in her *art*. But even Beejee and Chris had to admit there was something a little miraculous in it. Lily worked primarily in watercolors and acrylics. Everything she did seemed to express just those qualities that Lily herself lacked—pale, delicate, feminine creations, rather oriental looking and elusive.

"It's all *natural*," Doug emphasized. "She's had about six lessons in her life. From an old lady named Mrs. Gibson who paints nothing but flowerpots and apples, *crap*. I mean, you figure, if she's this good now, with no help, imagine what she could do if she went to art school! She's a goddamn *genius*."

It was a difficult summer. Beejee and Chris tried to get Doug to go out with them—off to honky-tonks, across the river into Louisiana, or even just for a drive. But he was strangely reluctant to leave the house. And if they hung around there Lily sooner or later would fly off the handle and begin screaming at them—at all three of them—barking like a wolfhound.

Part of the problem that summer was that Doug was in school. He had done badly his first two semesters—fucking off, he claimed—and so he was on probation and had to make up a couple courses. This was itself a betrayal. None of the three of them had been any kind of student in high school. But that was because it was high school—right? It was taken for granted that college was another matter. And, in fact, Beejee and Chris had both done pretty well, especially Beejee. So how was Doug flunking out of a goddamn junior college?

"Because that place is just another high school," Doug explained. "Just another prison where they shuffle you around from room to room to keep you off the streets. Listen, at the student center the kids all have special tables, you know? This high school at one table, another high school at another table. Walk over to the wrong table and it's like an ant wandering into the wrong nest. Everyone who has one wears a letter jacket so there won't be any mistakes."

Perhaps the most disturbing thing about the Doug Chris and Benjee found when they came home, however, was his passivity. Or apathy. He didn't seem to *care* that he was sliding downhill. On the one hand, he didn't admit it, but behind that defense was a kind of indifference. Whether feigned or not was beside the point. The point was that he was inactive, dull, he only smirked or shrugged. They couldn't seem to reach him at all. Like when Lily had one of her fits of rage. He didn't try to defend them, nor to defend himself. Later he'd explain: "You take the bad with the good. When she gets her blood up like that she gets *hot*. You should see what happens here after you guys leave—it's an orgy. She starts having orgasms almost before I get her clothes off."

If they didn't seem adequately awed by this sexual compensation, Doug would lecture them about "real life":

"You guys know nothing about it. Living with someone means making adjustments, compromises, tit for tat, so to speak. You look at me and you say, 'Doug, you've changed.' Hell, *I* know I've changed! I'm growing up! In a way college, going to school, is just a way of keeping us children for an extra few years, *floating*. But you wait, your time will come."

❧   ❧   ❧   ❧

The summer was just a little more than half gone when they tried to get up a little party. Beejee and Chris, Doug and Lily, and two others squeezed into Doug's old Plymouth and drove across the river about 11 one Saturday night. They were going honky-tonkin'.

The two others were friends of Doug's and Lily's. Jeff was a guy Doug knew from school, a rather extraordinarily homely guy, very quiet and shy, who was planning to be a music major. Pam was Lily's "bosom buddy," as Doug repeatedly called her with a leer. She was a tall, very skinny girl, with a slightly stooped posture, and a large bent nose that made you think of a buzzard. Pam seemed to wear a perpetual expression of sarcastic lechery, grinning and rolling her tongue around, and squirting out laughter in little high, whinnying jets.

Their first stop—and as it turned out, their last—was The Big Oak, just across the river into Louisiana. The shell parking lot was jammed with cars, the place was swarming with people, and every time someone opened the front door music blasted out with a roar like a jet airplane.

As they entered and paid the two dollar cover, they were stamped on the hand with a dye that showed up under ultraviolet light. Then they had to squeeze into the crowd surrounding the dance floor. There wasn't much light, and what there was was mostly a purplish blue so people's faces looked like cheap Halloween masks and it was hard to see what was happening more than a few feet away. Amazingly, as they wandered around the dance floor they came upon a table that appeared to be abandoned—at least no one was sitting at it; they scrounged an extra two chairs, and they all had a ringside seat. The band was so loud that the music seemed to reach them through the floor, their chairs, and their bottoms, as much as through their ears, which were soon numb. Everyone ordered beer, except Doug, who wanted bourbon and soda. He was already pretty far gone, having put away a half a bottle of Heaven Hill before they left.

Pam and Lily seemed to team up. They sat next to each other, exchanged glances and winks, and even laughed in a kind of grotesque harmony. Every time someone said anything to Pam she said, "Piss on you," and Lily began to echo her. Doug was soon furious. Not only that but both the girls were making eyes at guys on all sides. And The Big Oak was not the kind of place to do that. Even Beejee and Chris were nervous, but with the clamor from the bandstand and Pam's inevitable "Piss on you," they couldn't communicate very well.

Almost as though he sensed the tension building up, Jeff left. He said he thought he knew one of the guys in the band. Twice in the next half hour they saw him come dancing by. Once was with a decent-looking girl, once with a woman of about forty. Both times he gave them a look as if to indicate *he* didn't know how he had got himself in this position. Then, a little later, they saw him climb up on the bandstand. Someone pushed a trombone at him and he played.

Doug drank as fast as he could flag down a waitress. He soon turned pale and started to gag. Chris helped him outside where he proceeded to vomit on the great bulging roots of the Big Oak itself in the parking lot.

Pam and Lily waited about a minute after Chris and Doug left, then they got up and took off. Beejee called after them but they disappeared into the crowd, Pam, her back turned, curling a bird at him behind her back. Chris and Doug came back and Chris announced that he was suddenly sleepy. He cleared a place for himself on the table among the bottles and glasses and put his head down on his arm.

Doug was furious that the girls had gone. He kept looking for them, cursing. He had agreed to "taper off" to beer, but he downed the beers as rapidly as the bourbons. Then he stood up suddenly, knocking his chair over. "I'm gonna stash Titty's skrull in," he snarled, meaning presumably bash Lily's skull, and hurled himself into the swirling crowd. Chris looked up, Beejee shrugged, and they stayed where they were. It seemed as though a crisis at this point wouldn't be all bad.

About fifteen minutes later a commotion started on the other side of the room. Reluctantly, Beejee and Chris went over to investigate. It was just a couple Cajun girls in an argument. It fizzled when someone took away the penknife one of the girls was jabbing the air with.

They turned back, but their table was taken. They drifted around, trying to find the others. The only one they could find was Jeff, who was still on the bandstand playing, a dazed look on his face—a look he shared with the others in the band.

They went outside to get some fresh air. There they found Doug with Pam and Lily, all screaming at the tops of their voices into each other's faces. Doug's face was crimson when he turned to Beejee and Chris:

"Found this bitch sitting there, some greaseball wiping his shitty hands all over her *tits*!"

For some reason Pam and Lily found this hilarious. They both emitted high, squealing laughter. Doug whirled and shoved his finger almost into Pam's right eye.

"You can shove this right up your stinking cunt mouth, too, you shit-assing whore!"

"Blow it out your dingleberry fairy asshole!" Pam shot back, cackling. This sent Lily into a paroxysm, bending over double, holding her sides, howling, tears rolling down her cheeks. When she straightened she put both hands on her swollen belly as though to keep it from bursting.

Doug turned and watched Lily's head bobbing up and down as she abandoned herself to her laughter. His face was white. His eyes followed her head, which looked like a bouncing, hairy ball. Then just as she was making another bow toward the shell parking lot, he swung his arm around in a high arc and struck her on the top of the head with his fist, bringing all his weight into the blow. She went sprawling face first into the dust and shells. Pam shrieked. Doug turned toward her, both fists wadded tight, his arms tensed, but she kept a distance. She spat a steady stream of abuse at him and backed away. Doug circled Lily's prostrate form, waiting for her to get up, but she did not even try.

Doug looked up at Beejee and Chris, as though suddenly

remembering something. "I'll kill that fucking greaseball!" he said, and before either of them could grab him, he had run back into The Big Oak.

Beejee and Chris helped Lily up. She had small cuts on her face and held her big belly as though in pain. She looked frightened. They helped her to the car. Pam followed them, screaming.

"Big shots, tough guys, beating on a pregnant woman!"

Beejee told her to shut up and get in the car unless she wanted to walk home. They were going inside to get Doug and Jeff, and there just might be a little trouble. They might have to make a fast exit.

"Oh, such big shots," Pam sneered. "I hope somebody kills you shitty bastards. I hope they cut your fucking balls off!"

They put their hands under the ultraviolet light and went inside. It was hard to tell what was going on. On one side of the floor there seemed to be a fight. On the other side people were sitting and drinking as though nothing were happening, and on the dance floor people were still dancing all together in a crush. They moved as quickly as they could toward the scuffle, but by the time they reached it, it was over. They found Doug lying on his back under a table, but no one paying much attention to him.

"I showed those bastards," Doug said, when they sat him up.

"How many were there?" Beejee looked around. It was amazing, no one was even looking at them. "Where are they?"

Doug's answer was an incomprehensible mutter that brought blood to his lips. He had a deep cut on his cheek, too. They towed him out toward the exit. By the door a hand reached out and grabbed Beejee's arm, but when he turned there was again no one looking at him. "Meet us outside," he snarled to anyone who wanted to listen and pushed Doug out the door. Chris caught Jeff's eye and waved to him that they were leaving.

The five of them waited in the car in silence. Lily appeared to have recovered. She wouldn't look at Doug.

"You sure Jeff saw you?" Beejee asked Chris.

"He saw, he saw . . . How would I know? He seemed to."

"Maybe he wants to stay?"

"He'd come out and tell us, at least, wouldn't he?"

"Someone grabbed my arm on the way out."

Silence again. Five minutes. Finally Beejee said, "Let's go," and he and Chris went back inside.

They found Jeff nearly unconscious near the door, bleeding a lot from the mouth, everyone stepping around him, and ignoring him. He groaned when they pulled him up.

"Who did it, where are they?" Beejee demanded. Jeff merely rolled his head around and groaned again. They almost had to carry him outside to the car. They pushed him into the backseat with Pam and Lily, and Doug took off, sending a shower of shells behind him.

Jeff just kept rolling his head around and moaning, blood bubbling out of his mouth. He refused to open his eyes or say anything. Pam cursed him for smearing blood on her. Doug pushed the Plymouth as far as it would go—close to a hundred. Lily screamed at him to slow down and he snickered. Then she said he was trying to kill the baby.

"Damn straight," Doug agreed, turning to leer at her. "And you too. You guessed, you bitch, you stinking cunt. You think I want to be held responsible for bringing a piece of *your* shit into the world? And I haven't given up yet, either."

Doug hunched over the steering wheel as the car squealed around the curves in the highway. He kept turning around to look at Lily, but she said nothing.

"That's right," he said, "kill you both. Exterminate the vermin. Service to mankind. Glad to oblige. Make the world a cleaner place for everyone." He began to pull the wheel back and forth so the car made a zigzag from one shoulder to the other. There weren't any other cars.

"Cut it out," Beejee snapped. "Watch the road."

Doug turned and grinned at him. "As a matter of fact, why not kill us all? Who's worth saving? Not *you* guys. Whose side are you on, anyway? Never mind, I know. You're on your own. We all are."

"Cut it out!"

Doug pulled down hard on the wheel. The slick tires all

broke into a drift at the same time as the car slid down the road, turning slowly, heading for the ditch. Beejee grabbed the wheel and tried to straighten it. The car did a quick swing over to the other side, began to fishtail back and forth, and finally slid backward into the ditch.

No one was hurt, nothing was broken. Jeff still groaned in the backseat. He did not seem to realize that anything had happened. Beejee pushed Doug out of the car and got behind the wheel. Doug had to ride shotgun with Chris between him and Beejee. The car slid easily out of the ditch and they were once again on their way.

They went directly to the hospital. Lily was examined, found to be uninjured, the fetus intact. But Jeff's jaw was broken in two places. He was admitted, wired up, put under sedation. All he ever managed to tell them was that someone he didn't even see had suddenly hit him with a beer bottle.

❖   ❖   ❖   ❖

Doug and Lily patched things up. In fact, Doug seemed more passive, more acquiescent than ever. He seemed to blame Beejee and Chris in some way but refused to talk about it. He also refused to allow Pam in the house. And he began to drink a great deal.

Doug failed one of the summer-school courses—he was out. "Now no school will ever let me attend for the rest of my life," he said, as though it were a big joke. "I'm finally free. Anyway I should get to work, we need the money."

Doug drank, said he was having trouble getting enough sleep, and got thinner. Something was obviously boring into him, but he did not want to talk to Beejee and Chris about it. They even got the feeling they were not exactly welcome, although when they asked he denied it vehemently. "I just have a lot on my mind," he explained. "I didn't think I had to be polite with *you* guys."

The one night they did get him to talk at all he was so drunk he literally could not stand up and not really coherent. They got a long, broken monologue that seemed to be chasing itself and circling around itself:

"What do you think, you guys, what are you thinking about me?" he began. "No, no foolin' . . . I know, I know. But look, there's the kid, right? I mean, there *is*. No point talking about a maybe at this point, it's a fact. A life you know. Sure, you can say I didn't want him if you want to. A lot you know, anyway, but there he is in any case, right? Big as a bushel basket. Hey, you know sometimes when I'm riding that mountain I wonder if I'm pokin' the little fucker in the eye . . . or maybe it isn't a little fucker, maybe it's a little fuckee . . . . Maybe I *didn't* want to get married just yet, maybe I don't love Lily at all, maybe I hate her in fact, who knows? And what's the difference. Reality is what *is*. Got to deal with what you got. Anyway, maybe I did, maybe I even still do, too. She's a good fuck, buddy, one thing you can't take away. I mean, we all sit around with our fantasies, the girls in the Pepsi ads and so on. But that's not reality, that's not life, Lily's better'n you might think at a lot of things. But if you really want to know, the kid is the thing, what I call the inescapable. You think I should have got one of those butchers to fix it? Supposed to be one nearby, actually, which shows the kind of neighborhood . . . . Naw, I couldn't do that."

"You're doing the manly thing, right?" Beejee asked sarcastically. "You'll have the kid and everyone will be happy, right?"

"Fuck you Beejee! You don't know shit!"

And that was the last he spoke to them of his life, his fate, that summer.

*   *   *   *

When they came home for Christmas, Doug had moved; he had a job and a red-faced, mostly bald little boy named Arnold.

"Arnold!" Chris exclaimed before he thought. "*Jesus*, Doug, you got to be kidding. You named your kid *Arnold*?"

"That's right, what's the big deal? You think *Christopher* is such a great name? And as I recall Beejee's driver's license says his name is Bennet. What's the difference? I call him Arnie."

"Lily's *got* to have picked that name."

"So?"

When they came over Lily ignored them. She wasn't even hostile anymore. When they came in she gave them a smug, contemptuous glance and then pretended they weren't around. It was as though whatever there was about them that had irritated her had disappeared—and left nothing at all. She hadn't lost much weight with the baby. She still looked vaguely pregnant, and in the thin nylon blouse she wore her breasts looked swollen and enormous.

Doug caught them both looking at her. "Mother earth," he said. "She thinks she's got something the world needs. Cop a feel if you've a mind to, she won't mind."

Thereafter Lily stalked cockroaches with her slipper.

The new house was in a neighborhood more or less like the old, but it was bigger—half a duplex. There was a small yard in back, surrounded by a hurricane fence and overrun with weeds. It looked as though the place had not been cleaned since they moved in, and in fact Doug complained several times that Lily had become a slob. He seldom referred to her by name; rather it was "the cow" did this, or said that. And the baby was usually "the little shit-machine." But for all his sour abusiveness, Doug seemed to have made his accommodation. In fact the abuse seemed to express rather than deny it.

Doug was a "management trainee" at a loan company. The pay was bad, and Lily hadn't gone back to work. She was thinking about enrolling in art courses at the college, Doug said. Someone had seen her work and said he could get her some scholarship money. But it wouldn't even be enough to cover day care.

They didn't see much of each other over the holidays. Doug's job kept him working late. And sometimes Lily went off and left him with the baby. One time they did manage to drag him away, and they all went across the river. It was Tuesday night, between Christmas and New Year, and nothing much was happening. They played the jukebox and drank a few beers at The Big Oak. They even made a halfhearted attempt to pick up a couple of girls from Lake Charles.

Doug gradually loosened up a little. He told sarcastic stories about the people at work. The place survived by sucking money from blacks, mostly, he said. But *barely* survived. The margin was the aggressiveness they squeezed out of the collectors. "That's what they're training me for," he said, "to get my throat cut." He said he had taken a test for computer work and done well, but financing the training was another matter.

"I hate Lily," he said at one point, with a feeble smile. "I hate her guts. *Especially* her guts."

"So why the fuck don't you leave?" Chris asked irritably.

"I hate the kid, too. Most of the time. Because he reminds me of her you know. Same hair, eyes, same swollen gut. But I know that's not fair. I fight it, I do. You know she's not even good in the sack anymore. Except when she *wants* to be. She and that Pam—God only knows." Doug suddenly grinned brightly, "There's a nice dumb hot little number at the office, though."

New Year's Eve was a surprisingly warm night, a promise of April, the smell of the marsh lying heavy in the air. Beejee and Chris went by Doug's to help him celebrate—Lily had left him with the kid. Doug had almost killed a bottle of Heaven Hill, but he had another bottle in reserve. He was clearly trying to drink himself out—filling a big tumbler with bourbon and hardly bothering to splash a little water in. He seemed glad to see them but had little to say. In the long silences they could hear a scurrying sound from under the sink. "Roaches breeding in the paper bags," Doug explained.

Shortly after midnight they got up to go, and Doug walked, very unsteadily, with them to the car. It had turned quite a bit cooler, and the dampness made it seem colder than it was.

"I wanted to ask you guys a favor," Doug said, leaning down to the car window. "I thought maybe I'd go to computer school and one of you guys would take care of my cow and my little shit-machine for me."

Doug made a halfhearted attempt at a laugh.

"Seriously, I do have a favor." He peered in at them, then turned his face up toward the sky, or the streetlamp, that made a white mask of it. He swayed slightly and grasped the roof of the car to steady himself. When he spoke, it was in a quiet, dreamy sort of voice. "You may not believe me. But I think I could kill her. And get off, too. In Texas no one minds if you kill your wife, if she's ornery and not too good looking. What do you think?"

Beejee started the car. Chris said, "You couldn't kill Lily with anything less than a silver bullet."

Doug grinned, bobbing his head in and out of the window, in and out of the light of the streetlamp. "Hey, no, I'm *serious*. Only there's the kid, you see? It wouldn't be fair to do him. Remember *La Dolce Vita*, that guy Steiner? See, I could never do that, I'm not a philosopher . . . . But you guys are my lifelong buddies, right? If something happened, would you . . . sort of take responsibility? If you know what I mean. I never told you, Beejee, you're the kid's godfather-in-absentia."

"You're crazy," Chris said with disgust.

"Drunk as a skunk, that's all," said Beejee.

"Hey, no kidding? You guys wouldn't do that for me? Look, Lily and me have nothing to do with this, just the kid, just bald little Arnie."

"Look, Doug, if you really want to be serious," Chris said, "why don't you just dump that bitch? Let her take the kid too. It's not much harder to get cut free than it is to get tied up."

"That's where you're wrong," Doug said. "But you don't know." Doug paused, as though considering, and for the first time the smile on his face looked natural. "No, my friends," he said at last, "it can't be done. Ne-vair hoppen, cher."

"Why the fuck not!"

Doug shook his head, still smiling. "Cannot be done, ma fren'."

"You're out of your fucking gourd."

Doug seemed to bow to this, then rapped his knuckles in a brief tattoo on the roof of the car. The mask flashed at them and then he wheeled away, shuffling toward his front door. About halfway he fell down and waved his arms around as though warding off help. He regained his feet, and when he managed to reach the door Beejee drove away.

* * * *

Neither Beejee nor Chris came home for Easter. When they did come home in June, Doug, Lily, and the baby were gone. They had simply disappeared. Doug's folks said they not only didn't know where he had gone, but they didn't want to know. They wouldn't explain. They couldn't reach Lily's parents at all—they didn't know whether they had left town, or whether they had got the last name wrong. Finally they tried Pam. They drove to a pay phone at a gas station. Beejee waited in the car, watching Chris dial three numbers, then talk briefly. Chris came back to the car, shaking his head.

"You won't believe it," he said. "That scraggly cunt managed to catch herself a husband."

"Good *God*!"

"Yeah, some guy at the refinery. He didn't sound either insane or retarded. Maybe he's a triple amputee or something."

"So what did she say?"

"She knows."

"Yeah?"

"Yeah. She knows, but she ain't sayin'. She enjoyed the hell out of it."

"Out of what?"

"Talking to me. Knowing and not telling. Knowing I know, but that there's nothing I can do to her. What a bitch."

"Do you think maybe later? How did she sound?"

"No chance at all. Dead end."

Jobs were scarce. Beejee got a construction job for a few weeks, Chris never found a thing. The hot muggy days were long and oppressive. By July they were both looking forward to school as to salvation. They half hoped Doug would write, or suddenly show up, or *some*thing. But, as they expected, nothing happened. They felt that somehow they had been cast adrift, and it seemed likely that it would be the last time they would come home for the summer.

In late August they drove over to The Big Oak for a last "memorial beer." But The Big Oak was no more. The building—and the oak—were still there. But the sign had been torn down. Pieces of it lay about the parking lot. A small, hand-drawn sign in the door announced: "Under New Management." They went in for a couple beers anyway.

In the afternoon light the place looked like a big barn, or an empty warehouse, with light from the small, high windows making yellow bars on the walls. They were the only customers. They were served by a woman in pink pedal pushers and pumps, with dry bleached-blonde hair. She was too old and too sour to flirt with.

They sat at a table near the jukebox. By turns one or the other of them would stand in front of the box, reading and rereading the titles, and finally shoving a coin in and picking something more or less at random. But every time the music stopped it left the place emptier than before.

On the third beer Chris asked: "Why do you think Doug wouldn't just get a divorce?"

Beejee shrugged. "Maybe he did."

Chris shook his head. "Maybe he shot her with a silver bullet, too."

Beejee made a snort that was supposed to be a laugh. "Or a silver spike, at midnight. My money's on *her.*"

"Why do you suppose that is? Doug was always such a *mean* little bastard."

"One way or another she *had* him, I guess. I don't know. You can't live someone else's life for them."

"There ought to be *something* you can do!" Chris said hotly.

To this Beejee did not reply. He stood and wandered away toward the toilet. Chris put his feet up on the chair with a defiant look at the woman and nervously jingled the keys and change in his pocket. Beejee came back and flopped into his chair. They sat for a while in silence, occasionally pulling at their beers. Neither looked anymore to the jukebox that seemed to peer over their shoulders, like a third companion at this meager feast, as sullen and silent as they.

Finally Chris said: "He just lost his nerve, that's all."

"Not entirely," Beejee said.

"Sure he did. He didn't do anything. He hardly even said *ouch.*"

"I don't know, it took some nerve."

"What?"

"What he did to *us*."

Chris looked angrily at Beejee and then away. "If you want to call that nerve."

"Whatever you want to call it."

Chris watched the last, golden, guillotine-shaped bar of light rise slowly up the opposite wall. His face was grim—and pained. They both felt it. Something precious, as fluid and elusive as youth itself, was trickling away. Chris drained his beer and shook his head.

"Whatever you want to call it," he said.

The Assistant

It was like an egg, fried too long, fried till it's hard, dry, and dull pale yellow. To Ray Begnaud, sitting in the shade of the grandstand, mechanically waving at mosquitoes, it hardly seemed to move at all as it glowed sickly in the colorless sky. Through the stands, like enormous venetian blinds, he watched the children run and dance around in the hot glare. As long as possible he would remain sitting in the shade, watching the white T-shirts scatter and gather, watching the summer pass.

Nothing changed, nothing moved forward, there was no relief. Except that days did somehow tick off, and September, a sinkhole of dread, crept closer and closer. Two-a-day practices, the damp, still mornings, scorching afternoons . . . for which the whole summer was one long wait. In the meantime hiding from that eye, blistering the air, the focus of all the daily monotony, of all the boredom in the world.

"Begnaud!"

Ray brought the front legs of his chair down hard. He glared, then smiled, at the figure above him in the stands.

"You wanna get off your butt?"

"Sure, coach, whatcha got?"

"Wanna work the shot-putters? Kay's givin' you a life a Riley, huh?" Haller was trying to be chummy and sharp at the same time, and as usual he couldn't bring it off.

"Sure, coach, she's great. She don't need neither of us."

"I see you don't run with her anymore. She run you out? September's just around the corner . . . ."

"Yah . . ." Ray drawled the syllable in a faintly derisive

way. "Tell ya, coach, I try not to think too hard about September."

"Won't go away."

"I still work out, I just don't run with Kay is all." He paused, caught a mosquito in his fist that had been buzzing around. "There's no point. I mean, she's a girl. She's a strong runner and all but she's too slow. . . . I work out mornings now."

Haller nodded. Ray just caught sight of his grin between the seats before he turned away, saying, "I'd appreciate it if you could spare a few minutes for those shot-putters."

Ray muttered curses as he walked along under the stands. Mostly he cursed himself. What made him say that about Kay? Comparing himself to a *girl*. And bragging! Haller always did that to him, got him to say things . . . that didn't come out right. At least there hadn't been any others to hear. What a summer—Haller had spoiled it. With his goddamn sarcastic grins.

A wall of scorched air hit Ray as he stepped out into the sunlight. There was Haller with the T-shirts flocking around him. Looking like Moses and the children of Israel, for Christ's sake. Ray's gym shoes squeaked on the grass of the field and little spasms of pain shot up into his sore calf-muscles.

As he drew up to the four boys waiting for him he barked: "OK, enough crappin' around, time to do a little work, gents."

"Uh–oh," Henderson said, "Look who's talkin' about *work*."

"Hey coach, how's ol' Kay Hoffpauir doin' these days?" Jennings asked.

"Enough lip action. I haven't seen that fifty footer you promised me, Henderson." Ray accepted the ribbing easily. They were four or five years his junior and they had worked out a comfortable relationship that gave Ray less than the authority of a coach but something more than an equal.

"Aw, you should see how he's fadin'," Jennings said. "Three thirty-nines and he's almost splittin' a gut."

"I'm slippin' I tell ya," Henderson said.

"We gonna hear that after the meet, too?" Ray asked, and the others guffawed.

They told him they were loose, but he made them make some easy tosses anyway, standing flat-footed and pushing just with their arms, then some back stretchers. Ray had never done shot put himself in high school, never thought to try, but Haller had showed him how so he could coach them. And he'd discovered he was pretty good at it. Not good enough to try it at A&M, but he probably could have earned a letter in high school. Just another boat he'd missed: a three letter man!

"Hey, there he goes," Henderson said, turning toward the 220 track. "Look at that little bastard fly!"

All the others turned to watch, including Ray.

"Shit!"

"That sonovabitch is gonna be fantastic."

"Whattaya mean? He *is* fantastic. Hit 9.8 yesterday."

"Hey, did I tell you? I made a 10.7 myself yesterday. Coach says he may let me run in the 100."

"You'll look pretty funny, coming in a second after Le-Blanc."

"Shit, everybody'll come in a second after *him*. I might place."

"Yeah, and you might hit the moon with this shot put, too."

"Henderson, I just wish you'd hit forty feet," Ray quipped. LeBlanc's 220 was finished, and he brought them over to the ring. Ray had mixed feelings about the boy wonder. Fifteen years old and the paper was full of him. He hadn't even smelled a varsity football game and they were already touting him an all-state. He would bring in a state championship, that was the prevailing fantasy. As though one man could. Always the backs who got the attention—the publicity. When Ray made second-team all-state there was hardly a murmur. Who cares about guards? Even Coach Benton—Coach Benton knew damn well that his line was his strong point, year after year—but that time on TV, the Pasadena game, there was Ray Begnaud breaking into the other team's backfield, dogging down that quarterback, the announcer asking who that was and Benton said: "Oh that, uh, that's just a lineman, Begnaud . . . ."

"OK, loafers, I'll give you something to toss at," Ray said and took the shot from Jennings. His form wasn't by any means perfect—only what Haller could teach him in fifteen minutes, but he heaved it past the fifty-foot mark.

"Aw, c'mon, coach, give us a break."

"You ought to throw left-handed, coach, that'd be fair."

"Listen, you guys, I'm just an amateur, never even touched one of these things before a few weeks ago. *You* guys are the experts. So let's see some action."

They looked at him in an odd way, and it occurred to him he had said this too many times.

Henderson, who was the best, could do not better than about forty-seven. "That won't get you no medals," Ray told him.

At the other end of the field the T-shirts were converging on Haller from all sides. Ray sent the shot-putters down—the workout was over. He walked leisurely toward the starting blocks, taking his time. It was his job to dig them up and put them in the field house. And pull the hurdles in under the stands. As far as he was concerned, this was his *only* real job. Haller, a new coach, had taken Ray's title "assistant coach" too seriously, making him responsible for the intermediate and senior girls, and at odd times, the shot-putters. It was just to annoy him. Coach Meyer, who was Junior Olympics coach before Haller, and an old football coach of Ray's, had simply let Ray use the time for doing his own workouts. And then of course he had cleared up the field afterwards. They didn't pay him enough for anything more, a semi-job really. Luckily, the intermediate girls amounted to little—the number fluctuated between six and ten on different days, and they weren't very serious. Not the age for girls and track. And the senior girls amounted to Kay Hoffpauir, who was so good she was almost a professional. At least she didn't need any coaching from *him*. So Haller could make fun of Ray's "coaching" and still make him go through with it. He was simply an asshole. And he hadn't been around in Ray Begnaud's glory years here, he had no respect.

By the time Ray dragged in the hurdles the heat had eased. He had the field house to himself, showered and sang, and as usual the hollow sound of the shower room gave him an uneasy feeling. So familiar: the musty, sweaty smell, the old chipped blackboard—he could almost see Benton beside it, fuming over the Texas City game. Something had been left behind here, but it was hard to say what—or why. He was the same man. A little bigger, stronger, faster. And of course, in a faster league now at A&M. Somehow he just couldn't fight his way to the crest. In high school he had been the best. Among the coaches, the players, the few fans who really knew football, there had been little doubt. He had received the most offers, hadn't he? But at A&M he just labored among the middle range. He believed he was better, maybe, just an increment, but he couldn't seem to prove it. He still hadn't earned a letter. He certainly should this year but . . . but that wasn't enough. He wanted to be first team—no, that wasn't enough either. He wanted to be all-conference. He could aspire to that. No more, certainly, but to that. And then they would take notice of him again back home. Even Haller, maybe.

If he thought about it too hard—if he let himself brood too much on the sound in the empty shower, the smell of the locker room . . . he would be swept by a fierce determination to be in the best shape of his life, he would put his shorts back on and run, run till he was sick, even though he'd had a full workout in the morning. And this never helped in the least. You didn't get in shape like that, that was mere flailing the air.

When he was ready to go home at last each evening the air had a soft, dusty, forgiving quality, a light golden brown. He stopped at the door to the dressing room to glance at the sun, setting behind the stands, hanging over the black silhouette of the refinery—it looked like the company's official symbol in fact. And he inevitably thought: it's like they bought that sky, that particular portion, just to hang their symbol on it so there'll be no doubts of their ownership: land, sky, lives by the thousands. And if Ray failed, perhaps his life as well.

✿   ✿   ✿   ✿

August dragged along. Ray took his ease in the shade when he could, cursed Haller and the LeBlanc kid with his growing ring of worshipers, and played at being a coach with the giggling intermediate girls.

There was something criminal in how things were falling into place for Leland LeBlanc, he decided. They would canonize him before he performed a single miracle. The track didn't really matter in itself, of course. It was the promise for football that had everyone excited. And yet he was just a scrawny, pimple-faced, fifteen-year-old kid. It was particularly amusing—in an unpleasant way—to Ray, since he had known Leland LeBlanc years before, when he was still playing cowboys and Indians. His older brother, Tim, had been a friend. Briefly. Leland was always running around screaming in the most repulsive, high-pitched voice and being completely obnoxious. And one day Ray's patience snapped, he'd kicked the kid's tail a good one and stalked off, never to even say hello to his brother again. Now look!

The face hadn't changed, except for the pimples. The nose, especially, was as unattractive as ever: it turned up so the nostrils opened right at you. The body had changed, of course, lengthening mostly, especially the legs—like an ostrich's, knotty and a little big footed. And gradually, over the summer, from reading so much of himself in the paper and hearing so much of himself from Haller and others, his style had changed too, the way he carried his head. He was getting such a swelled head he didn't know *how* to carry it.

Ray believed that no one really saw what was happening but him. Leland had been an unpopular kid, a nothing, the kind who hangs around the edge of the circles that form . . . looking at the popular guys from a distance and not even dreaming of being one. And then suddenly his legs grow long and someone discovers how fast he is and that alone changes the universe: no longer a remote satellite but a sun. He was taking it in now, trying to adapt, to adjust to this. Leland LeBlanc was a *name!* You read it in the paper, heard it in the street, the barbershop. So some of the time Leland tried to act cocky and confident. And other times he retreated, obviously longed to return to the simpler condition, where all he had to do was hover and admire others—to be a kid and play cowboys and Indians again. The whole scene disgusted Ray. The kid, after all, was still the same. Obnoxious. And the process of rising to the top—Ray knew it all too well. He had never been such a waste as Leland, but he had risen also and felt—well, it was like a new responsibility on his shoulders. And now, now his shoulders were uncomfortably light, and it was hard not to despise this kid's pimples.

The intermediate girls were gaga over Leland, naturally enough, and Ray found himself sneering at their prattle. Leland hadn't the slightest idea what to do with the situation. Ray had to bite his tongue sometimes to keep from telling the girls what a twit Leland LeBlanc really was. He was a coach, after all, it wasn't for him to lower himself to the level of disputing with fourteen-year-old girls about their latest fantasy heartthrob.

In the mornings, when Ray came out to the stadium to run alone, the air was absolutely still and steam rose from the grass. Most mornings he ran a dozen fifties and a fairly fast mile, but others he felt listless and just jogged a bit and stood around, did a few chins and push-ups. Summer training was such a misery anyway. It was arbitrary. You never knew how much was enough. The first few days of two-a-days were going to wipe you out anyway, no matter how hard you trained, and the coaches, one or another of them, would say you weren't in shape, you hadn't trained. And yet training might just be the difference, the tiny advantage over the other guy that got you on the first team. Some sudden burst of effort late in a practice that a coach saw . . . the coaches formed their impressions early in September and were slow to change them.

After working out he came home, ate lunch with his mother in front of the TV, the soaps, then went back for the Olympics in the afternoon. By mid-June, nights were so warm he didn't much feel like dating, especially not with the girls around town. It was too sticky to neck—and what else could such girls do? None of his friends from high school had gone to A&M, and so they'd grown apart, although once in a while they'd tour the old haunts together—bowling alley, miniature golf, drive-ins—and watch the latest generation repeating their own stupidities. It all seemed stale to Ray, but what else was there? He might long for college—in general it was better—but first you had to get past the two-a-days, and there was no way to look forward to *them*. Occasionally he ran into an old teammate and they made noise about the old times, but it was hollow noise. Ray was the only one to have gone on to real big-time football, it was a different league than say, Sam Houston, or Lamar, and they knew it. They never pressed him for details on how he was doing—if he did well they'd know it, no need to ask. These meetings always depressed him, left him restless and anxious, feeling he wasn't getting anywhere. Should he quit? This was a dark thought indeed, but he entertained it, even at times courted it. But for what? Pipefitting at Gulf? Selling cars or something? No, he had to get his degree, had to launch himself away from this town; and besides, football, with all its disappointments, was still the most exciting thing in his life. He should make first team, and if he did . . . he was realistic. You might *dream* of All-American, pro-ball, but he wasn't good enough for that. If he made first team he'd have to fight hard to hold it every week, there'd be no resting, but—football was the only thing he had, the only future worth thinking about.

✿   ✿   ✿   ✿

The district meet of Junior Olympics was held near the end of August. For a while it looked like Ray might just surprise Haller. One of the intermediate girls started looking real good in the hurdles! Ray knew nothing about hurdles, but the girl was a natural. He'd thought nothing of her at first— she was too pretty, too feminine to be any kind of athlete, he thought. He encouraged her and timed her, and she was good enough to place, maybe to win. Haller had expected nothing from the intermediate girls—wouldn't he be surprised! And because he wanted to see Haller's face when his girl won points, he never mentioned it. He just ran her, encouraged her, timed her, and grinned to himself as she got faster and faster. But then in the last week before the meet she hit a hurdle hard enough to hurt herself. It wasn't anything really serious, she was running the next day, but it did something to her confidence. She started hesitating at the hurdles and this threw her timing off and she hit one every time she ran. After two days of this she came to him, crying, actually crying, and begged off: she was so sorry to "disappoint" him she said. And this moved him—to think she should feel that way toward him, that he was someone she didn't want to let down! But it meant he had nothing to offer at the meet, unless you counted Kay, who was her own coach.

It was a night meet and being on the field under the familiar lights gave Ray a spooky feeling. He couldn't watch the meet as a whole since he was a judge at the broad jump and then a scorer. Their team won though, Leland taking the 100, 220, and anchoring the winning 440-relay in his division. Kay won two firsts and a third. None of the intermediate girls even came close to placing, and even the shot-putters scored nothing.

As the winning coach, Haller would take a combined team to regionals. Theoretically Ray was to accompany him. But Ray had already decided to skip the trip. He would have his final paycheck. If they didn't like it, what could they do? He didn't need the job next summer—he could graduate by then, if he wanted, if he chose not to come back for the fifth year he had coming because he'd been redshirted. No, he'd use the time for relaxing, enjoying his leisure, maybe working out twice a day.

The last week—after the meet and before regionals—Ray loafed. His training slacked off. He arrived at work late, but Haller said nothing. After workouts in the morning he drove around—and sometimes instead of working out.

The very last day, a Thursday, Ray sat in the shade with the shot-putters. They weren't going to regionals, they continued to work out only because they all played football and so were "expected" to. It was one of those dull, hot days with a lot of dust or smoke or something in the air so the sky was almost tan colored, the sun orange and blurry. The grass—everywhere except the field—was brown from a dry summer. Across the field they could see the sprinters working with Haller, but they too looked sluggish and mechanical. It seemed abnormally quiet, probably because only a small percentage of the little kids were still coming. When someone did shout, it sounded far away, farther than it was, as though carried on the wind.

A typical "dog day," Ray mused. Common enough at A&M

during September. The kind of day that took every ounce of your energy and will to keep going, that no habit or discipline could carry you through. As the coaches said, a "testing" day; testing what? They were less precise about that. Your guts, your manhood presumably, what they called your "character."

Suddenly Ray found himself walking toward the sprinters. Haller was instructing LeBlanc, they were at the blocks. Haller had said that was where Leland needed the most improvement, in the start, he was still young and hadn't developed the power out of the blocks. This was interesting to Ray because it was here he was strongest. Ten yards are everything to a guard, for ten yards Ray was as fast as any man on his team.

He stopped and watched Leland break out of the blocks a few times. It was an odd stance, the ass way up high: he looked like an ostrich. Ray felt a slight tingle in his knees.

"Hey LeBlanc, what about a race?" He himself was surprised at the challenge that came from his mouth.

Puzzled faces turned toward him, including Haller's and Leland's. Leland honked: "What, coach, you and me?"

"Sure, why not? Just, say, forty yards? I'm no sprinter, but I've got a pretty good start."

There was no comment from anyone, which surprised Ray. He'd expected a little more interest. There was only puzzlement.

"I'm only about 10.5 in the 100," Ray said, shaving a few tenths, "but my speed is all in my start, you know? A guard only needs that jump. It OK with you Coach Haller?"

Haller shrugged in a way—Ray had a keen desire to step over and punch his face in.

"LeBlanc?" Ray inquired.

"Sure, coach, anything you say."

Haller walked down the track, stopwatch in hand. Ray jogged around and loosened his legs. LeBlanc seemed to be taking the race seriously at least, he was retying his shoes. This reminded Ray he only had on gym shoes and he borrowed a pair of track shoes from one of the other sprinters —they were tight, but they'd do for one race.

Ray tried the blocks a few times. They felt a little awkward but very fast. It would have been better without them since he'd never used them before, but he was in it now. Haller waited with the stopwatch in the air. Ray jumped too quick once and had to come back.

It seemed to Ray he was out of the blocks even before Haller's hand passed his shoulder. He rolled out smoothly, the sharp cleats biting neatly into the cinder, his legs hurling him forward with speed that surprised him. He thought he was ahead—but no, there was Leland right beside him. A sudden anguish seemed to cramp his heart, for he could see plainly that each stride Leland took was longer than his: *no chance!* The sense of power and ease slipped away from him, his strides felt rough, the cleats seemed to stick in the track for a fraction of a second. His whole body felt suddenly heavy, clumsy, fated, and the track, the whole earth seemed to attack him through his legs, jolting him with each stride as LeBlanc moved swiftly ahead, the long, long legs reaching out magically. Ray was several yards back at the finish, and he stumbled right in front of Haller and almost fell.

Ray stood catching his breath, hands on knees as Leland came walking back.

"How'd I do, coach?" Leland asked Haller.

"Same," Haller said and put the watch in his pocket.

"What about me, coach?" Ray said. "What was my time?"

"I only got one watch, Begnaud."

Back at the starting line Ray pulled off and returned the cleats, put on his gym shoes. He headed toward the field house and found himself walking beside Leland. Ray slapped him on the back. He felt a sudden warmth toward him, a former neighbor, a friend's brother—and a kid on his way into so much that Ray already knew all about.

"You're looking real good out there," Ray said. "You got a great career ahead. You're getting quicker off the blocks. It's not necessarily something that shows on the watch, you know, it's a matter of mental attitude, of character, something you don't develop overnight."

Leland nodded.

"I may have clipped you by a hair, right at the start," Ray continued. "You haven't come into your full strength yet, and besides the reaction time is a factor, a guard's got to have very fast reflexes you know . . . ."

Leland turned, a surprised, hesitant grin on his face.

"What do you think, Powell," Ray asked one of the kids standing near the field house. "Didn't I have him by a hair maybe the first couple steps?"

"Naw, coach, looked to me like he had you from the gun."

Ray stared at Powell as though expecting more, then nodded. He slapped LeBlanc on the back again, or rather, patted the opposite shoulder, wet with sweat.

"Anyway, you keep up the good work, y'hear? Hard training, discipline, that's the thing."

They walked a few more steps, matching strides.

". . . Yeah, *discipline*, I ought to know. But look, Leland, I got chores to do—last time this year! And some laps. We both got football coming at us; I got two-a-days in a little more than a week you know. So I'll be seein' ya, OK?"

"Sure, see ya, coach," Leland nodded, grinned, and walked on without breaking stride as Ray fell back.

He gathered the hurdles and threw them under the stands. He dug up the blocks and tossed them in a heap inside the field house. He was free!

Long, reddish shadows lay across the field now, the sun was a rusty color. On an impulse Ray set off on a mile. By the end of one lap, however, his legs were rubbery and his breath painful, so he quit.

At least he'd have the field house, the locker room to himself now, he thought. He'd had a heavy workout that morning, why push it at this point? No point running himself sick *now*. He had a week. A week all his own. The thing was to be methodical. In a week he could put himself in the best shape of his life; and he would.

The Home Country

It was as though the double bump of the drawbridge was to be the last sound they ever heard: the hot, thick silence of the marsh swallowed them.

The road ran straight over the marsh on a ridge of oyster shells, a gray black cord stretched taut across the soft pale green. Heat waves rose from the asphalt, making the air visible, palpable, quivering before them in a dance of defiance as they drove.

At first the marsh looked empty. Then, gradually, they noticed the cadaverous cattle slogging through the mud, the egrets jerking stealthily, stalking the slime, grayish blurs of mosquito swarms against the white sky at the horizon.

Fannett looked at his temperature gauge: the needle tapped at the red band. It was no place for an old car like this in July, but there was no turning back now . . . .

"We're out of beer," Santos said. Not for the first time.

"I heard."

"Well *fuck*."

The car hit a swarm of mosquitoes and a gray smear spread across the windshield.

"Jesus!" Hebert exclaimed.

"Got a few mosquitoes out here," said Benoit. He sounded a little proud.

"I want beer!" Santos insisted.

The two six-packs certainly hadn't lasted long. Not with Dina drinking—as much or more than anyone else. Illegal beer. Now they were legal. Louisiana didn't just have a lower drinking age than Texas, they had a different attitude.

"There's a place up here beside the road a few miles," Santos said. "Not far, I remember it."

"Just bet you do," Fannett said.

"Yeah. Just a bar, nothing else. All by itself."

"Why not wait—till Lost Beach?"

"*Wait*? Why?"

"I don't know . . . I just feel like getting somewhere first . . . ."

"Lost Beach is somewhere?"

"*Two* bars in Lost Beach," Benoit said. "That's someplace."

"Oh yeah," Santos said. "Really groovy gas station too. Three pumps. Hasn't seen action since 1902."

The needle nibbled at the red. Fannett tried to control his annoyance. When he went, he liked to go all at once, he hated this pulsing, these little jumps. It seemed like zigzagging. If Santos had his way they'd stop at every bar between the border and Bergeron.

"It's only a few miles more," he said, "what's the difference?"

"A few miles!"

"You'll live."

"Fuck, *fuck*, Fuck!" Dina screamed. "Let's just *get* it, stop all this *shit*." Her voice, piercing, suddenly glissandoed into a ripple of laughter. "Bee–er," she concluded, giggling.

"Looks like you're outvoted," Santos said.

"Oh Christ. What is this, granny ladies' election night? I'm driving, it's my car."

"Up yours, buddy! You can't bully us on that account. That's just *horse*shit."

Fuck him, the prick, Fannett thought. Fuck them all. He hadn't wanted to bring his car out here in the first place. The needle was definitely into the red now.

"My car's running hot," he said. "Once I kill the engine it'll have to cool a long time before it starts. *If* it starts."

"It'll start," Hebert said—he was the mechanic. "Your car always runs hot."

"Not this hot—look at the goddamn gauge!"

"It'll start," Santos assured him.

"Oh, if you say so," Fannett said. "You don't know the generator from the carburetor, you asshole."

The argument went no further. It was beside the point anyway. Fannett's reluctance to stop was only circumstantially aligned with the problem of the car. Part of it was a desire simply not to fall into Santos's design. Santos always assumed he was the appointed leader. They had been after each other like this all summer; it was monotonous.

Fannett turned his attention to the "scenery." He wondered: could any other place on the surface of the earth be as flat as this? As flat and empty? Certain deserts maybe, and the ocean. There were trees occasionally—oaks they looked like. They passed by about a quarter mile to the south, always about the same distance, as though they marked a line or frontier of something . . . . Yes, all summer it had been like that with him and Santos, snap snap snap. Do *some*thing, *any*thing—that was Santos's philosophy. It didn't matter what, anything but idleness, boredom. He attacked boredom as if it were a ferocious animal, clawing and kicking. To no avail, of course. It didn't matter what they did. Whether they sat around somebody's house, or around Gralino's over cokes, or got into one of Santos's "adventures" and had to run from the cops—what difference did it make? It was spoiled anyway. The freedom. Yes, that was it, the freedom of summer really spoiled itself, rotted on the vine. The nights for instance—sometimes it didn't cool till late, close to midnight maybe, the heavy heat, the leaden air just hanging still, and then when it came, the first breath, the first touch of coolness—it stank of the refineries.

Home country they called it. Everyone, no matter where they came from actually. Fannett's family came from the red dirt piney woods country, but even he . . . like when they were burning the marsh. You could see the gray plumes from town, one after the other on the horizon. Muskrat hunters or cattle growers did it. The wind would bring the smell in from over the lake and whatever you were doing you stopped when you smelled it, lifted your head like some sort of animal testing the wind. Wild, sharp, a little sweet . . . . Benoit had family still out there somewhere. Just south of Lake Charles he said. Maybe they still poled to town on pirogues? With muskrat and nutria furs.

Suddenly a building leaped up beside the road.

"There, pull over," Santos ordered.

Fannett braked. On the blank wall facing them "Bar-Lounge" had been drawn inexpertly in red. He steered the car cautiously off the paved surface down the shell slope. As soon as his tires left the road he felt a fear, almost a panic contract into a ball in his stomach. When the shells exploded behind the rear wheels the fear exploded with them, and then it was gone.

He stared at the small gray building, waiting for the others to climb out of the car. In the hot air it wavered and blurred like a mirage, seemed about to melt. When he got out, the sun on his head and shoulders felt more like weight than heat—a burden. The earth seemed to be held in tension by it, stretched tight as a drum top. There was a faint smell, not quite like the smoke, a little dusty, but sharp and sweet . . . .

It was surprisingly cool inside. The few windows were shuttered so the only light came through the screen door, and from a red and blue beer sign behind the bar. There were wooden stools at the bar and a few square wooden tables with folding chairs. In the dim light it looked as though the room was mostly empty. The floor was worn rough by dancing. On the far side they could just make out the huge squat shape of a jukebox, turned off, looking somehow sinister.

"Hello! Hidy! Anybody here?" Dina yelled toward a small doorway behind the bar. A man appeared suddenly through it and nodded to them.

"Five big cold ones, my man," Dina said.

The man, small, with thick shiny black hair, put five beer cans on the bar and without a word began to open them with a hand opener: each can sent a *whish* into the dark like an audible puff of smoke.

By the time they took the beers to one of the tables the man had silently disappeared.

They tried to talk—about Bergeron, the festival—but the heavy silence of the bar seemed to intrude. The longer they sat, the more force it seemed to accumulate, sucking thirstily at the sounds of their voices. Only Dina wouldn't give in. While the others gradually fell silent, she got louder. She laughed at nothing at all, scraped her chair viciously across the floor, and chattered, almost yelling at them. Finally, when no one seemed inclined to say anything to her, she jumped up restlessly, went over to the bar, reconjured the man, and demanded five more beers.

She brought the beers to the table pillowed against her soft breasts—she wore no brassiere—and grinning savagely. "*Shit*," she shouted at them, "this place is a *tomb*."

Coming out of the bar, Fannett felt the sudden sun as a blow. He waited, a little dizzy, while the others got in. He was a little high—and edgy. He thought of a hurricane—the eye. Something about the lack of pressure, they said, it made you depressed, suicidal, murderous. This was prime hurricane country of course—Bergeron had been wiped out only a few years ago. And the countryside looked like something had blown it flat, swept it clean.

Back on the road the others were more cheerful. Dina started singing and everyone joined in, including Fannett. They competed at making obscene verses for "Jamaica Farewell."

Lost Beach was a cluster of houses at an intersection with a dirt road. The houses were small, rectangular, single floor, wood frame, all graying, mounted on bricks. The first bar was closed. It was right at the intersection, all the windows were boarded up, and the roofline sagged dangerously in the middle. Across the highway was the gas station, its cylindrical pumps bleached of any color or identifying signs. The windows of the stucco building were also boarded up, had been for a long time, and there were large holes in the walls. The two ruins, facing each other across the narrow black roadway, made the village seem like something withered by the sun. The dirt road, perfectly straight in both directions, looked like an angry gash in the marsh.

The other bar was the last building on the Bergeron side. It was open, and Fannett pulled up in front. Just before he killed the engine he glanced at the gauge: the needle was right in the center of the red.

Once again they stepped from blinding glare into blind darkness and had to grope their way to the bar. A large man with an enormous bulging belly stood behind the bar. He watched them come in as though he had been expecting them.

Though his expression was grim, he looked a little like a Buddha. After serving them their beers, the man did not move but stood in the same place, staring at the door as though expecting someone else, his big fists resting on the bar.

They sat at the table nearest the bar.

"Hey, man, nice place you got here," Dina said to the bartender. "Nice town." He didn't reply.

Somehow it wasn't as cool here as in the first place; the air had a thick, dusty quality and seemed hard to breathe. The shaft of light slanting through the screen door hardly dissipated at all so the room lay mostly in gloom even after their eyes had adjusted. The silence, too, seemed even denser than before, indefinite, infinite, an emanation of the marsh. Fannett realized he hadn't seen any sign of life in the village as they drove through.

They drank their beers in silence, ordered a round for the road, and left.

"Hey, man, why do they call that groovy place 'Lost Beach'?" Dina asked when they were back on the road again.

"They had a beach once," Benoit said, "but then they lost it."

Nobody laughed.

"Actually, there may have been a beach once," Hebert said. "Mud and shell, you know. This here's what's called a *chenier*. The marsh keeps filling up the Gulf, moving the coast outward . . . ."

"You're talking about thousands of years," Santos said.

"No, much faster than that. In some places anyway."

For awhile no one said anything. Then Dina said, with a kind of awe: "It's one creepy place."

"Can you imagine living there?" Fannett asked, expressing aloud a question he had been asking himself. "I mean, your whole life?"

"Why not?" Santos sounded testy.

"Are you kidding? Talk about nothing. Jee–zus. What would you *do*?"

"Work. Like anyplace else. And you have nature, real nature, not just some pretty picture."

"Oh man," Fannett said, unbelieving. "Think of the reality.

The long days, the heat, everything soggy and steaming, nothing to do from one year to the next but watch a few sick cattle slosh around, the rice inching up . . . ."

"Yeah, they miss a lot," Santos said sarcastically. "Miniature golf, Bat-a-bat, Gralino's watery coffee, the bowling alley, and Walt Disney movies. Except they could drive in to the fleshpots on weekends I guess. And they got TV—you see all the antennae? We're lucky all right . . . . Listen, these people have something we *don't*. I mean, we're always hot to keep up with what's happening someplace *else*, right. Because we're not *any*where. Here—it's their own little world, really, they don't need to know what's happening someplace else . . . . And they have a beauty in their lives . . . ."

"Sweat," interrupted Benoit. "They got beautiful sweat. The bugs pass out in ecstasy from the smell."

"—and silence, real silence."

"They sleep good," Hebert said. "I mean, man, in Lost Beach you can really *sleep*."

"I'd go out of my fucking mind," said Dina.

"Put yourself in their place," Fannett said, arguing with Santos again. "Try to imagine it. You know, actually living it. Try to go through it in your head. I mean, it may all look beautiful from a far enough *distance*. If you see them as part of the landscape or something, like animals, like the cows or—"

"*Crap*," Santos snapped. "We're *all* animals if you want to look at it that way. Struggling to stay alive whatever way we can."

"No, but there's more. A man . . . plans things, builds things . . . ."

"Look at all the nice buildings they got in Lost Beach," Benoit said. "You s'pose they all have the same architect?"

"Maybe it doesn't matter much *what*," Fannett insisted, "I mean from some cosmic point of view, but he—"

"More horseshit," Santos declared. "No different here than with our folks. You take whatever way there is to stay alive. Look, my old man works his shift at the refinery—is that meaningful? And they ship the gasoline out and the cars use it to run around from one place to another. So what? I mean for *him* there's nothing but a set of dials to watch, sitting around about like we do at Gralino's, or watching TV at home, or playing checkers on Saturday, and drinking himself into a stupor."

There seemed no appropriate answer to this, so Fannett said nothing, and they drove a long time in silence.

Gradually he became aware of a softening of the sharp glare; the heat seemed to back off a few degrees. The sky lifted up, became less oppressive, and the color of the salt grass was an almost violent green. Fannett, becoming drowsy, picked out an oak tree far ahead of them, followed its slow approach, watched it pass by Santos's profile, then he looked for another . . . .

"Stop the car!" Santos shouted suddenly.

"What? What is it?"

"Just stop the car. Back up, slow."

"What for, what's the matter?"

"Back up goddammit."

Santos was turned around on the seat, staring out the back window. Fannett began to back the car down the highway.

"What the fuck are we looking for?"

"Saw a big nutria, he was right beside—"

"Christ! The boy's lost his marbles! A *nutria*."

"Gonna catch him."

"Oh boy! Just what I always wanted—a twenty-five pound rat!"

"Be the first on your block to own one."

"Maybe we'll sell it in Bergeron—for the hide. Or maybe I *will* keep it as a pet."

Benoit patted Santos on the shoulder. "He's all right, folks," he said. "Just relax, boy, till we can get this nice elastic jacket with the long sleeves on you. And look, in the meantime, why don't we just collect a nice big jar of mud for the folks in Bergeron. They need mud every bit as much as an extra nutria."

"Or mosquitoes," Hebert said. "Sell 'em by the ounce. We got a pretty nice collection back here on the back window."

"*Stop right here.*"

Fannett stopped and Santos jumped out. The others clambered quickly after him. Fannett hesitated but followed.

"He's right back there," Santos said in a loud whisper. "Everybody be quiet."

Dina whooped: "Hey! I see him!"

A fat brown shape scurried down the shell slope and into the salt grass. Cursing, Santos ran after him, followed by Benoit.

"Come on, form a circle around him," Santos shouted.

Dina and Hebert plunged into the shoulder-high grass after Santos and Benoit. The four of them made a loop around the spot where the nutria had disappeared. Fannett was left to face the grass from the bottom of the road bank.

"You're the bag man, Fannett," Santos said.

"Yeah . . . where's my bag?"

The four "beaters" moved slowly toward the edge of the grass. The footing was slippery in places, squishy in others, and the grass was dense and sharp. Hebert stepped in a hole into mud calf deep and cursed. Dina slipped and fell.

Fannett watched the four of them moving falteringly toward him through the grass. It all seemed rather strange and vaguely ridiculous, but still he kept his eyes open for the nutria.

At last Dina and Hebert reached the edge of the grass. There was only a small patch of grass for the nutria to be hiding in—unless of course he had slipped between them, which seemed the likeliest thing to Fannett.

"Ready?" Santos asked.

"Oh sure." Fannett crouched, rocking up onto the balls of his feet.

Santos leaned toward the last patch of grass. "Run, rat, *run*," he shouted and began kicking at the grass.

Nothing happened.

"If we lost him it's your fucking fault, Dina," Santos said. He and Benoit stamped heavily on the remaining grass.

Suddenly, to Fannett's amazement, it was there. It didn't seem to have moved, to have appeared, it was just suddenly *there*. Staring directly at him. Its eyes were tiny, little glittering yellow points of light. For a moment he seemed to lose perspective, the nutria looked enormous, the size of a buffalo, massive and shaggy. The eyes seemed to paralyze him, to nullify him. He felt his hands and feet turn cold, his knees go weak. It was as though something like an *understanding* swept over him, communicated to him from the savage breast of the nutria; as though there were just the two of them on the earth and some current ran between, delivering a message, not to his mind, but to each individual cell in his body, a message not of fear or anger, but of loss, doom, of sinking or drowning, some perfect hopelessness . . . .

Time froze, a moment of ice, the whole universe seemed to pivot in that instant on him, on the two of them . . . as though a film, thousands of moments flitting by so fast they give the illusion of action, of life, suddenly stopped, held a single frame so he could see . . . but before he *knew* what he saw the film resumed its motion, he took two quick steps and hurled himself.

He seemed to know in a kind of backwards cast, in retrospect, knew—*had* known—even before he moved, that he had waited too long; the nutria had instinctively taken the single most efficient path for escape and he had waited an instant too long . . . but he knew that he had known this only as his body violently struck the earth and his outstretched fingers barely grazed the wet, prickly tail.

He did not try immediately to get up. His head was spinning. The nutria skittered up the shell slope and disappeared over the road. *All is lost* Fannett thought, absurdly. What? What was lost? The dread and panic that had gripped him when he turned the car off the highway for the first time swelled up in him again, more intense than before. It seemed to tighten around his chest painfully.

—Sounds of music seemed to come to him from very far away.

"Hey, man, you all right?"

"You almost caught the mutha."

He looked up. Dina and Hebert were grinning down at him. Santos and Benoit moved toward him with a slow, floating motion that seemed incredibly graceful. He felt like a lump of something, inert, shapeless, impossibly heavy. He didn't want to get up at all.

"You did, you almost had him," Hebert repeated.

"I . . . I almost . . . . I hesitated . . . ." Fannett could not collect his thoughts.

"Did you see the size of the mutha?"

"That there must have been the king of the nutrias."

Santos looked at him strangely. "What did you wait for?" he asked.

"I don't know. . . he so suddenly, I mean it was so sudden, I didn't see . . . ."

Dina laughed. "Hey—what would you have done if you *had* caught him by the tail like that!"

He got up and slapped the dirt off his jeans. The others' voices moved away again, too distant to hear. Who were they? They seemed so alien, unreal. But he himself was befuddled. He stared—he didn't know how long—as though uncertain whose legs these were he was slapping. He started back to the car, suddenly in a hurry to get away, to be in motion again. It seemed to him a new vulnerability, a new *kind* of vulnerability had opened up like an old wound deep inside him.

The others trailed along behind, their voices chattering like birds.

As soon as the car reached highway speed he felt better. It was getting cooler—it seemed to him he could feel the heat draining from the air with a kind of flutter. Daylight was disappearing rapidly and a thick blue powder seemed to gather around them, filling the air.

Breezes riffled the marsh grass like a pool. The first lights began to appear far off in the marsh in the shadowy edge of the slowly approaching darkness. From right beside the road a flock of egrets suddenly exploded and passed over their heads like a low, humming cloud. Dina leaned out to shout obscenities at a cow browsing near the road, but the animal didn't lift its head.

Fannett turned on his headlights with reluctance: they made such an ugly yellow stain in the blue gray. The mosquitoes were everywhere now, they seemed to fall through the light beams like a shower of cinders. The needle of the temperature gauge was dropping, just out of the red now, which was a relief. Imagine if the car broke down! The mosquitos had been known to smother cattle to death.

He became gradually aware of a glow on the horizon ahead of them: Bergeron. They were driving nearly due east now, and the sky there was completely dark. But in his rearview mirror the sky was pale blue and bright. His headlights seemed to chew across the darkness, or at times they looked like something festering in the air in front of them.

They passed a sign: Bergeron 4 Mi. Then the first car coming toward them, and a second. A few buildings appeared beside the road.

"Hey!" Santos pointed toward one of the buildings. It was called Bayou Club and the sound of music reached the road. Fannett pulled up into a parking lot nearly full of cars and pickups.

The Bayou Club seemed on the point of bursting with music and people. They squeezed in at the door and then fought their way to the bar and ordered beers. The whole room—which may actually have been like the earlier ones—seemed to dance to the music coming from a jukebox in the far corner. This was an illusion. In fact no one was dancing —there were no women. The men simply moved about restlessly, shouting at each other, swinging their arms about, turning and staring across the room at each other, all in apparent rhythm to the jukebox.

A quiet seemed to spread out from them in a slow wave. More and more of the glances focused on them, and more particularly on Dina. She was the only female in the room! And Dina would not keep still. She laughed and shouted and squirmed around, and Fannett found himself cursing her for not wearing a brassiere. But why shouldn't she wear what she wanted to?

"Hey, man, you got a lady's here?" Dina shouted at a man behind the bar, wiping at the bar top with a rag. He didn't look up, but his lips moved and Dina immediately started pushing her way across the room toward the far corner.

She hadn't been gone long when Fannett noticed the bartender had moved down near him: he reached out and touched Fannett's arm. He grinned and showed bad teeth.

"That there your girl?"

Fannett shook his head. "Friend," he said. Then louder, "Just a friend, we're all just friends."

The man nodded, made a pointless sweep with his rag, before asking in a low, confidential voice. "You boys up here fo' trouble?"—he shook his head no, as if to assure himself in advance of Fannett's answer.

"No, no. We're just over here for the Shrimp Festival," Fannett said. The man nodded once, then slid away down the bar.

The jukebox fell silent just as Dina appeared again at the other side of the room. A strange hush followed her as she made her way through the crush of bodies. Now, at last, she was self-conscious and grinned on all sides. As soon as she reached the bar Fannett said "Let's go" and headed for the door.

The others were a little while in following. Benoit arrived at the car laughing. "Hooee! Did you see that?" he said. "Those guys' eyes 'most poppin' out of dey *heads.*"

The others were less amused. Dina didn't seem to have made up her mind what she thought.

"Oh, they were hot for your *bod,*" Benoit assured her. "They don't get young titties shook in their faces *every* day."

"Bartender asked me if we were looking for *trouble,*" Fannett said.

"Don't wonder. *Hooee.*"

"The swamp air has got to your coonass brain," Santos said.

"Those guys," Benoit said, ignoring Santos, "those guys wouldn't have been more shook up if the devil himself showed up in their bar and chased them around the room with a pitchfork."

❧ ❧ ❧ ❧

A line of cars was backed up at the ferry. Beside the road, near the landing, there had been some sort of accident. A pickup truck was on fire, the flames shooting high into the air, and people from the waiting cars had gathered around it, black silhouettes against the yellow flames. The crowd was strangely quiet, as though awed, and there was something a little ritualistic about the scene. The black shape of the pickup danced about in the heart of the fire, and the people watched it like an audience ready to applaud.

The ferry lights could be seen moving slowly toward the landing. A few hundred yards out, the ferry uttered a loud, low, mournful cry, but no one seemed to notice. It landed, the gate was raised, and a stream of cars—about a dozen in all—passed by the fire. Still no one in the waiting line moved. Fannett waited till all the cars getting off had cleared, then drove up the wrong side of the road and onto the ferry, the first car on.

As if Fannett's maneuver had been a signal, people ran back to their cars from the fire, then everyone tried to get onto the ferry at once. It looked like a file of ants stirred up by a child's stick. Some people tried to drive around the confusion on the road and got stuck in mud up to their hubcaps. Men got out of their cars and began yelling at each other. Two of them even came to blows, then were separated. From the ferry the whole scene looked to Fannett like something writhing uncontrollably in pain in the yellow red light of the fire.

Slowly, one by one, the cars began to come onto the ferry.

When the ferry moved away, the scene at the landing, separated by the widening black pupil of water, lost its frenzied appearance, seemed suddenly peaceful and even festive. An occasional car horn could be heard, like the cry of some injured, mechanical bird, but even this seemed to have difficulty piercing the thick, baffled air, the stillness the water breathed.

Fannett had gotten out of the car and stood looking back over the side rail of the ferry. Even as the retreating scene behind seemed to contract into a picture, a fiction, a change in the ferry's course suddenly shattered its perfect reflection in the water, scattering it into a thousand embers of light. He turned and watched Bergeron, a kind of heap of pale white lights, approaching from the other side. The warm smell of brine and decay rose from the water. . . .

"Ain't one of them Hackaberries, are ya?"—the voice sliced at him out of the darkest shadows beneath the bridge of the ferry.

"What?" He turned, tried to find the voice's owner in the dark.

"You ain't no Hackaberry?"

"I'm from Texas, across the Sabine," Fannett said, uncertain whether this was what he had been asked or not.

"Uh–huh . . . ." The voice was skeptical, perhaps even sarcastic. Something stirred in the dark, then a small figure —not much over five feet—slid into the lesser dark of the deck. A man with a visored, captain's cap. The visor turned to one side and there was the sound of spitting.

"P'lice a lookin' fer some Hackaberries—you wouldn't know nothin' about that, would ya." This was not a question but an ironical assertion.

"I told you, I—we're from Texas, just over the—"

"See that?" The man's arm snapped at an angle upward and past Fannett's head. Fannett turned and saw that one of the ferry's principal running lights was smashed. "That's them Hackaberries done that."

Fannett nodded. "Hackaberries, huh?"

"And that." The arm leveled, and Fannett saw a lifeboat that looked like one of its sides was stoved in. He nodded again. "P'lice a lookin' fer them Hackaberries," the man repeated.

Fannett turned to watch the Bergeron landing move swiftly toward them; the ferry hit it with a jolt, and the little figure hurried to man the chains that operated the gate.

✻　　✻　　✻　　✻

Bergeron was a fishing village of a couple thousand people, but, with its central square under a canopy of strung lights, alone in the surrounding dark, it seemed much larger. The square itself, a bare patch of ground, was crowded with tents and wooden stands, and at one end a raised platform. The whole area was full of people. Fannett parked a couple blocks away on a side street and they walked back. As they approached they could hear someone counting into a microphone: "One, two, three . . . ." There was a pause, then "*Un, deux, trois,*" and a cheer.

The square was packed with people. Some crowded around the dance area waiting for the bands, others milled about among the stands and tents, buying beer, plates of shrimp and crayfish, or playing "games of skill and chance."

There were two bands. On one side four boys in their late teens, wearing purple velveteen and long hair, adjusted the dials of their electronic equipment. On the other side there were six men in their forties or fifties, dressed in crisp new jeans, plaid shirts, and red bandannas. One of these, a tall, thin man with an enormous Adam's apple, was counting into the microphone and grinning at the crowd. Under his arm like a rifle was his fiddle.

Satisfied with the microphone, the man with the enormous Adam's apple stepped back and began to saw on his fiddle: "*Allons à Lafayette*." After a few bars he grabbed the microphone and bent over it to sing, but just then an earsplitting screech echoed across the square. The singer gave the microphone a savage wrench, which silenced it, and sang in a high, nasal patois. The crowd was pouring onto the dance area with whoops and shouts.

The waltz lasted only a few minutes before it was absorbed into a deep shuddering sound from the other side of the stage. A frenzied burst of piercing screams followed, and the Cajun band put down their instruments and smiled uneasily, tapping their toes as the youths in purple velveteen began to writhe.

Dina was asked to dance by several young men all at once and moved away. Fannett suggested beer and shrimp to the others. The shrimp plates were only a dollar, the shrimp highly spiced but lukewarm. The beer was a dollar a can, which annoyed them. They drifted from one tent to another, trying a few of the games. Nobody seemed to win at any of the ones that paid off. It was a small triumph when Fannett hit three balloons in a row with darts and won a ceramic doll —a woman in a hula skirt and no top, the nipples of her breasts little crimson points, Made In Hong Kong stamped on the bottom.

Bergeron's public buildings faced the square, four tall white buildings. Just beyond these was a street of bars, one after the other. In the first of these they tried, they found a pool table in the back, under a light bulb hooded by a copper sleeve. Around the table, about a dozen young men stood, leaning against the wall, watching the players who circled the table, waiting for a game.

They moved down the street. The bars were much alike, except some had pool and some didn't. The beer was only fifty cents. Finally, at the fifth bar, Fannett and Santos got a game. They lost. Hebert and Benoit played their conquerors and lost by four balls. They moved on.

By the time they found their way back to the square the crowd seemed much larger—and denser. It seemed to sway and surge like a container of liquid. Around the edges groups of high-school age boys prowled restlessly, as though looking for something. In fact it seemed to Fannett that the whole crowd bore an air of sullen expectancy, as though something that should have happened long ago had been unaccountably delayed.

The Cajun band played a sad-gay waltz, but only about a dozen couples were dancing. Several of these took advantage of the space to sweep around the dance area with extraordinary speed and grace, spinning as though flung by some centrifugal force. To Fannett's astonishment he saw that one of these couples was Dina and a fifty-year-old man.

When the number ended the bands changed again. Dina did not even reach the ropes before hands were groping for her from all sides, drawing her back into the center. She was evidently very popular. Crimson faced and sweating, she disappeared into a knot of bodies, her laughter floating up to drift among the jangle of chords.

Fannett watched Dina in fascination. He envied her the talent to fling herself into things with such obliviousness, as though in ecstasy. It seemed to him that she was entirely enmeshed in the hot, angry, lusts of those who surrounded her, staring, leering at her. He thought: when sex becomes just the opposite of love . . . .

He turned to Santos. "You think maybe we should get Dina?" he asked.

Santos stared at him, then laughed. "What for?"

"Don't you see? Those guys? I mean, I don't, uh, like that situation there . . . do you?"

"I haven't the slightest idea what you're talking about.

Seems to me she's having a ball. She's got tongues hanging out on all sides—she's in heaven."

"She doesn't even know. I mean, look at her."

"Yeah. I see her."

Santos was being perversely obtuse. Or so it seemed. He looked at the dancers and grinned and looked back at Fannett with a snicker. "She's having more fun than *you* are."

"I just thought—if we went over to her, you know, just to say a few words, so they could see that she . . . you know, that she's not alone."

"I wouldn't want to cramp her style."

"But—"

"Get off it, man."

"Fuck off!"

When Santos led the others back to the bars for more beer, Fannett stayed behind. Santos's presence had become obnoxious to him. He watched the dancing, watched Dina, not at all tempted to dance himself, then made a tour of the stands and tents, willing to pay double for his beer to be in the festival and not just in another bar. He returned briefly to the dance area. It was amazing how Dina made a place for herself—with her laugh it seemed. The boys seemed to swarm over her like vermin, dark and fierce.

Weaving through the crowd, he decided to try his hand at the darts again. Win a pair of hula girls. He was bumping into people, the swirl of the crowd made him dizzy. He found the place. It was in the open, the woman who operated the game enormously fat, wearing a bright red dress. Dark sweat stains marked her dress under the arms and on the back. As he waited his turn he ran a thumb over the sharp points of the breasts. Made In Hong Kong—for some reason this seemed an outrage, a cheat. A fine souvenir of the Bergeron Shrimp Festival!

His first throw missed the entire board. He heard the woman laughing, turned, found he was laughing too. The darts were greasy, the feathers nearly all torn off. He hit the board with his second, far from the balloons. The last he threw hard, and it seemed to take off on a trajectory of its own, high over the board and into a patch of long grass beyond. The woman retrieved the dart and brought it, with the other two, back to him. Try again? He nodded. It seemed important that he concentrate, that he win and not lose here. He threw carefully and just caught a balloon. Suddenly the whirl around him slowed. The second dart wobbled, hit a balloon and popped it, though it fell to the ground rather than going into the board. He glanced quickly at the woman: she seemed to be looking at him admiringly. The third dart flopped in midair and hit the board flat, dropping harmlessly. He watched the huge red rump bobbing above it. She came toward him bearing a string of plastic beads, but he shook his head and turned away.

He crossed over to the bars, looking for the others. He couldn't find them. He felt vaguely that he had forgotten something as he searched for them—did Santos tell him where to meet them? The hula girl! He forgot his doll back at the dart game! It didn't seem to matter anymore. He returned to the festival, the dance area. The Cajun band was on the stage alone, but they seemed to be collecting their instruments, quitting. The lead fiddler stumbled to the microphone, mumbled something, and then was led away.

The crowd was thinning out—he felt this with a pang of regret. Still the movement carried him along. He bought beer, tried a few more games. He bought another plate of shrimp but lost it somehow—he couldn't remember whether he had put it down and forgot it like the doll, or simply dropped it. He was searching—but for whom? For Dina, or the others? In any case he couldn't see Dina among the dancers awaiting for the rock band to come back. He was heading back toward the bars when suddenly a hand reached out and grabbed him.

"Hey! Where you been?"

It took a long time for his eyes to find Santos's grinning face.

"Hey, man, we met these guys, you got to see . . . ."

Santos's face would not come into clear focus. His eyes looked red rimmed, moist, his breath smelled of something. Fannett found a beer can in his hand. He took a swallow—it was warm and slimy, and he spat it out. He tossed the can onto the ground and watched the beer gurgle out into the grass.

"Hey, that thing was full!" Santos said.

Fannett nodded.

"I want you to meet these guys, locals, the real McCoy," Santos said. "Real Bergeron punks, tough guys . . . ."

Fannett allowed himself to be pulled along. Ahead, some two hundred yards away, across the square and a street near the Bergeron City Hall, he saw Hebert and Benoit. They were sitting on the street curb with four other figures, two on either side.

"What's going on?" he heard himself say.

"Oh nothing much. I told you, they got the hots for Dina, want us to help them out a little. They got what you might call a primitive mentality."

Something in a paper sack was being passed from hand to hand—a bottle. Each took a swallow from it. Fannett suddenly recognized the smell on Santos's breath. Whiskey.

"They want us to make a deal for 'em," Santos said.

"Deal? What the fuck are you talking about?"

"I told you, they got a primitive mentality."

Fannett stopped. The faces of the four strangers across the street looked all alike to him. A face and three mirrors. A dark, inhuman face, cruel and mindless. "No," he said.

Santos seemed amused. "No what?"

"No deals."

"Oh. OK. Glad I checked it out with you, otherwise . . . ." Santos didn't finish.

"You can't just *sell* her, you know." Fannett felt caught up in a feeling he could neither define nor control, something like fear, dread, revulsion, all in one. "You *can't*," he repeated.

"No, I suppose not. Guess we should have thought of that. Why don't you come explain to these guys—"

"What the fuck are you doing!" Fannett grabbed Santos's arm and whirled him around.

Santos looked at him sarcastically. "Calm down, asshole," he said. "I'm trying to tell you what *is*, OK? These four punks—actually there are more hanging around, watching us. They want to buy Dina. Just like that. They figured out she's with us, they think a bottle of booze, a few dollars, and they can stick her like a pin cushion . . . ."

"You can't do that!" Fannett screamed. He saw a flicker of anger in Santos's eyes, but then Santos smiled.

"Right. Very perceptive. I know that, and you know that, but the little bastards with the switchblades in their pockets are the problem. Can you understand that? They stopped Benoit, we got split up, they stopped Benoit and he was feeling good so he treated it like a joke and said something like 'Sure, what do you think she's worth,' and since then all they'll talk about is not *whether* but how much. Got the picture?"

"What are you, some kind of *pimps*!"

"Look, jerk, I don't have to take that shit from you! I'm telling you what we got. They're four, we're three, Benoit is zonked, Hebert can't even stand up. I need a little semi-sober weight. So come bring your righteous sword, OK asshole?"

"No!" Santos had grabbed Fannett by the elbow, but he pulled free. "You pimped your way into this, pimp your way out. You shouldn't even be talking about this . . . you're disgusting. She's a human being, you can't, you can't . . . ."

"I was hoping, you self-righteous fucker, that you might have figured out by now that we aren't *planning* to sell her. That's not the issue. The issue is—"

"But that *is* the issue! You can't talk, you can't *think* that way."

Suddenly, unexpectedly, Fannett found himself walking, alone, through the crowds tangled in the square. He had simply turned his back on Santos's curses and walked away. It seemed vital now to find Dina, to get her somehow under control, so that forces could be coordinated. But what forces? Everything was confused, beyond his understanding. Yet he was driven by an obsessive feeling of panic, of impending disaster.

The rock band had quit, the stage was empty except for the remaining equipment. Fannett climbed up, and as he did one of the figures in purple velveteen appeared unexpectedly from behind a speaker, his face a yellow smear, his mouth moving wordlessly. Then the musician stumbled sideways and he began to vomit over the side of the stage.

On the other side of the stage, where Fannett had not yet ventured, there was a parking lot, now less than half filled with cars. He moved toward it. It was as though something drew him, for he could not gather his thoughts well enough to think what he was doing. In the lot he began moving from car to car, peering in each, hardly able to see anything in the dim light.

After a search of the cars in the lot he moved along a narrow street that led away from the square, checking parked cars as he went. The light became fainter away from the square. He leaned against the glass of the car windows and each time it felt like a splash of cold water on his face. But he saw nothing.

He continued the search, randomly turning down this street and then that. He had to keep looking, no matter how futile, at least until his head cleared. He held, in his mind, a clear picture of the six figures on the curb—though by now Santos would have joined them—and this vision in itself seemed to force him away from the square, into this blind probing of the dark streets.

Then—in a kind of bright flash, events seemed to contract into a single moment, without sequence: his hand on the handle of a car door, something pale white, then yellow, on the backseat, and the darkness whirring past his face as he sprinted, stumbling through low bushes and over curbs. What? *What?* Something like a knot of maggots writhing in the maroon hollow of rotten meat, and a voice crying behind him—his own?—"Dina . . . ."

❀   ❀   ❀   ❀

He sat on the edge of the stage to catch his breath and gather his wits. The square, still bright under the canopy of lights, was mostly empty. A few workmen still picked apart stands and rolled up tents. The fat woman in the red dress was being chased by a short, thickly built man in white painter's overalls: he ran up behind her, slid a hand under her dress . . . then she bolted away giggling. Only a few feet from Fannett a half-dozen boys of about ten were methodically punching and slashing at a piece of sound equipment with pocketknives. They scattered at the roar of a big man

with a sunburnt bald head who appeared out of nowhere—
but then stopped to laugh and jeer when the man, quite
drunk, fell over on his face.

To Fannett the whole scene seemed to have a weird in-
tensity, not quite real, everything looked burned in, even
the colors were odd, distorted, the men's jeans almost purple, the flesh orange. He could see with perfect clarity all
the way across the square to the figures still sitting on the
curb. He watched them a long time—they hardly moved.
Hebert was leaning on one of the strangers.

When he felt sufficiently sober, Fannett stood and began
the walk. He watched them all the way across the square,
expecting at any moment that one of them would look up.
They didn't. He reached the street and paused, then crossed.
He was standing over them before they looked up. Then all
the strangers looked up at once, and it seemed they didn't
really see him even then; their eyes were like eight smoothly
polished stones.

"Hey, it's about time we got moving," Fannett said. "It's
late."

Santos stared at him as though trying to read something
hidden in his words, then said: "Why'nt you sit down here
ol' buddy." He wasn't as drunk as he sounded, Fannett decided. "Have a swif'." The paper bag was lifted toward him.
He shook his head.

"No thanks. I think we ought to get going."

"But these good ol' boys have been very hos-*spit*able,"
Santos said, grinning. "Very, very hos-*spit*able."

Benoit had not looked up. He sat on the curb in an almost
fetal position, his arms around his knees and his head on his
arms. Was he asleep?

Fannett noticed a wad of bills lying in the gutter by the
curb.

"Look, this girl, Dina . . ." Fannett began. What? He did
not know himself what to say. "She's . . . she's my, uh, sister,
see? She's my sister. So if anybody's responsible, I am."

He was addressing the strangers, but none of them was
looking at him. One looked at Santos, as though expecting a
translation, the others looked down into the gutter.

"You can't, I mean, she's really young and besides . . ." Fannett felt the anger rising again. He fought it down. "And besides that she's a *virgin*. To see her dancing you might not realize, but anyway you can't assume . . . ."

The one who had been looking at Santos turned toward Fannett. Fannett felt an impulse to simply step forward and kick his face in, and then the others.

"So there's *no deal*, see?" he said. "What kind of people are you anyway?"

He thought he saw just a hint of a smile on the face. But the dark polished stones were expressionless.

"No deal, y'hear?" he repeated and turned and walked back across the street. He headed vaguely in the direction of the car, although without Dina . . . .

Santos caught up with him only a few steps into the square.

"Are you crazy?" he demanded, hissing. Fannett pulled his arm loose.

"Break it off, I've had enough of this shit."

"*You*'ve had enough!"

Benoit arrived, laughing. "What a stroke!" he said. "Virgin sister!"

Fannett looked back. The four strangers were not even looking at them.

"They say if she really *is* a virgin," Benoit said, "they'll pay double. As for her being your sister . . . that doesn't seem to cut any ice."

"You goddamn pimps!"

Benoit sneered at him. "Listen to *him*."

"Did you find Dina?" Santos asked.

"No, I—I don't know."

"What the fuck do you mean, *you don't know*?"

"Never mind. I'll find her all right. You guys get to the car, she'll be there with me."

"Oh good, we get the *easy* part," Benoit said.

"You think they're gonna just let us walk away?" Santos asked. "Just like that?"

"Why not? You don't owe them anything. What the hell do you owe them? Just go. And stop this *talk*, this *pimp* talk."

"They got buddies, too, we saw them," Benoit said. "You

think Hebert can walk?" He was asking Santos, who shrugged. Then Santos's finger appeared suddenly an inch from Fannett's face.

"If I hear you say pimp one more time we're gonna get it on right here, you bastard."

"*Shit*. That's great. What a tough guy. If you're so hot to get it on, why don't you try it with those punks. Don't worry about the word, worry about the *reality*."

Santos glared at him. Fannett could feel the tension rising. Benoit intervened.

"Come on, let this asshole go," he said to Santos. "In a way he's right. We got to slip out of this *some*time."

They both turned abruptly and walked back across the street. Fannett picked his way through the debris in the square toward the stage and the parking lot beyond it again.

The village itself seemed darker than before. He could hardly see where he was going. After walking about a half a block he stopped, uncertain which way to go. Then, miraculously, he heard Dina's voice.

"Hey man, over here. Whatcha doin'?"

She was sitting on the hood of a pickup in a driveway on the other side of the street. He crossed over.

"Looking for you, damn you. Where you been?"

She laughed. "Oh, around. I been around."

"We got some trouble. A little bit. We better get on to the car."

He told her everything on the way to the car. When he told her about his last attempt to dissuade the buyers she let out a whooping laugh and began to spin around in the street. Then, abruptly, she stopped laughing and pulled her face up next to his as though to kiss him. Her breath smelled of cigarettes and beer.

"Hey, man, did you really do that? Did you tell them I was your virgin sister? Say, man, that's really *sweet*."

She studied his face a second, then broke again into howls of laughter.

In the car they sat together a long time in silence, Dina blowing smoke rings toward the windshield.

"I had a great time," she said at last.

"Oh yeah? Good for you."

"Yeah . . . a really, really great time."

After a few minutes of silence, she asked, "Hey, man, is it true what they say? That in Mexico, in the border towns, little kids come up to you and say, 'Fucka my seester for a quarter.'"

"Not for a quarter. A dollar maybe. I don't know. Fuck you."

"Fan–*tas*–tic."

Fannett began to get nervous. Should he go back and see if the others needed help?

"I guess you didn't get laid tonight, did you," Dina said.

"I didn't really come here to get laid."

"Bullshit. *Every*body came here to get laid. That's what these things are all about. That's what *every*thing's all about."

"Maybe I should go back and look for the others."

"Give 'em a little while, man, they'll get here."

"I don't think you realize, those guys were serious."

Dina chuckled.

Just as Fannett was about ready to go, the others appeared around a corner, walking slowly. They all got into the backseat.

"Now what?" Fannett asked.

"I think you'll have to drive by the square," Benoit said, "to get to the ferry. They might be looking for us there."

Fannett could not find a route that did not go by the square. But when he drove into the bright light of it, it was deserted. He followed the signs to the ferry. A block off the square dark figures appeared suddenly from the shadows, converging on the car from both sides—it looked like at least a dozen. He gunned the engine and sped past them. A big rock or brick hit the windshield and cracked it, others hit the car from the sides, but he had soon left them far behind.

"Broke my fucking windshield," he said.

"Count your blessings," Benoit said.

"Blessings shit. I didn't get us into this."

At Dina's prompting Benoit described the whole long evening of negotiations. He and Dina seemed to find it funny. Herbert went immediately to sleep, even before the ferry left the landing. Santos sat silent and sullen, staring out the window of the car.

Benoit said they had finally managed to get free by taking the money.

"Santos and this other guy kept pushing the money back and forth in the gutter," he said, "you know, with these I–hate–your–guts grins on their faces. So finally I decided, what the fuck, we might as well get paid for our trouble and picked it up. By that time I think everyone was so fucked up and tired no one knew what was happening. So I said we'd go get you and meet them at the square. They didn't really believe me—they wanted to keep Hebert—but I said no, and they couldn't be sure I guess. I don't know. Anyway we walked away."

Benoit waved the wad of bills in the air and Dina made a lunge for it over the back of the seat.

"That's my money, man," she said. "I earned it."

Benoit laughed. "Bullshit. You never did anything but grow big titties. We'll split it, have us a party. Everybody but the white-knight asshole here."

Dina put an arm around Fannett. "No, man, I got to be good to my brother here."

The landing on the other side was only a small circle of bluish light. Without the crowd, the fire, it didn't look like the same place.

The air that poured in through the windows of the car as Fannett drove into the great emptiness of the marsh felt cold. He shivered but did not roll up the window: it would help keep him awake. Within a half an hour the others were all asleep, and Fannett was left alone with the marsh, the dark, and the hiss of his tires.

Dina pillowed on his shoulder. But as she fell asleep she slid down, finishing the trip with her head in his lap, her hot breath flooding over him. Once he touched her hair gently but did not look down.

Arriving in town a little before dawn, with a pale gray already showing in the east, he dropped them off one by one, with nothing more said. Heading home, the moon, bright and gibbous, fractured in the cracked windshield, making it difficult for him to see.

He pulled into his side of his parents' garage and killed the engine but did not immediately move to get out. He thought at last he would be able to sort the evening out . . . but he was too tired.

He stopped in the yard. The moon floated just above the corner of the house where his room was; it looked like a bright light shining through a disc of ice. The whole yard was frosted by it: the rose bushes, the fig tree, clothes poles and lines, even the grass . . . the air seemed to be filled with fine, silver spores. He stepped over to the pecan tree that looked as though it were covered in a thin layer of fuzzy, opalescent mold. Touching it, he felt only the rough, cold bark. He pressed himself against the tree in a kind of embrace, to feel the hard, damp roughness of the bark on his face. For just a moment everything drew together inside him, as though into a perfectly still point, and tears started to his eyes. He tore himself away . . . .

Inside the house he moved as quietly as possible to avoid waking his parents. He undressed in the dark. He wasn't surprised when he found that his underwear was slimy with seed.

Roger Rath

The Sportsman

The Trim

The Model

*"The Young in One
    Another's Arms"*

Roger Rath

The Sportsman

I remember playing tennis with Carol Corley on the make-shift concrete court behind my grandmother's apartment house, Runnymede, on Bellevue Hill, in Sydney. Mother and I had just returned home from the States to sit out my Yank stepfather's tour of duty in Korea. The invitation for tennis and tea came to our flat from Carol's below, from her mother to mine: Wouldn't it be fun if the children renewed their perambulator romance on the old court? Mom said it was my invitation, not hers, she couldn't stand the woman. No way out. Best foot forward.

I had no best foot and Carol knew it. Still, it was a fine day to be forced out—the sky azure and high, cumulus clouds banked heroically in the west. I played with the sun at my back and by late afternoon the heat and exercise had soaked the Wasatch (Utah) T-shirt I wore against the exposure of my pale Yank chest to a girl as athletic and Australian as Carol. I was twelve; Carol blond, willowy, and thirteen.

She wore a cream-colored pullover and matching pleated tennis skirt and she was all competition, her long legs scis-soring goldenly as she rushed the net or raced after my lone-some, hopeless lobs. Time and again, she forced me back past the baseline to take weak-wristed swipes at her impossible shots. Going back was dangerous. There was no fence behind my half of the court and the concrete gave way there to a short, neglected lawn that sloped gradually, then dropped abruptly down a slick stone cliff. The drop was through a tangle of brush and low-hanging branches to the children's zoo in the city park below, about a hundred yards away.

The apartment-house children made a game of sliding down that cliff on garbage can lids, which they'd modified by prying off the handles. I had to make that slide to prove Yanks had it to Runnymede's mob of which Carol was the unchallenged chief: thirteen stitches across my left temple. I passed out and never reached bottom, and now I played at the tennis to make the great embarrassment of my stitches heal, scrambling, charging the net in chunky strides, finding wood more often than gut. My stateside black hightop sneakers loomed below me and I watched them nose each other whenever I neared the edge of the cliff. I thought death might be a clumsiness.

Carol missed an erratic bounce off a crack in the concrete, looked up, and elaborately shielded her eyes from the sun. We had agreed not to change sides after the evidence of the first few volleys; she'd taken the sun without mentioning the cliff. But my stitches should have remembered it.

"You've got the best side, you know."

"The sun doesn't bother me," I said. "Let's switch," and I started over.

One hand on her hip, the racket resting on her shoulder, she said, "I'm doing well enough over here, don't you think?"

After that, I let two new balls pass me down the cliff. She watched the last one dribble over and drop out of sight.

"All right, then. It's time for tea. Mother had me promise."

I had no idea escape would be this painless. On the landing outside her flat, I drew back my racket and popped her pleated bum in celebration. She whirled around; my eyes were blaming the racket.

"Learned that in the States, did you?"

"You won," I said weakly and followed her in.

Trophies crowded the Corley's small parlor. A large gold crucifix hung over the mantelpiece. It was flanked by two silver women, one tiptoeing up to smash her serve down my throat, the other poised arms straight back for a racing dive. Winners. Winners everyone. On every flat surface, cast figurines posed in champion form. Some of them had to be her mother's.

Mrs. Corley was in the kitchen fixing us a treat. "Jam tarts," she called in to us, "like the ones your father used to bring over of a Sunday, Roy."

Laurie's, my first father's, family owned a chain of Sydney bakeries. Laurie lived with Mom and me in Runnymede until I was three and he joined the RAAF and went to England for the war and never came back.

"They won't stand up to his, I wouldn't promise that, but I've still got his recipe." Mrs. Corley came to the kitchen doorway, a tanned, big-boned woman in a pleated tennis skirt and low open blouse across a generous bosom. She wore white nylons like a nurse's and white pom-pom house slippers. She had frizzy platinum hair and blue eyes that flashed. "Tarts for the tart and her beau," she said and handed me a small pan of unbaked, star-shaped pastry.

Carol plopped down on the daybed. "He's not *mine*," she said.

Mrs. Corley held out the ends of her skirt, let them fall, and nodded toward Carol. "Twins," she said, smiling broadly. Carol bit her lip, fiddled with the hem of her skirt, and watched her mother.

"Don't mope, Carol. It's very unattractive in a girl your age." She turned to me. "Tarts were your favorite and he made dozens and dozens for us. But I don't suppose you remember all that, do you, love?"

"Mom doesn't talk about him much," I said.

"Some does," Carol muttered.

"He was such a handsome customer, who wouldn't? Tall and wiry, kind of. Very high waisted." She made a wavy motion with her hand as if to shape him in the air. "And he was a great sportsman, too, you know. That's why he signed on for flying, I'd wager. Tennis, naturally, and cricket and swimming and hunting and soccer and Rugby and riding. Funny, though, he never tanned well, your da. You've got that in common. He and Regie were in the same lifeguard club at Bondi. I have a nice snap of him somewhere. Carol, do us a favor and see if it's in mother's jewelry box."

"*Where* in the box? I don't want to be in there forever."

"You'll see. The top little drawer on the left, I think." She touched her heart. "There's a dear."

Carol got up and slowly closed her eyes at us twice before marching out of the room. I heard her racket crash to the floor back there. Mrs. Corley didn't seem to hear a thing.

"We had gay times, your da and us. Your mother was off modeling always and he would take you and me and Carol to Bondi Beach and Regie would meet us after work when he could. Once we buried Laurie all the way up to his neck and gave him kisses till he couldn't stand it. How's this healing, love?"

She took my face in her hands and examined my stitches. I held on to the pan of tarts. I smelled flour and her perfume and the rouge dabbed on the tops of her bosom. I tried to keep the pan between us.

"Laurie would have said it gives you character, this scar, like an eye patch or a moustache. What a beaut, eh? He had a mark himself, right"—she slipped her hand quickly inside the top of my T-shirt and pinched my left nipple—"there." I jumped and almost dropped the pan of tarts. She laughed and took out her hand. "Got it running through the bush, tripped on a root hunting 'roos with the binghis."

"I don't know what binghis are."

"The aborigines, love, the blackfellows. They loved your father and he was one of the few whites could keep up with them. Or 'ad the sand to mix with 'em, for all that."

"How do you know so much about my father?"

Her stare went distant, blank, then angry down at me before she smiled. Her skin was not very good under the tan and now some blotches were spreading around.

"We were friends, is all," she finally said. Then her voice went smoky, kind of, and she touched my stitches again. "He saved you from drowning two times in one day, off the old pool at Bondi, the one the ocean fills up." Again she touched my stitches but this time it didn't itch as bad. "He said he couldn't let you die because he wanted you to be a priest. He said it funny, joking and smiling all the time, you know, love."

"I don't swim very well. Sometimes I think I can and I almost drown. Mom never said he saved me."

"She wasn't there. We never told her."

"I don't remember drowning."

She laughed, a high clear laugh I liked. "He saved you, Roy. You never did drown and that's why you don't remember it, love."

She touched my stitches again and we stood like that for a long time. Mrs. Corley was swaying a little. I kept my eyes on the tarts in my hands. In my mind or my eyes the tarts seemed to float, seemed to rise a little and float.

❀   ❀   ❀   ❀

"You'll get infection."

Carol was standing at the end of the hallway. Mrs. Corley took away her hand.

"I can't find it. The photo." Carol had changed into a flowered frock. There seemed to be something bumpy in the top of it. She looked like she was a bright flowered life jacket cut off at the waist. Mrs. Corley wouldn't look at her. My stitches itched terrifically.

"Your father was a religious man, Roy. You'd be a Catholic if he'd lived, but your mother's people were Church of England, so there you are." She laughed the high clear laugh again. Her eyes were shining. "There you are and *here* you are because of him."

"He was my father so he made me. Is that what you mean?"

"He told me once he wanted you to be a priest."

"You said that already, Mrs. Corley. Mom never said anything."

"She loves you very much."

"The photograph is not in the jewelry box, Mother."

Mrs. Corley turned to her daughter quick. "Who's deaf? Am I deaf? Are you deaf? Is Roy deaf? Is he? Answer me!"

"No, Mum."

"Very well, then. No. He's not deaf. I'm not deaf. So you won't be needing to shout at anyone." Her face was very red. She put a hand up to her bosom and took a deep breath, then turned again to her daughter. "He's got *something* to do with you, though, hadn't he? Do you know what that might be?"

Carol looked scared. She shook her head once hard: *No.*

"I'll tell you, then." Mrs. Corley looked away from Carol and back at me and down at the pan of tarts I was holding.

I wanted her to take them back and her hand was hovering over them as if she was checking their heat and I thought she would take them back. *Take them back. Take him back*, I thought. But she was thinking and it made her close her eyes so she couldn't see what I was thinking.

When she opened them they were a new color of red at the corners and wet. She said: "Well, he's got a mark from your childish games, for one thing." It wasn't what she really wanted to say and you could see that Carol knew that, too.

Carol looked at her feet. She still had on her tennis shoes. "I just thought it would begin infections if you touched it," she said softly, and her mother's face went blank again and lost its muscles somehow and all of a sudden Mrs. Corley had the tarts back and was talking about the way Carol looked.

"Are you off to a party, Carol? Frocks and stuffings? Why don't you show Roy to wash for tea? Don't smudge the towels, now. There's a good pair."

Carol twisted up her face and mouthed, *There's a good pair,* as her mother took the tarts back to the kitchen. "Through here," she said to me, pointing down the opposite hallway. When I didn't move, she came over and whispered in my face. "Mum doesn't play tennis anymore. You know that, don't you? She's got *veins*. She's only got on that outfit for you and your da."

I touched my stitches. "My father's dead."

"Don't tell *me*. *She's* the one's got his picture stuffed down her top."

I looked at Carol's top and it was bumpy and I took my eyes off it. I saw my father crushed between me and Mrs. Corley. "You're a liar."

"She said if I didn't bring you home to tea I'd get a thrashing. Does that sound like a lie, Yankee-Doodle?"

My father was a Catholic and a hunter. I would wear black robes and live among the aborigines and never speak to women. There were no women among the aborigines. I didn't think there was any ocean there, either.

"You don't think I let you quit just because you let those stupid balls go over, do you? Ask her. Go on. Ask her if it isn't true."

I couldn't move.

"All right, then. Come on."

Carol glided down the hallway toward the bathroom. She reached over to the left and turned the high handle of the door to it, then stepped back, and stood facing me in the hallway, her hand out to point the open bathroom door. A very slight smile was on her, and she was waiting.

I was standing in the middle of the parlor. It was like standing in the middle of a trophy case and not having any feeling in your legs. My father was in the kitchen with Mrs. Corley. I could hear them shuffling pans. One of them was hiccuping, loud.

"Come on," Carol said, smiling prettily. "You can watch me do something."

My legs were under me no matter what I'd thought and I looked down them and saw my black hightop sneakers walking me out of the flat.

❀ ❀ ❀ ❀

The sun had dropped behind the trees in the park below the court. I picked up one of the garbage can lids and carried it to the end of the lawn behind the court. I sat down in its cool, dish-like crater, blank and poised and ready for whatever, like a tart in a pan I'm thinking now, touching my phantom stitches, my scar, but I couldn't have thought that then— or at least I don't remember thinking it. I just sat there. After a while, I scrouched forward; and down there over the cliff I saw my father buried up to his neck in sand, in rouge and flour kissed to death. I pushed off down the cliff, rode the lid wobbling, wailing under me on the stone I wailed back to a little, the lid turning once completely and almost over on me past the spot I'd dumped before, slamming sideways into the darkness under the trees, down and down and down. . . .

I must have lost consciousness at the bottom. When I looked up I was at the base of a high steel mesh fence; beyond it in a wide green field, dozens of frightened wallabies leaped into the huge pale disc of the sun.

Flanked by naked blackmen who loved me for my strength, I vaulted the fence and charged my tiny prey; and grew up slowly and wrote this for my father in my thirty-third year.

The Trim

The bathroom mirror is specked with dots of toothpaste. The dots and their reflections rake this midmorning evaluation of his good looks like minuscule bursts of flak. Roy wipes at them with his hand; they smear. A red, raw-looking splotch of razor burn rings his throat. He powders this area gingerly and then, to cut down on the glare off his forehead, nose, and chin, he douses the rest of his face with the powder. It is not after-shave talcum and now he smells strongly of lilac. He does not understand how this could happen but to hell with it. He pours out a palmful of hair oil and massages it vigorously into his scalp. His hair has not been trimmed since his graduation from high school earlier this June. It is brown, the thick, oranged sideburns almost recovered from a halfhearted peroxide job. Cut in a "Hollywood," it is full at the temples where the sides of his black horn-rims disappear and crew cut on top. He places his palm on the bristly crown and runs it down the back of his neck. He feels a weird, electric sensation where the bristles collide with the length. The whole production is glistening and well underway now and he combs and brushes at it seriously.

He is wearing blue jeans which ride high in back, low in front, and one of his father's old khaki service shirts, starched to a sheen, the sleeves rolled neatly past his elbows. The cuffs of the jeans have been tucked under and just touch the tops of his shoes. They are heavy black dress shoes with wide menacing treads. They are called "snaps"; in place of laces and a tongue, a metal clip encased in leather closes over the throat and draws the sides up taut. The shoes are spit shined and glossy as a recruit's. Vaguely, Roy believes they, like the hair, will get him sex. He notices some powder has dusted them and he rubs them in turn against the backs of his legs. With a square of toilet paper he wipes the powder from his lenses.

He returns to the hair. He has the sides just right and is working on the top—which is too long to brush back and too short to comb down—when he hears a knock on the bathroom door. His father juts his head inside without waiting for an answer. This movement is sudden as the strike of a mongoose; he has a grin—quick and forced—to match it.

Slipping his metal comb into the hip pocket of his jeans, Roy says "Hi," and begins fiddling with the gig line described by the pleat of his shirt, his belt buckle, and fly.

"Phew! You got a woman in here?"

Handsome, chisled, reeking of bay rum, his father is self-consciously brusque in his weekend fishing garb: Hawaiian shirt (tiger lilies splashed on brilliant blue) hanging loosely over slick gabardine slacks. He looks like what he is: an Air Force colonel in civvies and determined about it. His voice is unnaturally loud.

"Hey, movie star, you need a trim, right?"

Roy's neck stiffens. "Could be," he says and tries to smile. His fingernails trace the outline of the comb against his wallet. His father points to his throat.

"Tried the electric razor again, huh?"

Roy admits this with a sullen nod, a touch to his throat.

"Use that pre-shave powder stick of mine next time. Look. Feel that." He takes Roy's left hand by the wrist and draws it up to flop limply against his smooth, iron-gray jaw.

"Smooth as a baby's bottom. Right?"

Roy can only grin his agreement. His right shoe seeks his left calf.

"I've got appointments for us with Bo and Gus. We'll be back before your mother's up."

Roy doubts this. His shoe drops from his calf to the tiles. The click of the heel tap startles him.

His father looks at his foot. "Get in gear," he says. He fakes a punch to Roy's midsection, then heads for the kitchen without closing the door, his thick crepe soles squeaking briskly. Roy closes the door himself.

For some time now he has been debating what to do about the top. He realizes he was in the process of deciding whether to trim it himself when his father caught him. Now he is going to lose the sides and the top does not seem important anymore. He turns his collar up. In profile his d.a. flares out behind him like the blade of a battle-ax. He takes one more swipe downward on the top and works a small curl into the uneven fringe, which frames his forehead. With nail-paring scissors he clips the curl, immediately to lament the barren white spot its absence leaves in the middle of his hairline. He quits the bathroom, thinking he has himself begun the mutilation Bo or Gus will complete.

In the kitchen he is running the hot-water tap for a cup of instant coffee when he hears his father backing the Olds out of the basement garage. The horn sounds impatiently for him, once. He obeys.

There is a shovel on the floor in back. Roy wants to ask about this but checks himself and climbs in. Nothing is to be gained by expressing idle curiosity when dealing with his father. The last time he did, his idle curiosity was told that the Olds was such a good deal because the last owner died in it. His father has a way of flooring him. Best to play dumb. Besides, he has enough to worry about already: Bo and Gus are butchers. Roy has never been able to come up with an excuse to avoid them which did not make him seem either frightened or pettily unimpressed by their all-cripple, all-veteran operation. There is a barbershop in the Officers' Club and one down by the PX, but his father religiously insists on Bo and Gus's.

Their shop is off base and his father drives toward the main gate. He is shorter than his son and he has the seat up so far Roy's knees are braced against the dashboard. The pressure is not painful. Oddly, Roy wishes it was. His father maintains silence as if under orders but he is grinning. The Virginia summer is muggy and hot and the stench of low tide off the seawall rolls in to mingle with the oppressive scent of the dying magnolias on the island that divides the boulevard. But Roy can still smell the lilac. The burnt grass on the island retains the dark, damp clumps of a recent mowing. They'll have the rakes and sprinklers on that by noon.

At the main gate the Air Policeman snaps their bumper sticker a salute and Roy's father snaps one back. Roy knows his father is in high spirits because of his capture. They are together in something his mother abhors and his father's elation is meant to infect him with the conspiratorial aspect of their mission. His father says nothing when Roy lights up a cigarette. He has quit smoking himself because the X rays taken during his last flight physical revealed a dark blur on one lung. He was smoking two packs a day, threw an opened carton in the trash, and never took another puff. Roy has always suspected such a display of self-control inhuman. He is careful to see that his smoke is taken by the open window vent. On the night of his graduation he flicked a cigarette out this window; it landed in the backseat where it burned undiscovered for several blocks. His father glances at his cigarette now as if this could easily happen again.

Bo and Gus's is a refurbished tavern pinched between a Laundromat on the left and a cut-rate hardware store on the right. It is a one-story, pink stucco box, the whole front a picture window bordered with cigarette and hair cream decals. A large sign stenciled high above the door announces "Servicemen Welcome," and below it hangs a mock-up of a bombshell spiraled in red and white. It is mechanized, and when spinning, as now, it creates the illusion of falling. The door is wide open, so the air conditioner is on the blink again.

Inside, three real bomb casings rest on their fins. Their noses have been unscrewed and inverted and filled with sand for ashtrays. Roy drops into the vinyl and aluminum chair his father points to and plants his butt deep in the nearest bomb. Bo has the only other customer chaired.

"Here's the Colonel now," Bo says. He is potbellied, moon faced, and in the mirror behind him his bald pate shines pinkly above the clear amber, yellow, and green bottles of his trade. His right arm ends in a stump. Below the short sleeve of his mint-green, creped-nylon tunic begins the strap of his artificial arm and its claw. It is stainless steel and gleaming. Bo often says it is better than the real thing, though his

wife complains it's cold. Roy believes it scares his wife shitless. Now it rests on the shaven temple of a boy whose wide
khaki trousers, black socks, and black shoes betray him as
an airman. With his good left hand, Bo wields his straight
razor high above the airman's natural hairline. The airman
flinches on the word "Colonel" and Bo nicks him behind the
ear. The airman does not complain. Roy notes the blood.
Bo slaps more shaving cream onto the airman's neck. La-
boriously, he works the razor up and down the length of the
strop.

Fresh sheet in hand, Gus waits by the second chair for
the Colonel. This means Roy will get Bo's claw.

"Bo. We late, Gus?" The Colonel snatches up a copy of
Air Force Magazine.

"The Colonel's never late," Gus says. He is Bo's natural
counterpart: Slight, weasel faced, he parts his curly red
hair precisely down the middle. It occurs to Roy that Bo
and Gus teamed up to make a whole man and failed: Half
of Gus's face is tight with beat-colored scar tissue.

He sweeps the Colonel in with his sheet. "The usual?"

"A little closer on the sides, Gus. That gray's beginning to
outflank me."

Roy does not believe anything can outflank his father.

"Do her right up," Gus says and commences to fix the
three fingers of his left hand around the clippers. He begins by shearing off two inches high above the hairline. Roy
knows he will eventually attempt to blend in the long top
with thinning shears. Gus is not always successful at this but
he knows the Colonel's primary interest is the gray; whatever errors the clippers commit him to are worth it. Once,
when his father was stationed in Japan, he took Roy to a
Yokohama barber who placed a bowl on his head and
snipped furiously at the air behind his ears. Roy, ten, bawled.
The bowl was removed, his father doubled with laughter,
then stern with shame. It was all a joke. Now Roy thinks his
father is unwittingly on the receiving end and he smiles to
himself—until he remembers the radiation burns on the
Japanese barber's face and neck. Why does his father insist
on entrusting their appearance to the care of victims? He

believes he owes his father some justice but he knows he will never get it.

Bo finishes stropping one razor, examines and rejects it, and begins on another. The airman fidgets. Roy picks up last month's dog-eared copy of *Argosy*. The gray has been vanquished and Gus whisks the evidence off the Colonel's shoulders and plants his feet to tackle the hard part.

"My boy Glenn'll be back from Germany next month," he says. His boy is Army, a staff sergeant. The mention of his name makes Roy think of maiming. He imagines the barber's son lost overboard in a shark-infested sea: feet gone, arms flailing, temples neatly trimmed.

"He's been recommended for OCS," Gus says.

"Damn fine," says the Colonel. "With the two of them in we might win the next one yet."

"Yours enlistin' too, huh?"

"The Point," Roy's father says. "Accepted last month."

Gus takes a step back to get the proper perspective on this.

Roy looks up from his magazine. It is a lie—at least, though it's true he has been accepted, he has decided not to go and his father knows it.

"Christalmighty!" Gus says. "You hear that, Bo? Colonel's boy'll be going to West *Point* this year."

"How 'bout that," Bo says. With the blunt edge of his new razor he wipes the excess shaving cream from the airman's neck. The airman bows his tonsured head.

Bo says, "Not going Air Force like his old man, huh, Colonel?"

The Colonel's grimace is not unkind. "The glasses," he explains. "Too many science-fiction novels in bad light." He shrugs. "I tried to tell him. Air's cleaner than mud." He winks in Roy's direction.

Roy blinks. When his father returns to his magazine, Roy stares at him for a long time, quits only when Gus spins the chair so the Colonel can see how things are shaping up. When Roy brings his head back up a few minutes later, his father is glaring at him for the length of his previous stare.

Bo is through with the airman—who pays for what's been done to him, pivots toward the Colonel, begins to salute, balks, and hurries out—and Roy is up. He would like to take his magazine with him so he won't have to talk to Bo, but his father knows he can't read without his glasses and they must go for the haircut. Bo snaps his sheet; Roy mounts. The chair is uncomfortably warm. On the wall between two huge mirrors opposite his chair, a naked woman straddles an undersized F–100. Her breasts resemble the noses of bombs. Head impossibly swiveled, the pilot has wide eyes on them. Below this calendar in a dime-store frame, Gus and Bo hold out on three-fingered hook and claw a magnificent stringer of largemouth bass.

"A career officer," Bo says. "It's a good life, son." He leans forward as if to confide a secret but his voice is louder than normal. "You can bet there'll be plenty of that, too." He leers, nods in the direction of the woman on the wall, and chuckles manfully. "Poontang aplenty, yessiree." The claw snaps. Roy notices a rough spot, like a hangnail, on one of the prongs. Bo moves behind him and turns down his collar. "How would you like it, Lieutenant?"

Roy ignores the commission. "Just trim it a little," he says, though he does not believe he is going to get away with this. "And follow the natural hairline." His mother's advice.

Bo laughs. "Not much sense in just a trim if you're going to the Point," he says. "Starts middle of next month, don't it? How 'bout that, Colonel?" He removes Roy's glasses carefully. The shop is blur.

"Right," the Colonel says and Bo has got the crew-cut guard fastened to his clippers. The claw positions Roy's head. He closes his eyes. The clippers whir. Bo's stomach pushes against Roy's elbow. Roy is afraid to move his arm; it might seem an insult for which he will have to pay with a closer cut.

It could be no closer. In a matter of seconds Bo gets him one quarter of an inch on the sides, one half inch on top. Roy looks at the long tuffs of hair in his lap and wonders how he has allowed this to happen.

He glances up. In the mirror opposite his chair the airman sits draped in white, as if up to his neck in snow. His features are blurred but Roy does not need his glasses. It is winter in another place. His father is leading him out onto the porch. They are in pajamas. His father points to the enormous drift piled up against the snow fence. Out there in the snow a boy is waiting. He is an obedient boy and very cold. He would like to come inside but there is only room for one good boy in the house. If the warm boy who lives in the house screws up just one more time. . . .

Bo runs the vacuum cleaner over Roy's scalp. Goose bumps rise, he feels chilled. His shoes shine up at him stupidly bright; he scuffs each one with the sole of the other. His father is talking about fishing.

"Where'd you two get that beautiful mess of fish? Big Bethel?"

Big Bethel is the Army reservoir where Roy and his father have consistently poor luck.

"Naw. No fish in there," Gus says. He is giving the Colonel's sideburns his final attention. "Went to Carolina. Bo has an uncle down there what owns his own boat dock."

Bo says the Colonel and the boy here are more than welcome to try their luck in Carolina.

"Thanks. Might do that sometime." Roy knows he won't.

Gus has finished up. He shakes his head once in admiration of his handiwork (white scalp ashine below oiled part and top), receives his payment, protests his tip, and gives the Colonel one more quick whisking.

Roy's father stands looking at him head-on, hands on his hips, grinning.

"That ought to hold you," he says and walks out.

Roy wonders if he has paid for them both. Bo tells him his father is one goddamn fine pilot, one of the old school, an officer and a gentleman in the true sense of them words. His men really admire the hell out of him. Wishing this were not all true, Roy nods and Bo has got the lather on him. It is hotter and thinner than he expected. He feels it oozing down to soak through his tissue collar. Bo eases his head forward until Roy's chin digs into his chest. The razor pecks fussily, then rasps down his rigid neck.

As far as Roy can tell, he has nothing left up there that requires attention. But Bo is a perfectionist. He buzzes lightly around the ears and for the fourth time gives the neck he has just shaved a firm sweep with the clippers. Because Bo cannot smack his hands together, thus letting Roy know what's coming, when he administers what he calls the "good smellum," Roy jumps. Bo restrains him gently with the curve of the claw on his shoulder. Roy's ear and neck feel inflamed, icy, then numb. Bo gets the other side. The stuff smells worse than the lilac. He believes he is going to gag and does.

"Wet or dry?" Bo asks. His father isn't here so Roy rubs his head once and asks Bo if he's serious.

Bo is releasing him dry as his father comes back into the shop. Perfect timing. He has one hand behind his back. Roy quits the chair, his jeans peeling wetly off the warm leather. Before he has time to reach his glasses and inspect the damage in the mirror, his father plops a straw hat on his head. Roy touches it. Bo hands him his glasses. He faces the mirror; the narrow brim is up all the way around; he cannot decide if he looks more like a farmer or a clown. The thing perches on his cropped head like a paper plate on a bush.

"Don't want to get sunburned up there, do you? Eighty-nine cents next door."

Bo and Gus proclaim this a real bargain. In fact, Bo thinks he'll get him one, too.

Roy makes for the door.

"Aren't you going to pay the man?"

Roy digs for his wallet. His comb comes out with it and clatters to the floor. His father beats him to the comb.

"You won't be needing this anymore," he says and pitches it into the wastecan on his way out. "Break a leg, boys."

Roy does not understand how his father can manage this without seeming to intentionally imply irony. But the barbers take it grinning broad as movie extras, and his father is gone.

"Don't be a stranger," Bo says as he gives Roy his change. Roy does not tip him. At the door he turns back to glower at the barbers. In their tunics he thinks them a pair of flimsy Cossacks. He reestablishes the height of his collar.

"Yeah. Hurry back," Gus says. "And good luck at the Point, son."

"Poontang," Bo drawls.

The sun is working toward noon. Roy rests his arm on the car window frame and jerks it away, burned. His father heads back toward the base.

"Those old boys sure jump to conclusions."

Roy doesn't answer. The crown of the hat touches the headliner of the car. He sits up straight, straighter, until the sweatband binds tight as a tourniquet and the cracking straw pricks at his scalp.

"I said, those two sure jump to conclusions. Right?"

"Yes." Up straighter.

"Couple of real characters. Think they know it all. I for one think there's probably some whoppers out at Big Bethel right now. What do you say?"

Now Roy knows why the shovel is back there on the floor. They are going out to the sewage disposal plant across the base where they will dig up four dozen of those hard, resilient bloodworms his father always says the bass at Big Bethel really go for. By the time they get to the lake the sun will be directly overhead, the metal seats of the boats will be hot as skillets, and if there are any fish they will be dozing on the bottom.

He sinks back down into the seat and loosens the hat from his swimming head. He hopes his father will at least stop at home for some breakfast but he suspects the gear is already in the trunk and he doubts they will stop for anything but the worms.

"Okay," he says.

His father reaches across the seat and slaps his knee.

The Model

After dinner the family disappears to their corners and Jason finds himself alone, leaning in the bathroom doorway in a swoon of reminiscence. The walls in there are a stark, emergency-room white, the two window sashes blinding orange. In each of the windows sit squares of orange, brown and white paisley on removable wooden frames to let in the morning light. These are the handiwork of his wife, Clare. Once they also let in the rheumy gaze of the retired lobsterman across the way because Clare thought a little innocent distraction might ease him through the sickness unto death. Jason remembers his pleasure when she confessed this sentiment. It seemed a generous thing for a young woman to admit and serve the fantasies of an old man, a harmless stranger removed from the ocean to a rented room. Jason bought her bunches of jonquils (*Narcissus jonquilla*) to suggest, teasingly, another motive, and though he never actually caught her consciously on show, she would sometimes ask him to wait a minute when he knocked on the bathroom door and he would hear the frames of brilliant paisley being slipped back into place. Those were her Foolish Years, she says, when the children were still in grade school. The lobsterman died when the children were in junior high and now, in her early middle age, there is no one across the way who needs to look, no one to serve. Now we are in the Years of Concern.

The nameless plant hanging in a pot above the claw-footed tub marks the transition between these two seasons. At the end of the first, Clare said she would burn off some of her nervous household energy taming this hairy, "Vincent Pricey" thing into a civilized shape, a sort of Rapaccini's-daughter project. "And you are the vain young man who doesn't love me enough to live on my poison and deny the world." He was already modeling suits and cigars then and it made sense, what she said, sense without injury. Jason built a shelf behind and framing the plant, which is now guarded by the irregular militia of her cosmetics: Deep Magic, Silk & Honey, Swedish Tanning Secret, *Lait Hamamelis Mercier,* a packet of Anti-Wrinkle Petals, cleansers, conditioners, removers and restorers, good soldiers all in defeat. The flourescent light on them is fierce, relentlessly tuned to her flaws, humming. He concocts a phrase about the signals soon-to-be packed objects transmit, *the distress of movable things.*

"I haven't done anything in here yet," Clare says behind him. "I want it all to jump into boxes and trail us to New York. It owes a loyalty to my youth. Or maybe I don't want to hold off the years anymore. Maybe I'm trying to tell myself something with this reluctance. What do you think?"

Jason turns and smiles down at her, a short compact woman with a little boy's clipped straw hair. The Bahama vacations meet the good works handsomely in her face. Once she was a star in summer stock; now she divides her time between long stints at the compressed version of the *Oxford English Dictionary* she bought to battle modern poetry until it yields, she says, what it promises, and late evening packing for their elaborate move to a small apartment she won with a bribe in a strange city.

"Take everything you need," Jason says and eases himself past the tiger moths on her kimono, the boxes stacked in the hall. Jason has no idea what these boxes contain. Nothing seems to be missing from the daily round, his own drawers are tidily full, yet the hallway is a maze of bulging cardboard.

"Our best battles are in these walls," he mutters, running his hands down the sides of the stairwell, bracing himself as if against a drop into darkness or water.

"I didn't hear you."

"Nothing," he calls back. "I'm going to have a talk with David."

He hears her tread solidly toward the master bedroom.

Pound for pound, inch for inch, she must have the heaviest footfall in the civilized world. She goes barefoot in the house to flout this talent. Jason's more serious moments with himself are often punctuated by her thudding heels and he believes his thoughts would scatter like leaves without these measures.

David is in the living room boning up on his French grammar. He'll be a freshman in an honors program at Harvard this fall. Jason has agreed to allow him to share the house with his older sister, Sharon, for at least the first year. David has clear skin and a shag haircut like the rock star Rod Stewart. He has overcome a mild speech defect and his inflection is without regional taint, like a disc jockey's. Jason often sees him picking up pencils, towels, socks with his toes, a talent he mastered at ten, "In case I lose a hand." He seems to have snared sanity, manners and wit from the times, a feat which baffles his father. Last week Jason caught him reading *The Sorrows of Young Werther* in translation under his stereo earphones. Jason lifted one earphone and received a faint blast of The Rolling Stones: "*I know you're only fourteen years old / I don't wanna see your ID.*" David grinned at his father's mock scowl, and Jason thinks now he was maybe set up for the moment. David is a young man with a lot on his mind. He plays chess and classical guitar. He plays hockey. He skis and hunts alone. He plays bridge and tennis and handball and he wins all the time, gracefully. His chess set, tennis racket, guitar, skates, climbing boots, ski poles, fly rod, and hockey stick surround him on the Brussels carpet, a citadel of his accomplishments at seventeen.

"I've just beaten fifteen irregular verbs and now I'm trying to decide which of these things I ought to give up. I have too many interests. There's no sense spreading yourself thin in an age of specialization. Could be ruinous, promote bitterness, underachievement, cultural disorientation. What do you think?"

Jason prods the hockey stick with the toe of his slipper. "This is a pretty battered stick. You should buy a new one."

"I think hockey is expendable. Overcrowded. Team sports require you to crank up group enthusiasm. Besides, I'm too light to last. Maybe chess could go, too. It's beginning to get a bad name since Iceland, going public, losing its etiquette, plagued by goons and cads. I need to excel in one, at the most, two activities. Maybe I should drop everything and take up boxing so I can visit you in Gotham without fear and trembling." He throws two almost invisibly quick left jabs at Jason's knee. Jason's reflexes are still good and his foot flies out and flicks back a wing of David's hair.

"I came down to talk about a dream I had last night. Listen up. I dreamed I was a middle-aged rock star. Women were chasing me, screaming for my blood."

"Jason, this is a possible alternative to your present situation, about which I have never heard you complain, but how could it be good in this vale of tears? Moving, the family in separate cities, a new a feary one for you and Mom. Hansel and Gretel alone in the big Cambridge Woods. This dream may offer a solution. We could get up a group. Jason and the Family Fleece. Mother can bang a tambourine and hum. Sister can do a topless number with police protection."

"It doesn't bother you? A dream like that in your father's head? I'm forty-six."

"Not every teenage son has a father who dreams of being a rock star."

"I don't dream of being one. I dreamed I *was* one. It was horrible."

"You'd have to do something with that handlebar. Too symmetrical. Too substantial. Looks like a muscle out there and this is a generation of peace. You'd need more hair, of course. And a sheep would help, something suggestive on stage."

"It was a pretty serious dream, David. Maybe I didn't make that clear."

"I am ears."

"They kept stepping on this chord I had stuck in me somewhere and I kept flipping over on my back and singing something that made my tongue swell up. I came out of it with the alarm clock in my hand, humming. Both of us, me and the clock. It seemed so stupid that I was angry for being frightened. And the night before I was a strong giant looking for a room I could fit into. Someone I couldn't see—I think it was lots of people—built a box around me. I was wearing a tight knit suit all humped over and staring down at my cross-country shoes, the new red ones."

"Jason In The Box," David says and underlines it in the air with his hand. "Someone is cranking your spring. You feel tense. The visual on this is whammy and memorable."

"I felt fat. I felt trapped and stiff. I kept worrying about them getting me with the nails."

"Sounds serious. Also sounds like one of Only Son's suits." David begins idly shuffling through his gear. He tests the tension of his racket strings against his knee, the drag on his fly reel, the C on his guitar. "I have a question which might alarm you. Don't let it. Are you ready?"

"I'll never be ready."

"Courage. Have you ever and did you recently *dream you were a complete wardrobe?*"

Jason answers into David's fly rod microphone in a voice much louder then he expected.

"Everyone kept putting me on!"

"Fast. That was fast. A little ferocious, but split second."

"I want to talk to your sister."

"Get another opinion, huh? You're too late. Freddy the Hindu with machismo has her helpless in the basement with the Hasselblad. I think he's shooting some glossies to peddle to your man Felix across the river. Surprised Fawn Frolics in Fun Spring Frocks. Put on . . . a sweater and a happy face and walk around the lonely block with your son. Say smart things. Talk to me of Joe Louis, Sugar Ray, Jackson Pollack. Inspire me with pugilistic legends."

"You might have to hold me up."

❁   ❁   ❁   ❁

The Cambridge night is blue and starless. The neighborhood has not deteriorated or grown in twelve years. Jason's feet are cold in his slippers. His son works the hockey stick through a Chaplin-quick waddle and twirl. He has on his gray Norwegian police sweater, pleated and wide-cuffed khakis, track shoes from Japan. Jason thinks he looks oddly European, a refuge from a bankrupt Slavic circus, a tumbler or an aerialist. In his heart he suspects the style of his son but he has no solid complaint to level. Felix in the Boston office wants David for a modeling job: feet shod in climbing boots and crampons, standing on a block of ice in a pair of grape-fizz jockey shorts, a coil of rope across his chest, gazing at challenge and danger, fearless, girded, prepared. For what? Felix is lonely and has his reasons but Jason believes David will not be amazed or unkind if approached. For a moment David's sophistication saddens him; his son does not need to get this contingency out in the open where fatherly advice might count. At seventeen, Jason would have thrown a punch or an insult, a recognition which dismays and thrills him still.

David leaps from the sidewalk onto Hersh Rainey's lawn. "Nureyev," he sings in fluted syllables and plants his hockey stick blade up in Hersh's peonies. Skating back to Jason's side with his thumbs in the waistband of his khakis, David grunts, "Bobby Orr." Jason is shaken by this precise and playful dramatization of his concern. As they pass under the next streetlamp, he tries to look David in the eye to see how much his son really knows. David winks, and Jason gives over to the charm of his son. Hersh will retaliate with a Wallace sticker on their bumper or a chopped cabbage in the morning mail. His son understands the neighbors. He is sensitive to their humor and foibles. At thirteen David carved a lobster out of soap for the old man who lived in the house Hersh bought.

He cried. When I gave it to him, he cried, Daddy.
It was a thoughtful thing to do, David.
Maybe not. Maybe it just said I knew he was going to die.
Jason is thinking about the war in which he did not die. In the final months of it, at nineteen, he was a tail gunner in a B–26 over Europe, 9th Air Force. That aircraft was famous for dropping on the approach to the runway like a stone. When he drives the dipping country roads which lead to the summer cottage the family rents on Newfound Lake, his stomach flies into his throat. He enjoys this foolish and nostalgic repetition of his warrior youth. He met his first wife in Nice after the war and lost her to that city while he was in Korea. In Indiana the faculty and students bought his paintings and prints for a song, Clare quoted pages and pages of Keats, the children were born. Now he is a male

fashion model on occasion and a senior partner in an advertising firm because he met a persuasive man in a bar in Chicago. He is grateful he is no longer a boondock painter with small canvasses to peddle, coeds to rescue, console and escape. He reads Chekhov and weeps for "the general idea," the shape of God in man. He knows what this means. He has messages for his son but he feels David doesn't need them and he holds them back without resentment fairly well.

"I feel blessed," he says to the night and wonders if this is true.

David places his hand on Jason's shoulder, then hooks arms with him and walks around the block without embarrassment, as though he has been raised in that foreign circus. Jason senses that they are being photographed from behind trees, parked cars. He laughs out loud.

On their stoop Jason follows the straight back of his son into the house. He remembers his own father, a master of sarcasm, telling him to tuck his thumbs into his fists if he wanted to break them when he hit someone. He understands and conquers without flinching the impulse to smash David in the kidneys. He opens his hands.

❋   ❋   ❋   ❋

Freddy and Sharon are in the living room. His daughter is wearing a simple beige dress, which reaches past her knees. She has style without wishing to be known by it. Her feet are not loud or dexterous. Revolutions and fads die in her blood. She will be an apprentice at the Impressions Workshop if freedom and melancholy don't win this winter. Freddy, a lecturer in quantum mechanics at M.I.T. on loan from New Delhi, is lecturing her in an intense whisper. Her gaze is lost in space. The Tarot cards lay scattered on the carpet at her feet. The flush on Sharon's face may or may not tell the real basement story. It was Clare who suggested Sharon put herself on the pill and, as far as Jason knows, she has not become a statistical sleeper. Jason likes Freddy because, as he has confessed to the physicist, Freddy is two inches shorter and ten years older than Sharon. He wants to remain in the States. He dresses like a cub reporter in the 1930s—bow tie, knickers, argyle socks. Jason suspects he has a tailor and debts. He signs petitions against détente and spoofs Indian nationalism in an Oxford drone.

"Good evening, Jason. We are discussing the recurrence of inverted Swords in Sharon's cards. She has taken all this a bit too seriously, I'm afraid."

"You told me it was nonsense then read them like a swami in a trance."

"The readings require a certain theatrical flare."

David puts Ravi Shankar on the stereo and Freddy looks at Jason with extravagant sympathy.

"I have taken the liberty of bringing you some studies of Sharon, Jason."

"He's got me inside and out."

David boozily tilts back his head, his fingers wrap an imaginary cigar; he drawls out the raspy deadpan fading rise of a W. C. Fields aside. "Science and the mysteries of the troubling East. The fakir physicist calls her shots."

Smiling with precision, Freddy asks Jason if he would mind taking a look at these photographs as a professional.

"I'll take my Swords into the pantry and mix you pigs a drink."

His daughter is nude in these photographs, faceless. She is bands of black and shadow, caged toes to throat by geometrically crosshatching tracers of light, which make Jason dizzy. He cannot imagine the circumstances of the posing.

"I thought you were trying to sell a few modeling shots to Felix."

Freddy is bewildered. Jason looks at David, who fakes a grin and shrugs.

"Have you thought of showing these?"

"Not really. I could, I suppose, though for the wrong reasons. Talented Asian, visiting physicist with a hobby. Et cetera."

"Freddy's got self-respect," Sharon calls in from the dining-room pantry. "You know that, Dad. He's a Brahmin, it comes with the caste. Self-respect, dignity, mission."

"The sister is disturbed," David says. "The father dreams of singing in a box."

Ducking Freddy's long look, Jason shuffles the photographs. He feels David maneuver behind him. He holds the photographs as long as he can, then turns them face down on the coffee table.

"What is your opinion?" Freddy asks.

Jason folds his hand over his moustache and speaks to the glass door of the bookcase beyond Freddy's shoulder.

"I think David should box, Sharon should marry for love, Clare should grow old, and I should go to bed."

"Your mind is on other things. I should not trouble you with my amateur handiworks."

"They make me dizzy. I'm sorry, Freddy."

"Ah, a coincidence. Sharon said the same thing."

Jason looks toward the pantry. Sharon has disappeared. David is on the landing, his arms around his gear. He opens his mouth wide, like a smacked clown, then clamps it shut and climbs out of sight.

"I hope you will not mind if I accompany Sharon to New York once you are settled. Clare assures me this would be possible. Perhaps after the spring semester, when you are reestablished."

"It's always a pleasure to have you over, Freddy. Right now, though, I'm a little tired. The movers come on Monday and tomorrow's a big day."

"I am available for reliable assistance with this move, Jason. My back is strong. My nation. . . . Right. See you in the morning."

Jason understands this means Freddy plans to spend the night in the house with Sharon. He has no strong opinion on this new development but he feels he has unwittingly sanctioned it by okaying New York.

Upstairs Clare tells him she has decided to do their apartment there all in white until a theme emerges to instruct her. Hersh Rainey called to say he and Grace would be only too happy to drop in on the kids from time to time. They promised to be casual and sly. Jason thinks of his wife as another child in his care, an intelligent child who mindlessly craves his attention. The story he tells her this evening concerns a large young man who falls in love, is changed into a migratory bird by a jealous god, and dies flapping in an oil slick. He apologizes for his subjectivity and lack of invention.

"It was sad and screwy and you made it for me." She

reaches for his hand and takes it tightly: She is going to quote a relevant line. " 'I married a vain and protean man.' "

He agrees and meets her demands.

❀ ❀ ❀ ❀

At 2:00 A.M. Jason sees his life as a series of erratic and expected moments, perpetually lobbed grenades, duds he neither dives on nor ignores. Rigging this image, he falls into a sleep of costumes and pursuit out of which he awakes furious and in terror.

He gets out of bed and puts on his bathrobe. The house feels poised, isometrically tuned to some irresistible, muscular thought. He steals downstairs. On the living-room landing he flicks on the light.

Sharon and Freddy have not had enough courage for the second floor, nor enough anxiety for the basement again.

"How could you!" Sharon screams.

Jason does not know how he could but the fact that he has is opening up.

Freddy wraps his sports jacket around his waist and stands at attention. In this position he maintains his composure and with feeling announces he has violated Jason's generous hospitality. "My apologies at this moment are perhaps of no interest."

"You little darkie worm," Sharon hisses.

Jason stares down at the waxed boards of the landing which squeak though he stands as still as he can. His daughter refuses to cover her breasts.

"Go home, Freddy. Go home," Jason says.

Freddy retreats to the foyer with the immigrant bundle of his clothes. Watching him go, Jason remembers his offer to help with the move and this somehow means now that the move has already happened. He is thick in the wilds of this thought when a hand falls on his shoulder. He looks back and up, expecting to see Clare. It is David, his face masked in appropriate filial concern. "Dad?"

Jason feels the torque rise through the arc of his elbow flying back to clip David across the shins, hard. He steps aside to give David room to fall past him, but the boy sits down on the stairs and hugs his shins.

"What did I do? What in hell did I do?"

"Dear?" Clare appears at the top of the stairs in an awkward squat, her hands tugging down the hem of her shortie nightgown. Jason sees her dark moss askant the white flesh of her thighs; as a crick in his neck protests his angle of vision, he thinks, and is amazed that he does, of the lobsterman dead and the neighbors alive to look in on his daughter and son when they live here alone. He looks away and addresses his wife with his eyes on his feet.

"Put on your kimono, Clare. And bring something down for Sharon." He does not hear her go but he knows she has gone.

David is whimpering. "What did I do? Jason it's already a bruise what did I do?"

Jason reviews to himself what his son has done to get hurt. In a moment Clare slips past David and Jason, trailing behind her fluttering moths the starched wings of a cotton kimono. Jason watches his wife spread out the wings like a screen for his daughter to enter. When she does not rise from the sofa, he helps Sharon to her feet with his eye on a line through the back of his wife.

Clare joins Sharon on the sofa. Jason feels them below and David behind him, waiting at the ends of his fingers. His elbow is a long corner of pain. He shuts his eyes.

"Can I go to bed now?"

As the decision not to answer David reaches his mind in a sentence, Jason thinks it should happen that he is photographed in this wisdom, in his bathrobe. He takes a breath he can hold without seeming to need it for balance. The women are his daughter and his wife, the question at his back is his son on the stairs ready for bed. He speaks to them.

"We are not going to live in New York. We are all going to live here."

In their silence he flicks off the light; then in the rush of a gasp, which surrounds him, he flicks it back on. He turns and steps up across his son, David, who at Harvard will be honored and handsome and home every night.

Roger Rath

"The Young in
One Another's Arms"

1

She said it was a good time of the month and this threw him because he had thought she would not need to worry about anything along those lines. She drank several gin and tonics to loosen up and Roy began to fear she might not come across. It would be unwise to take time out to undress her: He did not own a car that summer and he had to share the trailer with a graduate student who did, one whose hours were a mystery.

The fluorescent light over the lumpy hide-a-bed cast her legs in eerie blue shadows. She asked him to turn it off, and he did, though he had been counting on it heavily. She was tired and jumpy and drunk and he came in her at once, briefly. She cried quietly. She was all right when he asked her.

Turning on the light to find a cigarette, he was genuinely surprised to see a stain of blood on her powder blue skirt, a darkening wing of accusation. For a moment he believed it must be a false alarm, a mistake flapped loose from somewhere else. He could not be the one who had done this. She was twenty-three. "Look what you've done," she said, and he heard himself saying he was sorry.

❀   ❀   ❀   ❀

In the morning she drove back out to the trailer court and offered him a lift to class. The blue skirt lay neatly folded on the seat between them, stain up. He laughed to himself at the subtlety of this, then dropped his books on it to kill it. She talked about the trouble she was having in her German course, the wise, plump woman prof so patient with her grunt and whistle pronunciation that it made her cry in a class full of men, boys, talked quietly of this, as if she were speaking of a heroine she was meant to like but couldn't, until they pulled up in front of a dry cleaner's. In sentences so flat and precise she must have practiced them, she told him to take the skirt in there and see if they could save it. Sometimes they wanted to know what had caused the stain in order to properly treat it and if they asked he could just tell them what. "I'm not going to do that," he said. "Or take it in, either." She yanked the skirt out from under his books, toppling them to the floor, and marched inside with it.

When she came back he was sitting with his books in his lap. She threw the claim check onto his side of the dashboard and asked him if he was still here. He said he guessed he was.

That afternoon after classes they went swimming at Huelen's Lake, a private beach a few miles from the university. He swam beyond the plastic rope and buoys until a cramp convinced his right calf to quit. He heard her cursing behind him as he went down. Trying to cup his chin, she closed too close on his panic. His elbow clipped her low on the jaw and surprised him lightly thonking there. She cursed him, dove in a neat rippleless tuck he admired through the panic, then came up again behind him, the anger of her reach for him this time funny enough to make him grin. As soon as she held him under the chin the cramp in his calf vanished, though he heard himself decide to allow her to swim him in to shore.

They waded in the last few yards and she said she was very impressed, oh so impressed by his concern for others. She said she was an official lifeguard. He said he knew that now. In a high-pitched voice and more rapidly than what she'd used on him for the skirt's justice, she said she had never been able to dive for bricks and bring them up and she had almost flunked the course at sixteen when she was chubby and no one took her seriously and she'd read Proust instead. But she *had* passed the course, no matter what they'd thought, and earned her badge and why was she yakking like this, she didn't know, would he please kiss her. He said he knew that, about the lifeguarding, he meant, he knew that, damn it. He knew that now but there were too many people on the bank up there for what he wanted to do with her and he didn't have much wind yet.

In a while he added: "No one saves anyone in a black tank suit. It looks staged. Too professional," and he snapped the suit rim of her near hip with the pale rubbery tips of his fingers, which should have more of her on them.

"Ouch!" she shrieked and kissed him clumsily on the mouth in front of sunning drunk hundreds.

That Christmas vacation they agreed to see no one else. Roy took a job bartending three nights a week to prove his industry and character and on the other nights she drove out to the trailer and didn't mind much, after the first time, when the graduate student and whoever it was he had in there made the same noises she said he made to sound like a man when they "jumped the lumps" on the hide-a-bed in the eerie blue light she promised every night he could keep on.

The following June Susan graduated, passed her social-service exams, and accepted a position as a child welfare worker in a county far to the south, in the Ozarks, deep in them. Her first letter praised her luck in finding a roomy cottage in a resort trailer park on a lake. This coincidence of residence flapped like a wing in periphery as he read and passed on to the people there who needed her. She liked her work, sort of, most of the time—reshuffling the predictable miseries of the county's neglected children, unwed mothers and resentful foster parents—but the endless forms and errands exhausted her patience. "I'm so constantly confronted with the problems of others and then when I come back to the cottage I must be alone with my own." By July's letters her disgust with local doctors, probation officers, sheriff's deputies, and itinerant judges had blossomed into a mission-ary ferocity Roy uneasily remembered from the morning with the skirt's flapping stain his books hadn't killed.

Then in August she found sudden calm.

The old man who rented her the cottage was "fun com-pany," and she was getting in some practice cooking for two.

Roy wrote back hinting for more details about this man, Henry Simpson. He checked his impulse to ask just how old Simpson was, then scribbled the question in a postscript, which asked if he was young enough to need a trip to the cleaner's. During the week he waited for her reply, he thought of his nights at the tavern as slowly totaling up to the price of her complete attention. He began working a full-time shift. One night after closing up alone with a few mugs of beer, he called her long distance. It was around one on a Wednesday and she was not at home, or not answering. After another beer he remembered that she might be asleep, that people slept at night in their beds. Or slept in other beds beside telephones whose numbers did not match up to the one banging in his head.

The next morning he received a letter and he was grateful that he had missed her with a needy late night phone call. She had never asked Henry how old he was and she didn't see what difference it made, but she guessed he was in his mid-to-late seventies. He was divorced, childless, a retired light-verse writer for a Kansas City greeting-card company Hallmark had wiped out or bought up or something. She was getting in practice sharing with someone. Henry was sick and lonely and she was healthy and lonely and together they made a good pair. "I give him time. He keeps me sane." She, too, added a postscript: "For your information the nearest dry cleaner's is fifteen miles away but there are plenty of barns and garages around and they have men in them who should be taken there and sometimes early in the morning or late at night they knock on the door of my horny pink house and the witch gives them coffee and talk but that's all. I miss you."

He wrote back: "Getting in practice for what, when, how?"

And she: "You, swimmer. You. You. You. You," on a postcard that promised the lake she swam in was a retouched and impossible blue.

So a few nights later Roy drank himself into a dream in which a smiling blonde crone in a polka-dot bikini leaned over his booth and then knelt slowly to his ear, which was wet and whispered over and over again that she was healthy and clean and lonely as she kept reaching for a part of him too tiny to be grasped. He said it was not his fault and she cackled as he knew she would. He awoke terrified, in sweat on the hide-a-bed. The following afternoon he found his roommate and arranged to pay him double wages in advance to stand in for him at the tavern over the weekend. In another hour he managed to rent the cheap bastard's car. The graduate student was a business major with advice, standing in front of his shuddering Hudson Hornet and shouting above its cough to Roy dwarfed behind the enormous wheel that clunkers were reliable if nursed. When Roy told him that he would not be so goddamn rich and worried right now if anyone in hell ever knew last summer when he was coming in at night, the graduate student looked gratifyingly stupid. The clutch popped free and the oxidized black fender missed him and Roy stomped down hard south to surprise her.

He found Jefferson City and bought three extra cans of thirty-weight oil and a new red gas can from a slow-moving crook with gold teeth who quoted a law about selling used gas cans and watched whistling at the darkness dropping in the west as Roy filled it with white gasoline because he had faith in this offering and none in the Hudson's gauges, which were liars, liars, liars, and there would be no gas stations open at night in those steep hills that held her. From dusk through a coffee and candy-bar dinner the snaking Ozark roads held him under thirty-five. Although the Hudson held together and burned only one can of oil, he did not arrive until shortly after ten, a four-hour trip in six dreamily alive in his mind with the muscles of the slow, floaty way he'd won her, or *something*.

He had no trouble finding the court—there were dozens of luminous Burma Shave-type signs ticking off the remaining miles to Ozark Trailer Haven for what seemed like hours before he shot past the turnoff and U-turned furiously back to and down it—though under its high, prison-camp floodlights he suspected he had found the wrong place. Had come to the wrong rescue. At the end of a lane of trailers, which should not all be dark, a single cottage stood, a pink square one whose blue-glowing windows oddly signaled it hers. He eased into the driveway, honking once lightly to make it familiar, then cursed the roar of the Hudson's straight pipes.

A tall old man in a green smoking jacket and faded madras Bermudas stepped out under the porch light.

"Ah, you've found us so you must be Roy!" The old man waved his cigarette holder in greeting. As he stepped down to the side of the Hudson, Roy thought of strings instructing bones. "I'm Henry Simpson, owner and Ozark exile with nothing better to do than stay up past my bedtime for a taste of your intended's homemade bread, which she has just taken great pains to warn me might be a flop. You're just in time for sampling some hot if you don't dawdle."

Simpson thrust his face through the open car window. In silhouette beneath the floodlights it shone green and gaunt without a body attached, the white wild scientist's wings of his hair clamping it in place.

"Susan wasn't expecting you, was she?"

Roy failed to answer and Simpson danced back from the side of the car as if jolted by his reticence, perhaps expecting to be flung back broken by the thrown-open car door, a move Roy had considered—up to the moment he would have to help the old man off the ground. Simpson raised his arms over the Hudson in mock awe.

"A classic! Plump as an aging woman of the night. A hoodlum's delight."

Roy slumped in the boredom of too easily reading the old man's vaudeville diversion. Simpson patted the broad black fender, then fiddled with his cigarette holder, and finally loosened then launched a blackened filter out over the missle-head hood as if to christen or bless it. "Truly sinister. Yours?"

"Stolen," Roy said deadpan. "Hijacked. Nursed."

Simpson beamed his dentures. "This will be interesting. You must stay the weekend. Highly amusing. The weekend at the very least. I insist. You'll be my guest. Leave your things in the car for now. I'll tend them later."

The old man took a quick step forward and pressed the button on the car door that could have broken him. Roy did not know his hand was a fist on the strange talon of the handle until Simpson's grin clacked and the oxidized button clicked in, stuck; he half kicked, half shouldered himself free and swung out onto the gravel as the old man bounded ahead to the screen door.

"Your much enheartened host!" he chimed and held that one without trouble open to her, the management's treat. . . .

. . . Alive in there, standing at the sink in the kitchenette beyond the living room, a red-checkered apron floating gently about her hips in the warmth of baking for two, her back bare except for the twisted strap of her bikini top.

"Tourists or teenagers?" she asked without turning. "Are they going to stay over?"

Neither of the men answered her. Roy thought she might have some money in the business. And through the pettiness of that unlikelihood he mentally photographed the kitchenette alcove: two tiers of knotty, darkly varnished pine cupboards again mildewed beige wallpaper she'd brightened up with stick-on ocher and orange flowers the size of baseballs. The hill wife domesticity of her tunneled at him through the semidarkness of the living room and in the moment of her silence, her refusal to turn, the flowers hurled their fake cheer at him, at the thought that he would write this scene sad, chintz slease boondock sad, if he were not in it in anger. Simpson motioned him to a chair, a colorless plastic slide he would soon slip off if the pitching flowers didn't dump him first.

When she turned she did not say his name.

"You've quit your job."

"I haven't quit anything, thanks. Hello."

"I'll be leaving," Simpson offered but moved toward the kitchenette.

"Don't go, Henry. Please." She turned to Roy and lowered her eyes. "I just don't like surprises when I'm tired."

She stepped toward him, wiping her hands on her apron, and pecked him lightly on the cheek. Her lips were dry; he wanted to ask her about the sourceless blue light, how flowers or something in here gave off a blue light outside.

"Hello yourself." Over her shoulder Roy saw Simpson mixing himself a drink on top of the stove. In the interior light the old man looked less . . . magical. Roy heard Susan say he looked thin, his hair was too long, she'd just cut her own, the heat and the trouble. He pulled her to him as he stood. So he had been sitting when she kissed him. He had been able to stay in the chair.

"Watch out! My back. It's all burned and greasy."

From his new position in front of the icebox, Simpson said, "Don't fret. She won't peel. Although it took some time to convince her of the necessity—didn't it, Suz?—I oiled her down just this minute. Thoroughly." He raised his glass to salute his remedy or their careful embrace.

Roy smelled his fingers. "Vinegar."

"To brown it while the oil soothes, or so at least the theory goes and one hopes," Simpson called over.

"I'm sorry I was so antsy," Susan said. "I thought you'd call."

"I did, once. No answer." Roy looked at Simpson but the old man had discreetly turned his back to take a sip. Roy got his hand past her apron and the waistband of her suit for a second. "Salad," he whispered and heard Simpson convert a laugh to a cough of long and unconvincing duration.

There was not much more to it. Susan fed Roy chunks of hot-buttered bread that bloomed in his stomach like sponges. Simpson insisted they have a nightcap gin and tonic; he managed to refill Roy's twice. The talk was of cranky tourists who wanted city comforts or the backwoods Daniel Boone bit without chiggers, of bad drivers, corruption in local government, and loudly of the butcher quack down the road who cut welfare girls loose of their sins on speculation. There was a state trooper with a growing daughter and a temper and he would maybe have the abortionist *fixed*, Susan said. "She gives no quarter!" Simpson screeched and drank to it. Roy wished he had not joined in and grinned with Simpson so long at her.

Around two she allowed Simpson to put him up in a spare trailer, which stank, Roy thought as the old man sealed him in with "Sleep tight!," like retirement without ventilation. Like urine. Like defeat. He told himself that he had submitted to the accommodations under the mesmerism of driving fatigue, Henry's chatter, the gin. On the unmade top bunk he repeated variations on the line he should have delivered at the crucial moment in the evening when Simpson had stood, stretched, and yawned, "I'll take your bags over." It could have been almost anything, it could have been: "I'll sleep here, thanks." "The floor's fine." Or, "We've been fucking for over a year." But he had said nothing. Drowsy with lost alternatives and the gin, he began counting the luminous signs that kept popping into the right-hand corner of the windshield: Ozark Trailer Haven 35 mi., Ozark Trailer Haven 17 mi., Ozark Trailer Haven 8 mi., until he reached a string of merciful zeros and accelerated past the turnoff into a signless sleep.

✻   ✻   ✻   ✻

Susan made a trip to the Laundromat before Roy got up. Her note under the door of the trailer said she always went to the Laundromat on Saturday mornings, there really wasn't any other time she could. While he waited for her to return, he moved the Hudson from in front of the cottage to the boat-ramp parking lot, well out of range of Simpson's comments.

Breakfast was late and makeshift. There was no lunch. Susan sorted and folded clothes and linen and to be doing something Roy read three weeks of the county newspaper and shopper's guide: reduced rates and gunshot wounds, three women—or one sly woman with a different deal each week—on watch for a sober hired hand, the price of hogs down and the feeder pig man in Arkansas and the government and Kansas City responsible. Susan ironed her blouses for work and later took two of them from their hangers and ripped them up for rags. Roy made her a drink, which she didn't want just then and so he sat for an hour with a drink in each fist, watching her work and thinking about the ripped blouses, the skirt that had got him here. This was also her cleaning day, so she vacuumed the living room and scrubbed the kitchenette and bathroom linoleum. Roy walked down to the lake and threw stone after unskippable stone into its impossible blue before the thought that he might need his shoulder in its socket for whatever she was going to do without him next stopped him.

By three she was able to join him on the patio to sun. She claimed Henry's oil and vinegar treatment had done wonders for her back and, besides, she needed to even up her tan in front. She had washed a pair of trunks for Roy and when he asked her whose, she said Henry had dropped them off for him this morning just in case: Some forgetful tourist's years ago. They were tight, faded black, elastic, cut meanly like the kind he'd seen in photographs of lucky Russians wading in the Black Sea. He wore them to spare himself the explanation of why he did not want to wear them and her explanation of that. Susan brought out a tray of celery and carrot sticks from Henry's garden. They drank Simpson's gin on Simpson's patio in Simpson's sun and stared at the lake Susan said belonged to the state, so he could stop being funny any time now.

She lay on a plastic lounge chair, her bikini's polka dots glaring on her flesh like flesh-white eyes, jumping in the light. The sun hung over the far side of the lake and their side was getting most of it. Skiers churned by waving, pretty girls in suntans they had bought and dazzling orange life jackets, gaudy and remote on the blue green expanse of lake, which made the postcard a lie as the afternoon wore on below the cottage Simpson owned. Roy toyed with the idea of rescuing the girls from their fate, the mindless boy wonders who dragged them roaring the length of the lake. He would slip down to the boat ramps and cut all their tow ropes, sabotage their gas tanks with water or sand. Groggily, he lost the idea to the heat; weaves of it billowed up off the corrugated tin roof of Simpson's boat dock and through the waves he could see a ridgeline of pines on the far side of the lake dancing a chorus line monotony, rippling in its greenness. He hoped the pines would stop soon. Through them now—or through their wavering heat or out of the boat shack's shaded doorway—Simpson's scarecrow frame floated toward the patio. He had a bottle in his hand and as he bore down on them Roy saw that it was more gin.

"Spirits for the young! Spirits for the young!" he sang.

There was no help for it. Within a few minutes Simpson had snatched the topic "early marriage" out of the afternoon's thick air with the agility of a lizard, and Roy felt all the shape being sucked out of his weekend plans. He could catch no signal from Susan on how to end this, so he launched a line he had written last summer and immediately regretted it. "We marry the ones we've had: Some we get with guilt, some we get with child, and some just kill us with caution."

"Would you go through that once more, Roy. It sounds like something you wrote." Simpson winked. "Susan told me you were a fellow scribbler."

Roy grinned idiotically, then limply waved his hand in the air to cross out the line. He forced himself to look squarely at Simpson, whose face, though pale and clean shaven, reminded him—with its long hawk-Roman nose set high into the bridge of his tiny black sunglasses—of Ezra Pound's politics. Simpson had chosen for the occasion blue suede deck shoes without socks, a beige multi-zippered jump suit that would look good nailed to a wall with flowers hurling off it, a paisley scarf, and a Panama hat cocked back like a riverboat gambler's. Roy had mistaken the outfit for a fruity old fool's, a judgment he had been paying for since his second drink. *Fox*, he thought now. *Windy commando*. A sweet-sour odor wafted off the old man as if to pay Roy for this insight as the heat shifted.

"Again?" Simpson asked.

"You could both get too much sun," Susan warned.

"We'll be careful, love. Now, please go through it again, Roy." Simpson swung his glass to coax an encore. "I want to make sure I have it right." He was very much concerned with getting things right, as he had been last night when Roy pulled in, as if he were saving Roy's exact words to measure against future testimony.

"You heard it the first time, didn't you?"

"What difference does it make?" Susan wanted to know. "You said it once, why not say it again." Her polka-dots flashed as she shifted her position and squinted at Roy who was following the skiers and the pines and not thinking about the blonde crone, hard. "Go ahead. Please go ahead."

Simpson held out his glass for Susan to refill. Susan waited, her attention now strategically on the lake.

"Gin for my health!" Simpson bellowed happily and again raised his glass. Roy watched Susan free herself from the lounger chair, slip her index fingers under the rims of her suit and pop it over the excess flesh he'd once touched with fingers of water. She moved to service the old man. She did so with an air of feigned servility, like a waitress working for a rich uncle: Exaggerated curtsey, canned smile. It seemed a joke between them. Roy handed her his glass as she passed. She pursed her lips, accepted the glass, and mounted the steps to the cottage. On the backs of her legs the plastic lounge chair had imprinted a pink plaid any adolescent boy could wear. She might have gained a few pounds, baking bread for old men.

"Don't say anything good while I'm gone," she called back and stepped inside.

Simpson scrouched forward in his director's chair. "There are such distractions in these climes, eh? Now, please say your line for me again."

Roy looked to the shimmering pines across the lake. A girl shrieked above the roar of an outboard. "What's so goddamn important about it?"

Simpson coughed into his laugh. "Nothing, really, I suppose. My own intelligence has always entertained me but it's seldom done me any good. My mouth always at the mercy of my imagination, my imagination always at the mercy of my mouth."

"Sounds like something you wrote."

"Touché!" Simpson toasted Roy with his glass from which a drop of condensation flew.

Roy saw himself return, without will, the toast.

"And I was married myself, once. A terrible business if you lose command. No honorable way out of it."

"I'm not married."

Simpson bowed his head to the wisdom of this. A pair of grackles dive-bombed the lawn below, their wings and broad tails too coincidentally the iridescent black to green of old suits, caretakers.

Simpson snapped his head up in time to catch Roy double thumbing off rounds at the birds.

"Am I boring you, Roy? God forbid I should bore anyone but myself."

"There are other things He should forbid."

"Ah, the womens. She does have you rather . . . *cautioned*, as you say."

"Keep your mouth off it, old man."

"A feeble attempt at humor on my part," Simpson said quickly. He removed his hat and wiped his wiry hair with a colored handkerchief, then used it to blot a sudden fit of hacking. "An old man thinks he can say anything he pleases. One of the false luxuries of old age. Sometimes it's hard not to take deathbed license, fudge up on it a bit, you know." With a wave at the lake he added, smiling thinly, "You might not think it, but it becomes increasingly difficult to face the rather unfair obligation to die."

Behind Simpson the chorus line of pines shimmied frantically. Roy wiped his chest with his T-shirt, furious with himself for planting the image of the girlie pines in his head. He felt drained, all energy gone out of him to the gin and the heat, *to*, he thought unwillingly, this old bastard's death.

"Before or after dinner?" he said.

"What's that?"

"Are you going to die before or after dinner?"

Simpson looked up to the cottage door. Susan stepped out on cue with the drinks.

"When you're not here," Simpson whispered quickly. "I promise," then chuckled up at the waitress. "I believe I've been invited to dinner!"

2

Susan stood over them on the steps, the drinks equidistant from each other and her breasts.

"I'm off to relief," Simpson announced, hacking as he rose and aimed himself at his oversized trailer. He looked up to Susan; she and Simpson were taking him in shifts. She poured one of the drinks into the potted geranium wilting on the window ledge.

"What did he tell you?" she asked, extending the surviving drink. (He had thought it was his she'd dumped.) He reached around for her hips as she turned; she dodged him neatly.

"It's too hot."

Settling into the lounge chair she adjusted it up to a level in line with his slump, exposing shallow cleavage. For no good reason he could think of now, he had always believed small-breasted women were intelligent.

"What did you two talk about?"

"Nothing much. Death. Pussy. He told me he was going to die so I asked him if it was going to happen before or after dinner. A joke." It did not seem possible to explain the rest of it.

"Go on. I'm fascinated."

"You walked out and he said that about being invited to dinner."

"That's all? Well, I don't suppose it makes much difference."

"Something in your life sure as hell should."

"Something does."

She tried out her concentration on Simpson's Airstream. An air conditioner's gray snout drooped from its front end, dripping steadily. Roy strained to hear its whir, then did.

"There are . . . twelve trailers here people live in and they're all empty except for his. Once in a while someone stumbles in here for the night but they don't stay long because all the other trailers are empty and they think something's wrong."

"They're right. Something is. There's no one here but you and the patient."

"He *is* going to die."

"I know, I know. So is everybody. Ten to one he wants to be cremated. The literary way. Leave no trace. Ashes to the wind."

"What's wrong with that?"

Roy took another long drink not to waste it. The perfume of the gin burned his sinuses. He remembered the cramp at Huelen's rising through them as she took him in tow. Simpson tossed the gin down like water. He could afford to.

"I think it's got him stimulated," Roy offered her.

"What has?"

"Dying."

Ignoring him, she continued to stare down at Simpson's trailer. The shadows of the sycamores bordering the drive mottled her legs and shoulders and through the gin her flesh appeared bruised.

"He's lonely and he's been very good to me. He even had the bedroom painted eggshell for me."

"You're his Nightingale in residence. It's part of the fringe benefits."

"Talk. A little company. Is that so horrible?"

"He's sucking your blood."

"You're being theatrical. You sound like him."

"Anything else we have in common?"

"Don't be such a shit. He's a nice old man and we do owe him something. Besides, he probably really does think you invited him to dinner."

"You bet."

"Right now he's giving us time to make up an excuse so we don't have to have him over."

"The movies! We could go to the movies. A late-night swim in the raw."

"Sometimes he stays in there for days, brooding. You saw how pale he is. He frightens me, Roy. Oh, I know he might be locking himself up for sympathy, geriatric cases do that, but he still frightens me. I mean, what might happen to him when I'm not here. I always check in on him before I leave for work."

"So we owe him because he frightens you."

She took a deep breath and placed her hands out flat on her thighs. "He didn't tell you, then. Damn. I knew he wouldn't."

"Go on," Roy said. "I'm fascinated."

"You don't deserve to know. You don't deserve to know anything."

"But I'm *here*," he said. "And who else is there to tell, Susan?"

"All right." She made a temple with her fingers and locked them, he knew, for toleration. "Before you woke up this morning . . ."

"In the triple-A trailer . . ."

". . . he came over and said we could use his trailer tonight if it got too hot. The air conditioner gives him a chill at night. He was very nice about it."

"What was wrong with last night? You both seemed pretty anxious to lock me up in a hurry. In solitary. Change of heart?"

"He mentioned that. He said he thought it would have been embarrassing for all concerned. Besides, he didn't know you then."

"He knew me all right when I pulled up last night. He seems to know a lot of things."

"You wanted to sleep here," she said. "Why not over there?"

Roy gulped his or Simpson's drink. "I hate trailers, how's that?"

"You're acting like a child."

"Right. Wa wa. Just how much did you tell him about us and trailers?"

Her glance darted again to Simpson's doorway.

"Don't be shy, Susan. What did you tell him?"

She was up, straddling the sides of the lounge chair.

"You hate trailers so much, why didn't you think of that before you got one to fuck me in?"

3

The lake would cool him off, sober him up, maybe kill him.

He rolled toward the lakefront, the trunks riding uncomfortably high on the insides of his thighs where he had had trouble with boils before. The court was deserted, she was right about that, and in the glaring neatness of its tin and pastel siding he felt painfully tired, *blurred*. His crotch was tight and he took long strides to loosen it in the elastic trunks from Russia.

Skiers kept the lake choppy and he suffered real dread of the waves. He stood gazing out at them, at the cool blank joy of their thunderous skimming in pass after pass. Soon they began waving at him, the fish belly white Russian transfixed in their bleachers. They were all girls—Simpson's casting or crap coincidence. He did not wave back, and in their next passes they waved all the more gaily. It occurred to him that they might think him blind if he stood here long enough without waving. He bet some of them began waving even before they cleared the wooded point to his right where they could see him to wave at. They would get in as much waving at him as possible. He would wait here long enough to see one of them spill, bob in the life jacket above the stinky bait she twitched. Then he would wave back and turn out not to be blind at all.

Long after he had strayed from the thought, he found himself sitting on the bank, propped against a tree. "Susan," he sang to the lapping waves, "Susan, I think what you want is your cher–ry back, cher–ry back, cher–ry back!"

The sunlight off the lake scaled the smooth sycamore trunks in flickering crescents, a constant ascension that did not seem to be moving. Counting the light, he dropped off.

❋   ❋   ❋   ❋

"Beating our heat?"

Roy heard something else in the sentence and looked up furious to see Simpson leaning over him, a fresh drink in each hand. They were taking turns standing over him with the drinks. The old man had changed into white ducks and a lemon polo shirt, definitely beating the heat himself. A pink ascot bulged at his throat like a goiter.

"Rumor has it you might soon leave," he said. "I, for one, hope you'll stay."

"Is that what she told you?" Roy took the drink, sipped, and slowly poured it over his own bare feet. "Haven't said I'd do it yet, old man."

"What? Leave?"

"Lay her for you."

"Oh my." Simpson spread a handkerchief on the grass and stiffly eased himself down. "She's been very good to me. My offer of the trailer was meant to repay favors, nothing more."

"An odd way to put it, Simpson."

"Henry. My name is Henry. I'm not at all fussy about it but I'd like you to call me Henry. It sounds, oh, less institutionalized, shall we say, than Simpson. Anyway, she has plans for the future and they include you and sometimes she confides in me. Heaven knows why. We talk and I sometimes give advice. Her listening to it is her charity."

"Miss Charity," Roy sneered and watched his hand reach over and carefully remove Simpson's sunglasses. The old man did not move or flinch, but as Roy put them on, he stood. Roy shakily joined him at the height.

"I am a blind Russian," he said. He felt the phantom

pressure of Simpson's hand on his shoulder and before it could arrive he stepped off the bank and into the warm lake. The bottom was sandy and he waded out on swirls of it until the water reached his knees. He stood facing the far bank of pines, waiting for the skiers around the point to make another pass and see him with Pound's glasses on. His hope for this had been dead for several minutes when he heard Simpson ask in a distant voice if he was ready for dinner. He did not answer. He turned toward the near bank and tugged back the tight band of the suit from his thigh and popped it once and tugged it back again and emptied himself into the lake. Looking up and turning, looking up and turning from the startling purity of his stream, he could not decide if he was glad or angry that Simpson had vanished.

"She saved my life once," he said softly to all he had left, the skiers, two burned girls who waved and waved. He waded toward them.

He waded back and then back out again. "She's always *saving* someone!" he shouted to the now empty lake.

4

"Coffee. Lots of black coffee. Mr. Simpson, Henry, is a little tipsy."

Susan served them leek-green chunky gravy over Minute Rice and crunchy noodles. Roy shoveled it down for ballast. She was still in her bikini and coming with his order, instant ... and acidic.

"What say we take in a motion-picture show after dinner. It'll give us a chance to wear some clothes."

"Elvis Presley," Simpson said. "Walt Disney. John Wayne. The local theater lies in wait for desperate tourists. Also it is arctic."

"I thought that was what you two had in mind."

"Some of my cases go there."

Roy smiled in front of his chop suey or whatever. "They are cool and dark, that's what counts in theaters."

"Precisely," Simpson said. With a happy flourish he tucked his napkin in under his ascot.

"Or we could drive-in in the Hudson and preserve your

reputation as a chaste healer of the lost and unfortunate."

"The getaway Hudson?" Simpson grinned. "You might be ap–pre–*hen*–ded."

Susan puzzled this and Simpson's singsong delivery.

"A joke," Simpson explained.

"Everybody has jokes today and I'm not in on any of them."

"Yes you are."

"Might do you both good to get out," Simpson said and caught something in his throat, commenced his hacking.

Roy leaned back in his chair. "The best thing to take for that is bread and water." Simpson worked hard for a dry-heave effect. "Get him some homemade bread and a glass of water, Susan. If he takes some bread and water we can go to the movies before he does something permanent."

"Why don't you leave?"

"Rumor has it I soon might, Miss Charity."

Simpson kept it up. Wide eyed, overacting, or truly on his way out, he clutched at his ascot and napkin, ripped them off. The broken capillaries flamed in his cheeks, his neck went taut, the tendons quivering with the power to launch his head. Roy kept his eye on the feathery vise of the winged white hair loosening.

"Are you going to just *sit* there?" Susan, who wasn't, jumped up to pound the old man's back. "Do you want him to choke to death?" She was screaming.

Roy chewed and swallowed, slowly shook his head: *No.*

The hacking gained sonority. Susan reached into it and shucked out Simpson's dentures. On the table they looked very powerful.

Susan undid his belt. *Maybe we can disassemble him,* Roy thought. He bent to retrieve the ascot and napkin from the floor. Down there Simpson's blue sneaker stomped crazily in time with the spasms of his hacking. Roy realized he had been watching the sneaker too long for the strings on the bones in there to be sane. He came back up.

Susan shouted something and flapped her hands. Roy felt his feet under him, the wing of her blood alive in his eye as he pushed her aside and began pounding the old man's back. It echoed like a hollow gourd, one, he found the frightening time to think, with a little water in it. The pounding did not seem to be doing much good. He was frightened that his pounding on Simpson was too hard or not hard enough.

"Get him on the couch! Get him over here on his side!"

Roy had him under the arms, lifting. He was remarkably light and dry.

Simpson did not want to go. His mottled hand rose: *Please. Leave me be.*

With a resonant belch he came out of it gulping, quickly turned his head to replace his dentures.

"Are you all right?"

The old man nodded. His mouth opened and held agape; Roy checked an impulse to reach out and lift his jaw back up to his face. Simpson coughed; the dentures clacked. "Fine."

"I didn't know if I was hitting you too hard or not hard enough."

Susan glared at Roy. "What difference does that make?" she snapped, then ordered Simpson, "Open your mouth." Roy watched Simpson obey: *You must keep your fingers to yourself*, he thought at her but couldn't say.

"He seems okay," she said officially.

Through fits of wet hacking Simpson apologized for spoiling everyone's dinner. "You two finish up and see your film. I'm going to take a little nap." He stood. Roy did not want to take his arm in front of Susan. "I'll lie down here and you two spend the night in mine. The least I can do."

"You don't owe us anything," Roy said.

"Help him go back," Susan said to Roy before he could tell Simpson what he owed him. "I'll clear the table."

Following Simpson into Susan's bedroom, blurry in their sudden calm, Roy again held back his support.

He did not expect to see Simpson flop down on the bed in the eggshell room. He saw his fingers untying the sneakers. Simpson fiddled with the buttons on his polo shirt.

"Hand me the sheet and comforter in the wardrobe there, will you? I don't want to muss her sheets."

Roy balked.

"I know they're there because I've collapsed here before." He hacked, though mildly.

Roy took down the comforter. He did not immediately see

the sheet. When he did, he could not touch the stacked bulk of milky blue plastic on the top shelf.

"Where's the other? I don't want to muss her sheets. I've explained this."

"Don't worry about her sheets."

Simpson closed his eyes. Roy thought of the sunglasses, coins. "I didn't mean to embarrass you, Roy. It *can* be an unpleasant mess for her, though."

It looked heavy. As he cleared it from the top shelf he was surprised to feel it try to rise from his hands. His eyes decompressed with thunderous red and he sucked a huge breath that could have been blue. On his way back to the bed he stumbled over one of Simpson's sneakers and recovered.

"Watch yourself."

Roy spread the sheet lengthwise on the bed. It crackled and struggled in his hands. Simpson rolled onto one half of it and pulled the other fold out over the bed, then slipped the comforter under his legs and back. Dapper and prone on the muffled crackling of the bed, his long fingers fussing with lumps in the comforter, Simpson looked terrifically pleased with himself, as if he had at last accomplished something secret and good.

"Yes," he whispered hoarsely. "That does it nicely. Tell her you should go to your film now, Roy. It doesn't have to be a decent one, does it? She needs to get out. Away from all this. I promise not to croak without an audience. Go."

"We could probably pass it up."

"Don't be silly. Let me rest. Close the door and don't think about me."

Roy stood at the door considering this.

"One more thing."

"Yes?"

"Remember to turn it down at night or you'll freeze to death over there."

"Thanks. We'll be careful."

"Yes. Do," Simpson said and waved him off.

On the way to the kitchen Roy saw Simpson's sagging twin lungs fill with blue water, blue light he shook off to face her at the sink washing dishes in noise.

"Well?"

"He'll be fine. He said to tell you we should go to the movies. He'd like us to."

"And leave him? You go. I'm staying."

"What about that air conditioned comfort over there?"

"I think we should do whatever he wants."

"Me too. He said to go to the movies."

"Let me finish the dishes and we'll see, okay?"

"You'll go," he said. "And he'll be fine without you."

"What makes you so sure?"

"We'll go to the movies and prove it. That's what he wants."

"Did you get him his sheet?"

"Yes. He's all set up."

He reclaimed his coffee before she could dump the cup and as he turned from the sink she touched his cock lightly through the elastic trunks from Russia.

He handed her the cup and watched her fingers slowly wrap it.

"I'll bring the car around."

He stepped outside and eased back the screen door. The grackles had given up and so had the skiers. Beyond the edge of the court the pines on the far bank lay inverted and calmed in the dark mirror of the lake. He stood for a moment facing Henry's trailer. A few sooty clouds were gathering in the west and he held himself against the cool air moving in off the lake. We won't need the air conditioning, he thought, and swung his head back to the bedroom window of the cottage. Standing there, chilled and waiting, his attention cocked toward the old man's rest, he felt himself completely in focus, as if a perfect likeness of him was about to be taken and kept.

He would look over the trailer and then he would bring the Hudson around to the front of the cottage and take her to the movies. They would have to get back early and check in with Henry and not jinx the night.